WASATCH WITCHES

A COLLECTION OF UTAH HORROR

In memory of Jaren Rencher

CONTENTS

WITCHES ARE REAL

AN INTRODUCTION BY GABINO IGLESIAS

My grandma was a witch. It took me years to get comfortable writing that line and even longer to learn that whatever people make of it after reading it is none of my business and I shouldn't care about it.

You see, when I was growing up, my grandma was my grandma. She was small, incredibly thin, and sweet. She carried weird necklaces with her, whispered strange things every time we drove past a cemetery, and always had milagritos hanging from the inside of her clothing, usually her bra, with big clothespins. In her house, the hallway bathroom was for the spirits, so no one could use it. She kept it closed if anyone came to visit. There were lots of candles in there. They made creepy shadows dance around on the walls at night. There were also many figurines of saints in her room that looked like something pulled from a horror movie at night. I didn't like that, or the shadows in the bathroom walls, but I was never scared; I was at grandma's house, so I was safe.

The Caribbean, where I grew up, is probably the global epicenter of syncretism. Everything came there and everything goes. The mixture of what the indigenous people like the Caribes and the Taínos believed, the religion the Spaniards brought when they got lost and ended up there (no one "discovers" a place where people already live), and what the Africans brought with them when they were stolen from Africa as well as the myriad ways in which all of that mixed and morphed into new belief systems and practices is amazing. Growing up in the Caribbean usually means you're exposed to things like voodoo, Santería, Palo, and Mesa Blanca as much as you're exposed to Catholicism and Christianity. People who go to church on Sunday morning also go get a limpia on Saturday or get their palms read after church. People who wear a cross around their neck throw salt over their shoulder and pray to Changó when they need something. With that crazy, beautiful amalgamation comes acceptance, and with acceptance comes the good and the bad as well as the need for education.

As I grew older, I realized that my grandma wasn't like other grandma's who merely went to church on Sundays or never talked about religion. She talked about conversations with dead people and spent days worried every time a pigeon landed on the old AC unit under her window at night and cooed for a while because that meant someone was about to die. In any case, some of that stuff eventually made its way into my fiction, and doing so was hard because despite knowing I was only writing about my life, I also knew that anyone who acted like her was normally called a witch, and witches are evil green ladies with giant warts on their noses and pointy hats who eat kids and ride brooms at night.

In the last few years, I've witnessed a bit of a renaissance in terms of religions and practices that reach above and beyond the usual. It seems like people are starting to accept that there is something behind the veil and that there are many ways of getting in touch with it. What some call the supernatural is, for a lot of people, everyday reality. Unfortunately, soon after noticing that small shift in the tide of acceptance, I also saw that everything was becoming diluted and watered down. Anyone who lights a candle they bought online calls themselves a bruja or brujo. Anyone who owns a tarot deck and watches a tutorial on how to do a reading on YouTube claims they can see the future. Anyone who buys a Santa Muerte candle at the grocery store thinks they're in touch with something scared and strange. Anyone who practices yoga twice a week is enlightened and can see beyond the veil. Bullshit. The one thing I know about the supernatural is this: it's real. Thankfully, fiction is often a tool that allows us to reveal truths and educate people. That's why we're here.

The importance of books like the one you're holding is immense. Here are stories that offer a diverse look into the plethora of perspectives that grow rhizomathically from the supernatural. The list is long and we often hear about things like pagan religions, Wicca, occultism, witchcraft, brujería, druidism, shamanism, candomble, Thelema, and many others and, unless you're in the know, it's easy to think it's all the same. It's not. Every single witch out there has a story, roots, and a unique perspective and approach to the supernatural. We need stories that explore these religions, these practices, these cultural spaces, and these people. The stories you're about to read do just that. Read them carefully. Enjoy the horror, but also pay attention to the narratives and the stuff they're made of. In the immortal words of poet and mystic Isaac Kirkman, a good friend who now walks with the Orishas, "If you haven't seen shit you can't explain, you haven't spent enough time in the streets." Open your eyes and read about things you haven't seen.

Gabino Iglesias

January 2021, as the world burns

WASATCH
WITCHES

THE PESTILENCE

VINCE FONT

They came up the mountain with their torches and their bibles and their godly heads held high. Boots plunged into snow-packed earth and scarves drew over ears as winter's icy breath blew down the Wasatch Range. At the end of the path where the Devil dwelt, the men stopped and formed a hard line.

Within the darkened cottage, nothing stirred. The serpent lay in wait.

Jeremiah Howard was the first to speak. He always was. Even the most outspoken of his flock deferred to him with heads held low, and tonight was no exception. None dared be the first to call out the evil they'd come to face.

"Mary Creed!" Jeremiah shouted, struggling to be heard above the howling wind, but his lungs were heavy from the mountain climb, and his words fell from his lips like cracked leather. With a silent prayer, he cleared his throat and spoke again. This time, his voice cut like a foghorn through a squall.

"Mary Creed! Open your door and stand before us."

One of Jeremiah's men heaved a terrified gasp as light blossomed from inside the cottage and spilled out through the single window, casting the whole of the mountainside a ghastly red.

When something hideous moved across the light and disappeared, only Jeremiah's presence kept his men from racing down the mountain back to town. If they failed to carry out their duty, everyone they loved would die.

It began, as most things do, with a single word.

Witch.

Followed, inevitably, by another.

Curse.

The sickness had arrived with the stealth of a black cat on a starless night. It spread among the aged and the weak like wildfire, stealing their eyesight and rendering them paralyzed. Filling their lungs with fire. Jellifying their internal organs and turning their bones to sand. Not a soul who fell ill lived longer than a month.

It landed in the autumn and by winter showed no signs of stopping. Yet not until the death of seven-year-old Abigail Young, who on her fevered deathbed stammered claims of late-night visits from an entity half-human and half-pig, did the townsfolk demand something be done.

Jeremiah knew, as all who worshipped did, that witchcraft was the cause. He also knew that for the pestilence to end, the guilty had to die. And so he knelt and prayed and waited for a sign. When finally it came—delivered to his waiting ears from the tongue of the Lord—Jeremiah knew who was to blame.

Mary Creed. Spouseless. Childless. Harlot. Monster.

Steeling himself against a blast of wind so cold it could only have been summoned by the Devil himself, Jeremiah watched his torch flicker and nearly go out.

"In the name of God," he shouted, "I command you to surrender yourself!"

But Mary did not comply. Jeremiah had expected this. At his instruction, the men removed truncheons from their coats and advanced on the cottage, raining savage blows against it.

When something inside screamed, "Go away! Leave me be or you will die!" the men stopped, but only long enough to turn their eyes to Jeremiah.

"The witch lies," he told them. Then, in defiance of the demon's curse, he shouted, "Your powers will not work this time! Your spells have no effect! We come under protection of the Lord."

They resumed their assault, and in seconds the cottage door, long on the verge of falling in on itself, gave way. It did not splinter into pieces but instead crumbled inward, sagging from its hinges like a hanged corpse. Then, the men reached inside and tore Mary from her home.

"Don't touch me!" she cried. "You will die! All of you!"

Her voice was thick with astonishment and rage, but if they heard her warning, they paid no heed as they threw her at the foot of a nearby tree.

"Please," Mary wheezed, "I am ill..."

Blinding pain flashed across her jaw, and she shrieked in agony when a boot came down against her ankle, shattering it. Mary sank to the snowy earth.

"Death to the witch!" came a voice.

"We'll burn her alive," declared another.

"No," growled a third, eerily calm. "Let's string her up and watch her beg for mercy as she chokes."

All voices fell silent when Jeremiah spoke. "Mary Creed, you stand accused of murdering the innocent with your evil spells. Admit your guilt and die with a clean conscience."

She had known they were coming, had seen the flicker of their torches long before their arrival. She'd even hoped to reason with Jeremiah, to somehow talk him into sparing her life, but now, as she observed the stony set of the minister's jaw—that inimitable way his lower lip stuck out impossibly far, indicating he'd made up his mind for good —Mary knew nothing would save her.

She prayed for a quick and painless death. Her prayer was not answered.

First, they stripped her of her clothes. Then, they pummeled her with fists and feet until her body was reduced to a broken, bloody lump. Finally, they burned her alive.

Not one of Jeremiah's men had ever heard a human being make the sounds Mary Creed made when they strapped her to the willow tree and set fire to her, and if any of them had lived longer than a week, her screams would have haunted them to the end of their days. As it was, they were walking dead men. The sickness upon Mary's clothes and flesh and breath had already been passed on to them.

It was long after midnight when Jeremiah led his men down from the mountain. By then, the snow had reached the valley, and the town lay blanketed in white, but in the morning when the killers woke and kissed their wives and held their children, the sun rose warm and bright. Soon, the snow was gone. By springtime when the town lay dead, vultures from the northeast came to feast.

Vince Font is a writer of words and a righter of wrongs (the typographical kind). A fulltime freelance writer and editor, he co-authored the award-winning book *American Sons: The Untold Story of the Falcon and the Snowman* (2013) and is the creator of the *Shadows on the Page* book series (2020). He is the founder and chief editor of Glass Spider Publishing in Ogden, Utah.

THE WITCH'S HOUSE

JESSE N. WHITE

D oors slammed shut. The couple left their vehicle parked on the side of the road and started climbing the stairway to the so-called Witch's House. "Why are we here, again, Angie?" Paul complained, not for the first time. The coolness of the late October evening raised the hairs along Paul's spine. At least he hoped it was only the wind.

"You said you wanted to do something relaxing, and it is almost Halloween, so we're here for a float session," Angie explained for the fifth time that day. "Please, can we just do this? There might not be another opening for months. It's supposed to be relaxing and still in the spirit of the holiday. Plus, it is kinda non-refundable..."

"Yeah, yeah, sure. Fine. Whatever," Paul said, raising his hands in mock defeat. "But this is the last time you get to pick one of our dates." Paul looked at Angie with what she knew was some level of disgust. *So weird and weak,*

Paul thought to himself. *She's lucky to have such a great man like me in her life.*

Angie was worried her nerves would show and Paul would start to ask more questions. *Please, please, please,* she repeated to herself. *Please just let me make it through tonight.* She crossed her arms and huffed up the stairs. It seemed like an unusually long climb. Long enough that Paul asked another question. "Why is it called the Witch's House? Shouldn't a respectable relaxation slash luxury spa have a different name?" he asked as he made air quotations. They reached the door. The house was huge, spooky, and old. *Definitely fancy and nice, though,* Paul conceded to himself.

"What? Oh." Angie gasped and pushed her hair out of her eyes. "Well, I'm pretty sure Miss Weitchzel was just making a play off her name and she does really enjoy the whole Halloween vibe. Remember? I showed you the pictures of the inside," Angie said nervously. She was afraid of making Paul upset. It was exhausting.

"Still kinda weird though, right?" he pushed.

"Oh yeah. Of course. But appropriate for the time of year," she responded, disheartened.

"Whatever. Let's just get this over with. Don't say I never do anything for you, either. Got it?" Paul motioned with a jerk of his hand for Angie to knock on the door and then shoved his hands into his pockets and shuffled his feet. As Angie reached out to knock, the door opened. Before them stood one of the most stunningly beautiful, while simultaneously odd, women Paul had ever seen. Her raven black hair flowed around her face and down her back. Her piercing blue eyes seemed to swallow Paul's soul. He was momentarily taken aback by the strength of the feelings. He couldn't say what he found odd about her, just that he was sure there was more to her than he could perceive with his eyes or senses. Power.

"Hello," she greeted them cheerfully, her voice magical. "I am Olivia Weitchzel. Welcome to the Witch's House! You must be Paul Olmstead and Angie Pines. I hope you're both ready for a relaxing and therapeutic experience." She motioned them into the foyer and smiled broadly. Inside, the couple was greeted with a wondrous display of macabre decorations and knick-knacks. The interior, even without the decorations, gave off the same vibe as the exterior. Fancy, but old and creepy. The walls were lined with horror movie posters, fake cobwebs, and some obviously expensive pieces of ghastly art. Some of the decorations looked like genuine occult paraphernalia, whereas some others just seemed like kitschy trinkets. There was even a large mannequin dressed as a stereotypical Halloween witch. Paul might even call it a slutty witch mannequin.

"Quite the spooky place you got here, Miss Why-chel," Paul remarked, purposely mispronouncing their host's name as he walked over and casually cupped the mannequin's breasts. " I love the decor."

Olivia smirked at Paul and gave Angie a wink. "Not quite what you were expecting? Nothing here frightens you, Mister Olmstead?" She cackled as she swirled and allowed her dress to fall off her shoulder. She motioned the couple further into the house. "Well, not to worry. A float session is meant to relax. The decor is just something I like." They passed a large window that had one of the most amazing views of the Salt Lake Valley that Paul had ever seen. He paused and looked at the city lights below.

"Ah. But this does catch your attention, I see," Olivia observed. "I like to keep an eye on the growing sickness in our lovely valley." Olivia winked and smiled again.

"Sickness?" Paul scoffed. "Lady, this place is one of the top destinations for tech companies and outdoor-loving people around the world. I'd be careful what I called a sickness, if I were you, lady. A lot of powerful people make their homes here."

"I'm sure," Olivia responded sarcastically.

"I'm so sorry. He didn't mean it like that," Angie tried to quickly explain.

"No. No, dear. No harm done. The young man was just expressing his opinion. I am sure. Not to worry," Olivia cooed as she patted the air in a calming gesture and brought the couple to the back room. "Now, tell me. Have either of you used a float tank before?" Olivia asked as they neared a huge egg-shaped apparatus. She went over the procedure for showering prior to entering the float tank and explained how the salt water was used to make one float and feel suspended in the body temperature water. "It is pitch black in there, so I hope you aren't afraid of being alone in the dark, Mister Olmstead," Olivia chided.

"Ha! No one is afraid of being alone in the dark," Paul responded snarkily. "They are afraid of *not* being alone in the dark. But I haven't felt that way in years." He pointed a thumb at his chest and puffed it out as he said, "I am the scariest thing in the dark these days."

Olivia barked out a sharp laugh. "Ah, my child. Think

about all of the terrors that you cannot see. Like a poor frog being boiled slowly. He sees no danger, but the danger is, nonetheless, very real. Anyway, I find that people are often more afraid of what they discover in the light when it comes back on. Sighted people, at least. The mind finds other ways to terrify those poor souls that do not see light the same way we do. And I can assure you, there are many more terrifying things in the dark than a petulant child."

Paul's blood began to boil when he realized their hostess was patronizing him. Whenever people started using words he did not fully understand or only read in science books, he knew they thought he was stupid. His feelings were readily displayed, and Angie began to pale and cower back, sensing the storm coming. Now, or later at home.

Olivia's disarming smile somehow instantly removed all feelings of anger and fear from the couple, and she raised her hands and said, "Now then, we're all friends here. And this is a time for relaxation and enjoyment. Nothing to stress about." She explained that because there was only one tank, they would have to take turns. Paul announced that he would go first, and he was left to shower and get into the tank.

"We'll be in the living room. At the end of your session, a soft light will come on accompanied by gentle sounds. This will let you know it is time to come out. Shower when you are done and join us in the living room," Olivia explained as she motioned to the shower and float tank. She winked as she closed the door.

"Yeah. Fine. Whatever." Paul decided to follow the procedures Olivia outlined, even though he hated being told what to do. It was his choice to follow the directions this time. Paul rinsed himself off and climbed the wooden steps into the tank. He closed the lid as he lay on his back in the salty water.

All sounds and light disappeared once his head was resting in water, his body floating on the top. It *was* very relaxing. A nice change of pace from the hectic racing thoughts and constant stimuli of the modern world. Floating in the water even seemed to mask some of the sensation of touch. Paul had his eyes open, but there was nothing to see. Just blackness. He closed his eyes and was greeted by the same inky blackness. The lack of stimulation began to dredge up a feeling of unease and brought back vivid memories. How long had he been in here? Surely, only a minute or two, and this was supposed to go on for an hour? Paul reached out his arms to see if he could touch the edges of the tank. It would be nice to get a mental picture of the space. The edge was not there. He pushed his legs down to stand but found no bottom. He reached up for the release latch and again found nothing. Panicking, Paul began to thrash and choked on some water. "Get a hold of yourself!" he shouted angrily at himself. The sound of his own shaky voice calmed him down enough to remember he was in salt water and could just float if he wanted. Somehow, he was now in a space that should not have been so large.

It seemed to be getting warmer too. Paul couldn't be certain because the change in temperature seemed to be very gradual. But both the air and the water *did* seem to be getting warmer. He took a few deep breaths and reached out again for the edges of the tank or the release hatch.

Nothing above him. Nothing to the sides. He reached down and felt nothing at first, but then he felt something. His brain told him the object he was touching was hair. But that couldn't be right. Paul grasped the object and pulled it up, the water splashing as the object broke the surface. He felt it again and screamed as he felt what he was certain was flesh and bone. A smell assaulted his senses, and the object floated next to him. Paul frantically pushed the object away and then decided that he should swim to find the edge.

As he began to swim away, a hand grabbed his ankle. "Son," a rasping voice wheezed. "Don't leave me. I'm scared." Those were the same as the last words of Paul's father. The man who had instilled so much fear in Paul and gifted him a hatred of weakness was afraid and weak in the end when cancer claimed him. Paul screamed and kicked out against the object, and his feet connected with swollen, bloated flesh. A ring of light appeared above Paul in the blackness. The brightness blinded him temporarily. He felt more hands grasping at his legs, and he continued to kick and scream, trying to escape. The light showed Paul that he was in a large body of water with black edges. There were indeed rotting corpses around him, grasping at him. When he looked up, he was even more shocked to see Olivia's face. It was huge and smiling. Next to her was Angie.

"Oh, my sweet child. Don't be afraid. I thought you were the scariest thing in the dark?" Olivia laughed. "No? Well, no matter. Soon this will all be over." She cackled and threw large chunks of onion and potatoes into the water. Paul screamed as the water began to boil.

Jesse White is a Georgia-based author who dreams of the wonders of the American Southwest. An avid reader of steamy romances, mindless poetry, horror fiction, and bad puns, he loves writing the same. Jesse is a Gemini sun/Libra rising.

THE LADY OF THE LAKE

LEVI ROBINSON

"I don't think I can go much further," Beatrice groaned, her buckskin boots beginning to fill with blood. Her back ached, and her stomach seemed to scream at her, but what hurt most of all was her feet. With every passing step, the pain radiated up her legs and into her knees before finally settling in her lower back. She tried not to think about how her heels were rubbed raw or about how cracked the balls of her feet must be. She pushed all these things out of her mind and just focused on putting one foot in front of the other, doing her best to stay in the shadow of her husband, Henrich, a man she had known for a little more than three months.

It took all her power of will not to think about the comfortable covered wagon she had taken for granted just a few nights prior. If she had known then what she knew now, she would have been grateful for every second behind those stinking oxen. She tried not to think about how scared she was without the comfort of the others around their campfire. She tried not to blame Henrich for getting them lost—it was her duty as a wife to support him, after all—but with every agonizing step, she struggled to find a reason not to curse his name.

"Just a little while more," Henrich breathed back to her, his heavy pack slung over his shoulder. If Beatrice would have taken her eyes off the ground in front of her and looked up, she would have seen the beautiful, tree-covered mountainside cropping up from all around her. Their peaks were jotted with the first white speckles of winter, and their sheer stone faces looked down upon them. Towards the west, the direction they had been heading for weeks, the fiery ball in the sky threatened to disappear below the horizon, bringing them another frightful and cold night.

They walked on for what seemed like an eternity, Henrich's shadow stretching back farther and farther behind them. One foot in front of the other, they marched on.

"Beatrice, look," he said and stopped dead in his tracks. She barely had time to register the abrupt stop and nearly ran right into him. Pain surging up her legs and across her sweaty face, she looked at him, ready to finally let him know how she felt. But just as she was about to unload days and weeks of pent-up anger and stress, she saw his smile. And past him, what he was smiling about.

Beyond the mountain crests, a massive valley spread seemingly all the way to the horizon. At the far side lay a great lake, the orange sky reflected upon it. She didn't have long to ponder at the amazing view because something more pressing caught her eye almost immediately. A thin column of black smoke.

As they strode onward with their newfound sense of purpose, she couldn't help but imagine the scenarios in which she would be saved from this nightmare that she only just now started to admit to herself could have very well ended up in both of their deaths. Perhaps when they got back to others, they would have fresh mutton stew for them? She had been fighting her creeping hunger for the last day or so, and suddenly she was ravenous.

It was hard not to be distracted by the wonder of the great lake. Never in her life had she seen such a large body of water. If she didn't know any better, she would have mistaken it for the ocean since it seemed to have no far shore.

As they climbed out of the steep embankment leading from the high mountaintops down to the flat expanse, it became more and more clear that whoever was generating the smoke, it was not their traveling companions. Perhaps a wagon or two lost from the rest of the party such as themselves. But she had been with the rest of them long enough to know what their camp looked like and the path they left behind them. In fact, the path ahead looked pristine, as if they might have been the first humans to set foot in this land. Of course, she knew that wasn't true. There had been men through here to explore and map the land, and native tribes had lived here for God knows how long, and yet the place seemed still. Unnaturally quiet and dreamlike. The only thing she heard was the sound of their footsteps. The only thing she saw was the thin black crack in the sky.

Henrich only spoke once the sun had finally sunk below the vast horizon.

"It looks like a hut," he said, wiping sweat from his tanned brow. She squinted her eyes and tried to see what her husband could. In the distance, near the edge of the lake, was a small wooden hut, not much larger than a shack.

Her heart sank, and she hated herself for allowing hope and hunger back into the forefront of her mind. She tried to stay positive. At least it would be a place where she could sit down for a bit and give her aching feet some much-needed rest. And a roof over their heads was miles better than the dark, damp woods.

As the shack grew closer, it suddenly didn't seem quite as small, though much smaller than the house she and her family had inhabited back in Vermont, when times were easy. Still, maybe a small family lived out here near this enormous lake.

Beatrice didn't know an awful lot about the strange western expanse they were crossing, but she knew it was mostly uninhabited by civilized society until you got closer to the coast. She knew there were natives out in these parts but had only seen them once from afar. Could this hut be theirs? It seemed they were inching closer to the wooden structure at a snail's pace due to the vastness of the landscape. She tried her best to remove all thoughts from her mind, lest she drive herself mad with anticipation.

Eventually, they came upon the hut and its gently smoking chimney. The structure looked primitive, held together with various branches and clumps of mud, and yet it looked as sturdy as a boulder. Like it was just another part of the terrain that had been there century after century. The last rays of light trickled towards them across the shimmering lake, only a few short yards away from the structure. There were no trees. Only sagebrush and rock surrounded the water's edge and accompanying hut. Beatrice wondered just how long it would take to walk around such a magnificent lake, and her feet screamed out over the mere thought.

"Hello?" Henrich called, un-shouldering his heavy pack and setting down next to the rickety door. "Is anybody here?" As he approached, Beatrice stood back and watched, too exhausted to do much of anything else. Henrich, clearly not as transfixed by the dreamlike nature of their surroundings, banged on the front of the hut with an open palm. There was a faint shuffling sound from inside, and then a voice, as soft as a whisper.

"Come in," it said.

Henrich stole a glance back at her as if looking for some kind of reassurance, to which she simply shrugged.

"Come on," he said in an almost hissed whisper, seeming suddenly nervous. She took a few tentative steps forward, and together they opened the creaking door to the home and peered inside.

At first, Beatrice couldn't see anything at all, it was so dark. But then, after just a few seconds, her eyes adjusted, and she noticed a small fire against one wall. The fire was barely more than embers, but she was able to make out the shape of a woman hunched down next to it, tending to it as gently as one might care for a newborn babe.

Right away, Beatrice was hit with the enticing smell of something cooking. Over the fire was a small pot, and from it, the smells of carrots, onions, potatoes, and various other aromas wafted their way to her. Again, her stomach cramped, and all at once her mouth was watering.

"You must be hungry," said the shadow in the gentle voice of an old woman. Beatrice, not thinking in her hunger, took a step forward past the man next to her.

"Yes, ma'am. We are very hungry," she said, sounding loud in the stillness of the dark hut. Henrich grabbed her arm and squeezed, enough to make her wince.

"Well, there is plenty for the both of you. I don't have as much of an appetite as I once did."

"Ma'am," Henrich started to say and then stopped. "We are a bit lost. We got separated from our group last night."

"Come in. Come in and close the door," said the old woman, still not looking at them.

He did as he was told and shut the door behind them, plunging them both into the still blackness of the hut. As her eyes adjusted further, Beatrice noticed that the space was much larger than it had appeared from the outside. In the center sat a large wooden table with three chairs.

"We don't want to impose," Henrich muttered.

"Oh, nonsense. You'd be doing me a favor. I rarely get any company all the way out here."

"I'd imagine not," Beatrice said and smiled. Her father had always told her that her smile was her best quality and that it radiated joy to everyone who saw it. The woman finally turned to face them, and she smiled back. Her skin was wrinkled but not cracked, her features loose but never threadbare. Beatrice thought she looked surprisingly well put together for living out here all by her lonesome. Back home, she had known of people who lived all on their own out in the hills. It was a hard life. One that took its toll. But you'd never know it by looking at this woman's kind face. To Beatrice, she looked like someone's sweet grandmother.

"What a lovely smile you have, dear," the old woman said, returning her smile. "Contagious."

"Thank you."

"Sit. Let's get some food in you. Then, you can tell me all about how you became so lost."

Clearly exhausted, Henrich slowly made his way to one of the chairs near the wooden table. Taking this as her cue that she was able to finally sit, Beatrice accompanied her husband and pulled up a seat. They both sat, and Beatrice couldn't help but let out a satisfied groan as she got off her feet for what seemed like the first time in decades.

"Thank you, ma'am," Henrich quietly said as he sat. Beatrice didn't know her husband as well as some, but she knew he was a stubborn man. A man who didn't easily take help from others, no matter how badly he may need it. Pride, it seemed, was one of his defining features. So she was glad to see him relent somewhat. Glad for the both of them.

"Smells absolutely wonderful," Beatrice said, trying to be the polite young lady her parents raised.

"Why, thank you," she returned brightly. "It's a special recipe."

The old woman slowly and deliberately grabbed three bowls and three wooden spoons from the nearby mantel-piece, slopped hearty portions into each, and set them down on the table without spilling so much as a drop. Beatrice's stomach cramped with anticipation.

"Eat up," the old woman offered, giving the go ahead to begin without her. Beatrice was vaguely aware of how boorish she must seem as she dug into the piping hot bowl of goodness, but she cared little. She lived in that moment. The stew was great, but she would have eaten just about anything at this point. Her stomach cramped from the pace, and she had to take pause for a second or two. When she did, she noticed Henrich eating his, but at a much slower pace, like a penitent child forced to finish his dinner or go to bed hungry.

"Do you enjoy it?" asked the lady, now sitting across the table with her own bowl of steaming soup. The corner of her mouth ticked upwards in the vestige of a smile as she raised the spoon to her mouth and silently slurped. The hovel felt warm now. The fireplace and two oil lamps that hung from a rafter offered a hospitable glow, slowly erasing any of the harsh shadows that may have been previously present.

"Very much. Thank you again. We haven't had a hot meal in days," Beatrice said between spoonfuls. She had slowed down to savor the remaining liquid at the bottom of the bowl as well as to try to conjure her manners once more.

"And you?" the elderly woman asked, turning her attention to the man sitting at the end of the table.

He simply replied, "Yes. Thank you," then went back to slowly eating his meal, not looking at either of them.

"So tell me, now that you have had some nourishment, how it was you came to find yourself out here? In the middle of nowhere?" the woman asked, sweet as a pea.

"Well," Beatrice began as she wiped a thin stream of

gristle from her chin. "We were traveling with a party west towards California when we got separated from our group." She looked nervously to her husband, waiting for him to jump in, but when he didn't return her look, she continued. "We had fallen a bit behind the rest of the caravan. We only had our one ox and pack, but it was getting late, and we were hungry. Henrich isn't the most familiar with riding, so we didn't think we would catch up with the others until after dark. So, when we saw a rabbit bouncing through the brush, he decided to try and kill it with his rifle."

"I see," the woman said, nodding. Beatrice looked at Henrich again, expecting him to jump in and scold her for saying such disingenuous things about him. But he sat silently, plucking slowly away at his meal, seemingly oblivious to the two women conversing before him. "Don't worry about him," the lady said, regaining Beatrice's attention. "He is just hungry. Go on."

"Uh," Beatrice said, suddenly feeling a queer sensation rise up in her gullet. Maybe she had eaten too fast. "Well, determined to provide for us, my sweet Henrich jumped off the ox and gave chase to the bunny hopping into the woods. It was a fat rabbit. Big and brown. It would have been more than enough for the two of us. After I heard him calling, I went into the trees after him. To make sure he was all right. Of course, he was fine, but he had gotten a little turned around in the dense thicket of trees. Neither of us are familiar with the land here, so naturally, we got turned around. We were beginning to go in a canyon, so it was hard to tell which way was which. But it only got worse once the sun set."

She trailed off, thinking about how scared she had been once she realized they were truly and utterly lost. About how afraid she had been when she had heard the coyotes howling in the woods. About how difficult it was for Henrich to start a proper fire, so it was her that had to step in and complete the task. Which of course only served to further hurt the man's pride. They had found some berries that they were able to eat along with some jerky that remained in the single pack they had brought with them.

Suddenly, her stomach cramped with such intensity that she actually let out a harsh whimper.

"Everything okay, sweetie?" the woman asked, her smile still glued to her face. Beatrice realized she felt very strange indeed, that her creeping nausea had worsened, and she felt a bit like she was drunk. Her vision swam before her eyes, and her dizziness made the room feel like it was beginning to spin.

"I..." she began but stopped, closing her eyes shut in an attempt to shut out the spinning sensation. "I actually don't feel very good all of a sudden. I'm dizzy."

"Oh, honey, you've had such a long and exhausting trip. You just need some rest. That's what you need," the woman said, rising to her feet and making her way around the table. "Come. Come lay down."

Like a sick girl being led away by her attentive grand-mother, Beatrice went with the woman. Slowly, as not to stumble and fall, the woman led her to a corner of the room that had an inviting-looking bed with a straw mattress. Beginning to sweat, her sense of time began slipping away from her. Heavy and with no grace at all, she plopped onto the bed and almost immediately began to slip into unconsciousness. Above her, she could see the silhouette of the old woman, her face obscured by shadows now. Beatrice was certain the woman was still gently smiling, and that made her feel a bit better, if not just a little uneasy. Behind the figure, Henrich still sat at the table as if frozen, his spoon clenched in his hand and his eyes staring off blankly in front of him.

———

BEATRICE WASN'T sure how much time had passed, but she was certain it must have been days. Maybe even weeks. She had spent the time in a feverish dream state, only rising up from her sweaty and unrestful sleep to eat, drink, and relieve herself. All things the kind old woman was able to help her with. She must have gotten some kind of food poisoning either from the berries or from the stew. Either way, time passed in a haze.

Sometimes she dreamt. She dreamed of home and about a time that was simpler when very little was expected of her. Often though, her dreams would devolve and become corrupted. The childish, happy memories would melt into paranoid realizations of unseen danger lurking out of sight. These dreams would often turn into panic for seemingly no reason at all. She dreamt of the lake, the exceedingly endless mirror that lay like a jewel at the edge of the harsh mountain shelf. About something calling her out across the still and shallow waters. A sense emanating from the mirage that lay between the false sky and the heavens above. A place between worlds.

More and more often, she would find herself awake for

longer periods of time. The old woman fed her fresh fruits, porridge, and dried meats. She drank crisp water, and slowly but surely, began to regain a bit of her strength. She saw the woman attending to Henrich sometimes, no doubt afflicted with the same illness that plagued her. Sometimes, he would call out in pain, and she wanted to go to him, to comfort him in his time of need. She could hear the suffering in his whimpers through the darkness. Even though it had surely been days, she seemed only to wake during the night. She would like to see the sun again and feel its rays on her fevered gooseflesh, but sadly, dawn never came for her.

One perpetual night, she found herself standing on the shore of the lake, gazing out across its expanse, hypnotized by the shining stars that found themselves caught beneath its placid waves. She thought she might be dreaming once more, except she could smell the acrid salty smell of the lake in ways she had not before.

Again, something enchanted her towards it from deep beyond the blackness. A small light appeared where the horizon would have been had there been one, and she took a tentative step towards it. The calm seemed to grow stronger, more vibrant, with each passing step. Growing more pleasant and seductive as she grew closer.

Her old life—her life back home, her journey westward towards a new future, her falling sick—seemed to belong to another person. They were just a series of moments, barely remembered, like a dream of a dream.

Closer still, she drew towards the light. It began to fill her up, to replace everything that made her who she was. It was all that she ever wanted.

———

A TORTURED VOICE called out behind her, shattering the calm and causing the black midnight to come crashing back down. The pleasing glow was ripped away. Beatrice was standing on top of the surface of the water somehow for a brief moment before she fell into the murky lagoon up to her waist. The cold shocked her fully awake as she caught a gasp in her throat. She turned back to the shore, which was surprisingly far away.

She became hyperaware of just how quiet everything was. Dead silent. She again was overwhelmed by the salty smell of the water and the way it burned in the cuts and scrapes that covered her body. She hurt. She hurt all over. Her joints ached. Her skin crawled.

She could see Henrich lying in a darkened heap near the water's edge. As she was about to make her way towards him, she heard a slight sound above her head not unlike a crow taking flight. She looked up.

At first, the fear only crept in, bit by bit. But it crackled from her stomach and throughout the rest of her body, making her nerves flare red hot as she saw the woman floating above her, her face twisted and snarled to the point it looked barely human. The homely looking old woman who had helped her before was nowhere to be seen. Instead, floating ten feet above her head, was a cruel and hideous old hag staring down at her with such hatred and contempt that the gaze itself threatened to petrify.

Beatrice tried to scream but could not. She was frozen.

"RUN!!" Henrich managed to yell at her, sounding muffled and strained from his spot near the beach. That snapped her out of her daze, and she started sprinting towards him as fast as the water would allow her. She didn't want to turn her back on the evil floating woman but saw no choice. Adrenaline and panic had taken over, and she finally screamed, her voice carrying out into the desert for no one to hear.

As scared as she was, she still managed to feel the splash of water behind her as something fell. The water was to her knees now, and despite the strange ache in them, she pulled them high above the surface, hoping to gain some advantage. Screaming again as she felt the spray on the back of her nightgown, she tumbled forward next to Henrich and turned around.

The water rippled from all the splashing, but nothing seemed to be giving chase. She looked up into the moon-less sky and saw nothing insidious lurking there either. Breathing heavily, she turned her attention to the broken man that lay before her.

Horror and pity filled her as she gaped down at the barely recognizable man she had been so close to for the last several months. He looked up at her and drew slow, pained breaths. His face had been nearly peeled from his skull, leaving a red mask of drying muscle and infection. He was missing other parts of his body as well, including his left arm below the elbow and his left leg below the knee. Bits of flesh had been carefully removed from all over, slowly and over time, then tended to the point of finally healing. Some places were too damaged to heal properly, even though it was clear much time and attention had been given to each unique wound.

His wide, lidless eyes never left hers as his breathing grew shallower and shallower.

A cackle came from the darkness to her left, and without thinking, she jumped to her feet. She ran towards the hut, looking over her shoulder and seeing the pale eyes and flash of teeth kneeling over Henrich as he too disappeared into the dark behind her.

The thing in the shadows wore Beatrice's smile like a mask over its own.

The light from inside the cabin grew bright as she opened the door. The lanterns were lit again, and the flames in the fireplace roared gloriously.

The veil had been removed, and only now did she see things as they truly were. The cramped and cluttered hut was hung with strips of meat and fat. Mud and gunk covered the walls. Flies buzzed and crawled across every surface. The smell was enough to nearly take on a texture of its own. A bowl of dark brown sludge drew more flies on the table. It took all her strength to not vomit or scream. To not imagine the contents of the black stew. To not think about who it was that had been eating from it not long ago.

Her mind raced.

Frantic, she began to look around the mess for the rifle that had been with them on their journey to this godforsaken place. How long ago that seemed now. Almost another life. And yet it was impossible to actually gauge the passage of time. Henrich's wounds suggested they had been here months, but the reality was impossible to decipher. This was a place outside of time, where the watchful eye of God was blind to its terrors.

Against one wall sat a large Victorian mirror she hadn't

noticed before, and what she saw in it shook her to her core.

At first, she thought it might have been her mother, but as she stepped nearer, it was clear she was looking at herself. Somehow, she had slipped into middle age. Her once beautiful face was wrinkled. Her breasts sagged, and her hair had gone grey and wiry. Again, her bones ached. Her joints creaked. But the expression of horror on her face remained the same. Not only had the wretched witch taken her smile, but she had also stolen her youth. Fed off it like a parasite. She felt reality folding in on itself, like déjà vu times a thousand. She couldn't think. Her mind threatened to snap.

A loud pop from the fire made her start screaming. The damn had broken, and just like a dam, her screams had no choice but to come flooding through the cracks. She screamed so loud her vision began to shake. Her shrieks were only broken by the occasional sharp intake of air. She closed her eyes. Slammed them shut as hard as she could to get away from everything. If she was capable, she would have wished to be unconscious once more. Anything was better than this feeling of having her mind turned inside out.

"Shhhh…" A voice said, and she felt a leathery finger against her lips. The screaming caught in her throat, but she did not open her eyes.

The last remaining shred of instinct still working within Beatrice must have been just enough, because as soon as she felt that touch— that cold, dead touch— her immediate reaction was to strike back. Her fight or flight instinct finally realized there was nowhere else to run. No escape.

So she lashed out, immediately and without any sense of deliberate thought.

Her eyes shot open, and with one hand, she grabbed the flaming oil lamp that hung next to her head and smashed it down on the malevolent crone standing distorted before her. The remaining oxygen was ripped from her as both she and the old witch burst into flames with a magnificent whoosh.

She didn't know if it was the other woman screaming or herself, because the howl they produced seemed to become one. The white nightgown she was wearing, now muddy and disheveled, frayed and burned around her, as did her grey crown of hair. Beatrice had barely enough time to see the old woman's flesh begin to slough off her bones before she ran for the open door and out into the cool, dark night.

Her animalistic will to live was what drove her to the lake. She plunged into its salty waters, and the fires were extinguished with a ghastly hiss. Agony shocked her once more as the salt filled up her burns. Had she not barely had her head above the shallow, stinking water, she surely would have gulped a mouthful deep into her lungs.

The scream from the brightly burning shack diverted her attention from her own suffering. Slowly, she stood up and gazed at it with the half-sleeping eyes of a dreamer still not fully sure whether she was dreaming or not. Dead or alive. Not sure there was still even a difference. With great effort, she dragged herself to the front of the burning bungalow and sat down crossed-legged in the dirt before it. With the hint of a smile, she watched the evil woman and her home burn until the sun finally and mercifully rose in the east behind her.

That's how they found her.

The Marshall family and the rest of their thirty or so traveling companions came into the valley the next day. But when they saw the smoldering wood structure and the badly burned woman sitting on the ground before it, they did not think of Beatrice Caldwell. For they only saw a muttering old woman holding sun-bleached fragments of a skeleton long since stripped of its flesh, the incoherent whispers being her most memorable characteristic when people later spoke about the lady of the lake.

Levi Robinson has been deeply passionate about storytelling ever since he was a young boy. He spent his life dreaming up fiction. From screenplays and comics to song lyrics and short stories. He is only happy when he is creating. He has lived in Utah most of his life, where he has sought out like-minded individuals to share and collaborate with. He is constantly compelled to use his imagination to tell stories as a way of expressing himself and to share his voice with those around him.

WASATCH WITCHES

C.H. LINDSAY

The witches here
sing lullabies
to bulbous toads
with googley eyes.

They walk their cats
up mountain trails,
paint fallen leaves
to hang on nails.

Drink lemonade
with pinkies out,
eat custard tarts
and treacle stout.

Make candy floss,
then dye it red,
to build a house
of gingerbread.

But once the sun
has gone to sleep,
they stalk the night
'mid shadows deep.

In graveyards cold,
through darkest night,
they harvest names
while moon is bright.

With cat and toad
and teddy bear,
they tell the tales
that no one dare.

C. H. Lindsay is an award-winning poet & writer,
booklover, and housewife—not necessarily in that order.
She spent thirty years as an event planner, helping
organize and run science fiction, fantasy, and horror
conventions, and a decade acting in community theatre.

Now she prefers to stay at home with her family and write poems, short stories, and novels. This is her twelfth anthology. She's a member of SFWA, HWA, SFPA, and LUW. Mostly blind, she lives in Utah with her "seeing-eye husband," son, and a cat who thinks she's another child.

UNTIL NEXT TIME

K. SCOTT FORMAN

There are as many strange legends told of the Wasatch range as there are snowflakes in winter. To the Utes, the name means low pass over high range. The Shoshoni believe the mountains take their name from Wasattsi, one of their leaders now lost to time. The real origin is much older than the Indians, older than the Druids in Europe, or the ice covering Antarctica. Even the Old Testament prophets knew little of the doing of Wasatch the Sorceress, Wasatch the Giant, Wasatch the Bride, or Wasatch the Curser of Cain.

There is no reference to this woman in any known literature, not even in the obscure literature of the Jews, other than a vague mention of a witch that resided in a place called Endor, a place named after Wasatch's home when Pangea was the only continent.

Endor was a real place, a place where all witches trace their origin, a place that many still make pilgrimages to, a place found in the heart of the Wasatch Mountains of Utah.

I had been there. I had felt summoned to the place. That was where I met Dalca. That was where I started down the dark path.

I had gone to the woods often as a child, into the foothills. As I grew, I also grew brave enough to go deeper, to climb higher and enter the dark forests of the mountains. That was where it all began. Where I learned the story of Wasatch. .

To those of us who practice the craft, the more obscure arcana sometimes referred to as the dark arts is misinterpreted by many as being evil. The truth is, they are called the dark arts because they are hidden and unable to be seen by most. These, however, can be a steppingstone into the real darkness, the evil of murder, the sin of soul selling, and will eventually lead to finding Wasatch and the Curse of Cain.

I had heard as a child that Cain still walked the earth, that he had a mark set upon him by the God of the Old Testament, a mark that many believed looked a lot like Sasquatch. It had always been a speculation of religion or, at a minimum, a good campfire story intended to scare even the bravest. The thoughts of Cain walking, hidden and marked, in my lovely forests and mountains, was always at the back of my mind. And then it wasn't.

This is that story too.

It starts with a naked woman.

Almost naked.

I met this woman in the forests of the Wasatch, met her when I had almost completed my apprenticeship to Rahab, an old crone who fashioned herself a high priestess of the Uinta coven. Her name was Dalca, a name I found interesting but would have much more meaning later, but I am getting ahead of myself.

Dalca was one of thirteen witches in the Uinta coven. It was Halloween. It was approaching midnight. I was to perform a ritual that would demonstrate my loyalty to the high priestess and would allow me to replace one of the thirteenth witches in Rahab's coven. The ritual required the sacrifice of a living soul. The standard virginal female. I was fine with the idea in general, but there was one problem: I knew the sacrifice.

The shape of her body was familiar to me, or so I thought. We had become friends, spent time together, and did what friends do. Now, she was tied to the altar and clothed in sacrificial linens that left nothing hidden, even in the dull torchlight held by the twelve witches that surrounded us. Looking at her body, I could feel my face flush vermillion. I had mixed feelings. By sacrificing her, the thirteenth spot in the coven would be open for me to take. Destroying her would destroy a friend. I feared it might even destroy a piece of me.

"Take the blade. It is almost time, girl."

I was overcome with feelings, some familiar, most I wasn't sure where they came from or what they meant. I had felt the mists of magic, the dark and the light, and I knew that I was darkness, that it was my destiny. Even in the ebon, friends matter.

"It's almost time; ready the blade."

The old crone was irritating.

"I have the knife. I know what time it is."

"Good," said Rahab. "When the storm reaches its zenith, it will be time to strike."

The storm.

I had to admit, the old witch's powers were greater than I had anticipated, although I doubted her skills had conjured the storm. From what I had read, the demons she had called forth for the ceremony were more likely the influencers of the weather.

That's not to say I had not learned a lot from Rahab. The only reason I had submitted to her tutelage was to learn things I did not know, which mainly meant gaining access to whatever tomes of hidden knowledge she had on hand. I had read her few scant volumes, her single grimoire. Now, she had nothing left to teach me, and her plans were not my own.

"It's growing! The storm is growing! He is coming!"

He indeed.

If everything happened according to Rahab's plans, Azrael would appear to do her bidding. I seriously doubted Azrael would show up, and even if he did, nothing as powerful and malevolent as the Archangel of Death would serve a witch as inconsequential as Rahab.

"Ready yourself, girl! When the lightning strikes, you too must strike."

"I know what to do," I yelled.

I had read the spell she was using and doubted its accuracy. Before submitting myself to her instruction, I had read widely and studied deeply. Most texts about summoning malevolent beings warned about the consequences. I was certain Rahab would probably not make it through this night, possibly all of us, but something else was troubling me.

The sacrifice was Dalca.

Without warning, the storm grew in power and almost knocked me off my feet. I braced myself on the altar and jumped when Dalca's hand grasped my wrist. I looked down to see her smiling at me. She let go and then seemed to relax, closing her eyes as if waiting for death.

"Strike the blow! Do it now or all is lost!"

Despite my mistress screaming in my ear, the storm howling around us as if it would kill us all, and the sacrifice stretched out and secured on the altar stone, I paused. This wasn't at all what I wanted. I wasn't keen on killing an innocent, and Rahab herself had said to strike after the lightning.

"Explain to me exactly what will be lost," I shouted.

"You stupid girl, this is not a time to be talking or thinking. It is time to act. Give me the blade."

"What about the lightning?"

The air buzzed, and my hair stood on end anticipating the electric flash, and then it struck. As if by magic, the bolt hit the altar and illuminated the circle of witches. Thunder was immediate and jarred my bones. I blinked. I could see the autumn grass, the altar stone, Dalca tied to it, her lack of clothing. It was impossible. How could Dalca still be there. How could I see so clearly after—

"Strike now! Strike before it is too late!"

Another bolt of lightning. Thunder. My teeth hurt, and my ears felt like they were bleeding. Somehow, in the pain and confusion, I made a decision. Before anyone's eyes could adjust from the blinding blue electricity, I struck.

"What are you—"

Those were the last words the old sorceress would utter, at least in her mortal form. The crone's head separated from her neck. The blade was sharp, and it sheared the flesh and bone as easy as a razor splitting a hair. The head seemed to float, to hover, moving slowly to the altar, and then it dropped. It bounced on Dalca's chest, rolled onto her belly, and then between her legs. It just sat there, the eyes staring back at me in dumbfounded shock at what I had done. Dalca was still, frozen in the torchlight. I thought I could see her lips moving. The storm raged, thunder sounded from everywhere, and then lighting flashed again, striking the head between Dalca's legs, exploding it into a fine mist of blood and bone.

It was a sacrifice.

Despite dabbling in the dark arts, I would never betray a friend. Rahab had tricked Dalca, had given her a sleeping draught, had prepared her to be sacrificed. It wasn't right, even to someone as black-hearted as I believed myself to be becoming.

The thunder had deafened me, but I could feel a change in the air pressure, in the storm. Ozone saturated my nostrils but dissipated with the dying tempest. I was waiting for something to appear. Maybe the demon Rahab had summoned. I looked to the altar. The old witch's exploded head had covered Dalca's lower regions and made her look like she had had a rather bad—

"We need to get you dressed and cleaned up," I said.

"I knew you would do the right thing, that you would sacrifice the virgin."

I looked at Dalca. She was smiling. So calm, as if she—

"What? What do you mean?"

"Look at me, Rosalyn. With a body like this, do you think I would really be a virgin?"

"I, I…"

"You are now the thirteenth witch in my coven."

"Your coven?"

"Rahab's gone. I think she knew in the end who I was."

"Who you…"

I was confused. Dalca was a witch, I had known that, but I had never suspected she was anything but a pretender, a young, dumb girl with no gift for magic whatsoever, let alone dark magic. Now, especially after seeing her in a state of undress, she was much more than—

"A stupid girl?"

"Are you reading my mind?"

"Maybe. We need to go now."

I looked around. I hadn't noticed, but the remaining eleven witches had somehow disappeared. Had the storm, the lighting, what I had done to Rahab, a combination of it all—

"Yes, I'm sure they were frightened away, Rosalyn, and you think too much."

Dalca was smiling.

"Well, too much at the wrong times. Times you should be acting."

I was speechless. And thoughtless.

"We need to get going before the idiot that Rahab mistakenly summoned shows up."

"What? Azrael is coming?"

"You know the answer to that, at least part of it."

"Who then?" I asked. "Who is coming?"

"That would be me."

A dark, accented gravel sound filled the air. I could feel it run up and down my spine, the vibrations oozing some dark power. I turned to see a very tall, very hairy, very scary creature. It stood within a few feet of us holding a torch. It looked like it might have once been human. I felt Dalca's hand on my shoulder. I could feel her strength.

"Nice to see you, Wasatch, or are you calling yourself something new again?"

"What's it to you?"

"Just curious," said the giant thing. "Why would you summon me?"

"It's Dalca, and I wouldn't summon you if you were the last man on earth."

"Lovely. I always liked Romanian names. Lightning. How very fitting."

I stood there. I thought I felt myself going into shock, nausea in the form of acid coming up and into the back of my throat. Dalca's hand on my shoulder somehow gave me the strength to not fall in a faint or puke.

"Rosalyn, let me introduce you to my brother-in-law. Most think he's Bigfoot or Sasquatch, but to those of us who love him, Cain will do."

"If her hand was warm, the words from her lips would freeze more than Hell."

"Cain? You mean the brother of Abel?"

"The very same," said the beast.

At the mention of Abel, Dalca's grip on my shoulder turned painful. I flinched, and she relaxed, but the warmth I had felt earlier turned to a cold that filled my soul as if her fingers could freeze my heart in mid beat.

"My husband's brother."

"Your husband? What are you saying? I can't—"

"You can't believe it. Why not? You've read the

grimoire. The part about me and the Curse of Cain was almost true. Unfortunately, Rahab got the whole summoning part wrong and brought this."

"So, you were the first witch? Wasatch? You, not God, cursed Cain to walk the earth, put a mark on him?"

"You could say she put a spell on me."

The monster sounded like he was laughing at his wit. I wondered if I was dreaming.

"Yeah, I did, and what's left out of all the good books is that I was cursed too."

I paused. I couldn't really make sense of what was happening, let alone believe it.

"You expect me to accept that both of you have been walking the earth since the time of Adam and Eve? How did you survive the flood?"

"Two by two," said Cain.

There was evil in the creature's eyes, and he looked at Dalca as if he was going to eat her.

"By the time the flood came, I was considered more of an animal than a man, and Wasatch, Dalca, whatever, was supposed to be my mate."

"And look what the millennia have done to someone who hasn't been getting any. It would almost make them want to destroy the souls of women."

I was caught off guard by a sudden waft of stench that smelled of death and decay. It was as if Cain had done it on purpose.

"Only one woman," said Cain.

"Only one man," said Dalca.

"Thou shalt not suffer a witch to live."

"Begone murderer! There is nothing left here for you!"

43

At this, the beast laughed again.

"Just like my parents."

Cain looked at me now and continued.

"Do you know what it's like to be ignored by your parents? Tricked into marrying the nag of the herd, and your sister at that? Betrayed by your mother, hated by your father, cursed by the love of your life who chose your brother as her husband?"

"But it was your choice, wasn't it?" I asked.

Cain said nothing. He looked off into the darkness somewhere as if remembering something forgotten.

"And choices have consequences," said Dalca.

Her voice had become softer, as if sadness or longing was there.

"You are so right, sister, but what you fail to see are the consequences of choices that happened long before I killed my brother. My brother was my only friend, and I loved him, but the others, they drove me to it as surely as Lucifer himself."

"It is time to go, Rosalyn. Time to continue your training."

"Good seeing you, Wasatch. Until next time."

Her hand was still on my shoulder. I thought I could feel her heart miss a beat, her breath catch. I looked at her face. There was a yearning, and for a moment—

"Until next time, brother."

K. Scott Forman is the author of several short stories and poems. He is a member of the Horror Writers Association, enjoys long walks, sunsets with blood in them, and Metallica at volumes determined unsafe by the Surgeon General. You can find him at fearknocks.com

THE CRAZY CAT LADY

JO SCHNEIDER

"Where are you again?" my sister asked over my cell phone.

"I'm interviewing the Cougar Lady."

"I know, but where are you?"

"I can't say. She doesn't give her address out. Client privilege and all that." I stepped along the stone path that led from the driveway, across the pristine lawn, and past the meticulously manicured bushes. Three low stairs led to the door.

The porch swing and railing practically glowed white, as if they'd been painted the day before.

My sister snorted "You work for the university paper. I'm pretty sure client privilege is not a thing, Jackie."

"It's a thing." I checked the address in my notebook against the stacked numbers on the side of the door. "I'll have to call you back in an hour."

"Fine, but I want to hear all about the crazy cat lady."

"And I want to hear all about Brad." I hung up, slipped my phone into my purse, and knocked on the screen door.

A high-pitched yowl came from inside. I leaned forward. Was that a cougar cub? Or a regular cat? The sound stopped abruptly, and the door clicked open. I jumped back, straightened my shoulders, and smiled.

The Cougar Lady had never agreed to be interviewed before. Her stipulation to let me come had been that I kept all of this a secret until I published the article. I'd violated that with my sister—sort of—but no one else. Not even my editor at the paper.

None of that had seemed odd until this moment, and as the door opened, my heart sped up. What if she was legit crazy? What if I spent the next hour in a house that smelled like cat pee with cubs crawling all over me as I ate stale fruitcake to be polite?

That train of thought brought forth the image of a woman wearing a housecoat with her hair up in pink curlers into my mind.

Much to my relief, the screen door opened to reveal an elegant woman in her thirties. Curly brown hair hung past her shoulders, and she wore a refreshingly normal yellow blouse with blue trousers.

She smiled. It was radiant. "You must be Jackie."

"I am. You must be Marie." I held out my hand. "Thank you for seeing me today."

Marie clasped my hand firmly. "My pleasure. Please, come in."

Instead of plastic-encased couches and a layer of cat fur on the floor, the tidy sitting room Marie led me to held Victorian-inspired furniture and lights.

47

"Sit." Marie indicated the couch. "Would you like something to drink?"

I didn't, but I also didn't want to be rude. This could be my big break at the paper. I didn't want to ruin it. "Water would be great, thanks."

She nodded and left.

I took a moment to look around. Not what I expected, but in a good way. The pattering of small feet on the wood floors drew my attention, and I turned to find a single cougar cub peeking around the archway.

What was it about baby animals that made them so adorable? This one was a little bigger than a normal house cat, with brown fur and black spots. The markings around his nose made him look like he had a little mustache. I leaned forward. "Hi."

The cub cringed back but didn't run.

"Now, Jake, be polite." Marie returned with a glass of water. The cub followed her into the room, and she reached down to scratch his ears as she sat.

I accepted the offered glass and took a sip. "Is he purring?"

"He is. You can pet him."

Jake stopped purring as I lowered my hand. I let him sniff me and then scratched behind his ears. I expected his fur to be coarse, but it was soft. He butted his head against my hand, and the low rumble from his throat resumed.

Two more cubs peered around the archway.

Marie sat back. "So, Jackie, what did you want to ask me?"

I regretfully took my hand away from Jake's head and

opened my notebook. "First, thank you so much for allowing me to come over."

"My pleasure."

I looked away from her alluring smile and focused on my notes. "How did you get into raising rescue cougar cubs?"

"I just love animals." She picked up a new cub and put it on her lap. "I worked for a veterinarian for a while, and one day, someone brought in a cub whose mother had been killed. She was so cute, how could I resist? I took her home. That was years ago, and now I get rescues from all over the country."

"That's amazing. What made you think of loaning them to the university?"

"A friend from the office suggested I offer the cub as a mascot for a university function. It only took one volley-ball game, and then everyone wanted one at their event."

"They seem to like people." I reached out to pet the fourth cub to wander into the room. This one batted at my hand playfully. The oversized paws somehow made him even cuter.

"Oh yes, most of them wouldn't survive in the wild, so they end up in zoos. The more human contact the better."

I'd never heard that before, but I wrote it down anyway. I'd fact check later.

"How many cubs do you have?" I asked.

"Anywhere from three to seven."

"How long do you raise them?"

"That depends."

"On what?"

Marie leaned toward me. "I feel like I can be honest with you."

"Of course you can." I held my breath. I'd already proven most of the wild speculation on campus about some sort of cougar compound wrong just by walking into her house, but the more she gave me, the better.

"How old do you think I am?"

"Mid-thirties?"

"You're a doll. I'm over fifty."

I blinked. Flawless skin, perfect body. She must spend all her time and money staying beautiful. My mouth opened, and more came out before I could stop it. "Really? How?"

Marie laughed. "I've never had any surgeries, if that's what you're thinking."

"Now I'm torn between asking you about your beauty secrets or the cubs."

"What if I told you the two were related?"

"Oh?" Marie was probably one of those new age people who believed feeling youthful kept you young or something. Still, it was interesting.

"Yes. You asked me how long I raise them."

I nodded.

She crossed her legs—the cub fled—and put one hand on the back of the couch. "These little creatures have expiration dates."

Did the wildlife people have some sort of timetable for getting them to zoos? When she didn't elaborate, I asked, "What do you mean?"

"I mean, I raise them until they grow out of their cute stage."

My brain struggled to keep up. "So, you only keep them until they're too old to be seen as cubs at the university?"

"Oh, no." Marie patted my arm. "It's nothing like that."

Her words slurred a little. I felt like I'd stayed up all night. One of the cubs meowed, and it sounded as if it were underwater.

Marie picked Jake up and put him on her lap. "He's just a few weeks from expiring. Notice his spots are fading. When they do, I'll kill him."

I blinked, trying to parse her words and failing. "I'm sorry, you said you kill them?"

"The adults are ugly." She kissed Jake on the top of the head and let him go. He bounded after two others who were wrestling nearby. "I prefer to surround myself with adorable animals. Once they're not cute anymore, I kill them."

A drop of cold sweat ran down my back. I tried to put my notebook in my bag, but my hands wouldn't work. I dropped the pen and then my phone as I tried to get it from my purse.

"This is how I stay so young," Marie said. Her voice slurred, and her face blurred. "But I've had fewer cubs than normal this year, so I'm going to need a little more."

The strength drained from my arms, and my legs refused to work. A voice in my head screamed that I should run, but I couldn't move. I barely got my next question out. "What did you do to me?"

"Just a little potion." Marie stood and gently took my bag. "You won't feel a thing."

One of the cubs jumped onto the couch and curled up

in my lap. "Why?" I managed.

Marie leaned closer. Her eyes glowed green. "Because, my dear, you're almost to your expiration date. If I drain you now, your youth goes to me."

"My—my sister knows I'm here."

"Does she?" Marie put her hand on my chest. A white glow lit under her palm. My toes and fingers went cold. "Not to worry. I have a spell for that."

"A spell?" The cold crept toward my core, leaving numbness behind.

Marie smiled one last time. It was still painfully beautiful. "Yes. I'm a witch, you see. I've lived for generations. I don't normally kill humans, but I like you. Pretty, smart, ambitious. I'm doing you a favor. Your life will go downhill from here."

I opened my mouth to protest, but I'd lost feeling in my tongue.

"Now relax, Jackie, it will all be over soon."

Jo Schneider grew up in the wild west, and finds mountains helpful in telling directions. Goals include: travel to all seven continents, become a Jedi Knight, and receive a death threat from a fan. She's still working on the death threat. Jo writes science fiction and fantasy with amazing characters that she's not particularly nice to. You can find her at joannschneider.com

PERSONA NON GRATA

LEHUA PARKER

The doorbell won't stop, not for God or love or money. I open the door just wide enough to scowl at the woman on my front porch. She's not alone, but doesn't know it.

I've rehearsed this moment over and over, but seeing her in the flesh, I realize this is going to be harder than expected.

"Go away, Maggie," I say. "There's nothing here for you."

"Kiki, wait! Don't shut the door."

Maggie hasn't slept, and it shows. Since last Wednesday, I've watched her TV persona rotate between national press conferences and HallelujahNet, Salt Lake City's streaming megachurch channel.

On TV, in her televangelist power suits and sensible shoes, she stands next to her camera-ready husband, Reverend Phil. She cradles a picture of their missing daughter as he calls upon viewers to unite in a Power Hour of Prayer.

On my porch, she's wearing oversized sunglasses, sweats, and a hoodie pulled low.

Incognito.

But I know the real her.

She whips off the glasses. "Please. I'm begging. You've got to help me."

I cross my arms. "I don't have to do—"

"I know we've had our differences—"

My jaw drops. "*Differences*? Is that—"

"—but Celeste is your family, too!"

My eyes narrow. "As I recall, you and Phil made it very clear that I am *not* family. Admit it; you erased me from the photo albums. That's cold, Mags, even for you."

Maggie bites her lip so hard it bleeds.

"Kiki," she says, "please."

"I'm not in the family albums, am I?"

She dumps her glasses in her purse. "How would you even know something like that?"

I shake my head. "I know things, Maggie. You know I do. That's why you're here."

"I'm here because blood is thicker than photos," she says.

I sigh. We haven't spoken in nearly twelve years, but I know my sister well. If she's here, she's beyond desperate.

I state the obvious. "Phil doesn't know you're here."

Maggie shakes her head.

I glance up and down the street. "No reporters? No media?"

"No. I told the Reverend—"

"You call Phil *the Reverend*?"

"Only in public. Things—"

"Oh. So I'm public?"

"No, you're—" Maggie pauses.

I put my hand on my hip. "Well, which is it? Family or public?"

Maggie finally tastes blood on her lips and digs in her purse for a crumpled tissue. "It's complicated."

"Ya think?"

"Look, be mad at me. Hate me. But I know you love Celeste."

"And the Right Reverend Phil?"

"Fuck Phil," Maggie spits, spraying bright red droplets. "His way isn't working."

I throw the door wide. "Well, if it's fuck Phil, come on in."

As Maggie crosses my threshold, I grab salt from a nearby bowl and surreptitiously reset the warding. Stuck outside, there's an immediate wave of frustration from the invisible beasties trailing Maggie.

I swallow a snort of laughter. *Tough titty said the kitty. My house, my rules.*

They howl, but I just grin and shut the door. Nothing's coming in that's not invited, that's for damn sure.

Gran slips to the door, presses her eye to the peephole, and gives me a thumbs up. She points at Maggie, and I turn in time to see her aura leap, shining brighter and taller.

It's a good sign.

How much brighter, how much more herself would Maggie be if she could stay free of those beasties for an hour, a week, a month? I can lock them out of my house, but Maggie will always call them back. She can't banish what she doesn't recognize.

"How does it feel to be home?" I say.

"This was Gran's house, then yours. Never mine."

It's my turn to bite my lip.

Her eyes wander. "You changed the carpet for stone."

"Stone's easier to clean."

"Gran never let anybody wear shoes in the house," Maggie says.

"Yeah, well, now you don't have to worry about it."

"Painted, too."

"Lots of things change," I say.

"Hmmm," she says.

Maggie stands in the front parlor where I do my client readings. It's tasteful, but I admit it aligns with certain expectations. The table is shrouded in a long purple table-cloth embroidered with mystical suns, moons, and stars. It's flanked by a couple of heavy high-backed chairs. Dozing under fringe-trimmed silk are tarot and oracle decks. More for atmosphere than anything else, Gran's old Ouija board lies propped against candles and leather-bound books. Along the far wall is a bookcase filled with baskets of empty drawstring bags and collections of crystals, oils, and herbs.

And the odd skull or two.

"Have a seat," I say.

I don't have to see her face to know Maggie closes her eyes, says a prayer, and counts to ten before turning to me. "I'm sorry. I can't—"

"The kitchen, then. It's fine."

Disappointed, Gran throws up her hands and leads the way down the hall. She knows she won't be part of the spectacle there.

Nestled at the back of the house, the kitchen is bright and sunny. Herbs in pots line windowsills. On open shelves are canning supplies, a pickle crock, and jars of spices labeled cinnamon, ginger, and star anise. Beside the open-hearth fireplace are Gran's knitting basket and rocking chair. In the middle of the room is a big farm table with a bowl of red apples on a hand-crocheted doily.

The kitchen is another kind of stage, but one Maggie associates with childhood, not parlor tricks. As she draws closer to the room, I feel relief wash over her like a waterfall. The farm table and benches worn smooth remind her of Gran's Sunday towers of mashed potatoes, gravy, biscuits, and ham.

I see the farm table and remember the day I lovingly washed Gran, the shroud linens sheer and damp, sticking to the table as I rubbed potions deep into her skin. When I asked what to dress her in, Gran said since she was meeting God, it ought to be her Sunday best. When I asked whether to serve cake or cookies, Gran said it didn't matter to her. The dead don't eat.

Memory is a funny thing.

Halfway to the kitchen, I pause to consider my cards and crystals. I don't need them—no real witch does—but clients do. Regular folks need tangible things to shuffle and caress; it's what makes the ephemeral corporal, the magic real. To my clients, our time together is not about me; it's the cards.

In truth, all I do is tell them what they already know.

But Maggie doesn't believe in trappings or tricks. I nod to myself. Cards would only get in the way; she'd ignore or dismiss them.

As Maggie sits in the kitchen, bathed in lemon-yellow sunlight, inhaling fresh basil and mint, when I speak, I want her to know it's me and not cards or crystals.

Belief is always a choice.

I walk into the kitchen empty-handed, grab the cutting board and knife from the counter, and sit across the table from Maggie. With her back to the hall and fireplace, she's looking down at her lap and worrying her lip raw.

"Here," I say, pushing the board towards her. "Apples and cheese. Eat something. You're too pale."

"You cut the skins off."

"So?"

"That's how Celeste likes them, remember? When she'd come here, you'd always spoil her by cutting off the skins." Maggie reaches out, but doesn't pick up a slice.

"Skins can be bitter."

I glance down the hallway and spot a shadow hovering near the door to the guest room. I shake my head at it, but it doesn't retreat.

Stubborn.

Fine. But eavesdroppers seldom like what they hear.

Maggie's hand still wavers over the apples and cheese.

"Oh, for hell's sake!" I snag the unsliced half of apple and bite. "See? No poison."

Maggie lifts an apple slice and takes the tiniest nibble.

I choose my words carefully. "I don't know what you want from me, Mags. The police are looking for Celeste. Hell, the whole country is looking for her. I have nothing to offer. In fact, I'm a dangerous influence. I'll lead her straight to hell. Just ask Phil."

"Kiki—"

"And that's another thing. Twelve years! You don't get to call me Kiki. Only family calls me Kiki. Call me Janet, just like the UPS guy and the lady who does my taxes."

Names have power.

"Okay, *Janet*. Or should I call you *Madam Janet*?"

A sliver of apple sticks in my teeth. "No," I say, "Her Serene Celestial Royal Highness will do." I take a bite of cheese to keep myself from saying something I'll regret.

Maggie takes another nibble, then shoves the whole slice into her mouth. "Janet," she mumbles around the apple, "Janet, Janet—Janet is the name on your driver's license. That's not who I need. I need Auntie Kiki."

"Auntie Kiki is dead."

"Don't be like that."

"That's what Phil told her," I say.

Maggie nods. "She cried when he told her, cried and cried until he said you'd gone to heaven to play with Jesus."

I snort and roll my eyes.

"Phil made a game of it. He'd send her outside to watch the clouds, saying good girls could see Auntie Kiki playing the harp. She never did, of course."

"That's sadistic, even for a self-righteous son of a bitch like Phil."

Maggie dabs at her lip. "Phil was right, though. She only cried for a couple of days. The young are resilient. They bounce."

"I didn't bounce."

"No," Maggie says. "You remember, don't you? You remember it all. How Kiki was her first word. Not Mama or Dada. *Kiki*. How she loved digging in the garden with you. Tarrwots, remember? She called them tarrwots."

"Of course I remember. Tarrwots and green knees." I don't dare blink. No matter what she says, I will not cry. I'm done with tears.

Maggie leans forward. "And after her dinner, remember how she smelled fresh from her bath?"

"Like marigolds and starshine."

"Remember how she snuggled when you read her a story and how she loved thunder and lightning, but only if she was with you?"

"Yeah."

"You two had a connection. It was like you could read each other's minds. You always knew what she was thinking and feeling. When she needed a snack. When she needed a cuddle. When she needed to be brave. In some ways, she was more your daughter than mine."

"Celeste is *your* daughter, Maggie. None of this is on me."

"But do you remember how it was? How tight you were?"

"Yeah, I remember. I remember it all. I remember how Phil took Celeste away from me. And how you didn't stop him."

She shrugs. "I'm not going to lie. It was easier without you around."

I open my mouth to say all the words that will end this right here and now, but I don't. Ending it now won't actually end it. Eventually, Maggie will be back, seeking the answers she can't find anywhere else.

But I can't let her think I'm a pushover, either.

I raise an eyebrow and say, "Sister, if this is how you kiss and make up, you need to leave. Now."

Lost in memory, she says, "Without Auntie Kiki, Mama reads the stories. Mama dries the tears."

I can't believe my ears.

I say, "That's the most selfish, asinine thing you've said in a lifetime of assholery. There is always enough love to go around."

She snaps back to the present. "It wasn't selfish to keep her safe."

"From me?" I cross my arms. "You've been drinking Phil's Kool-Aid too long."

"Get over yourself, *Janet.* There are real dangers in the world. You're just Phil's excuse."

From her purse, she pulls out a toy.

I snatch it.

"Miss Kitty!" I turn the cat over and over. "Miss Kitty! I thought you burned."

"No. Toby Tiger burned. Phil never noticed the difference." She slips another pale apple slice between swollen lips. "While he raged, I hid Miss Kitty in a shoebox. I couldn't give her back to Celeste, even though she cried longer for Miss Kitty than for you." Maggie tilts her head. "How does that make you feel?"

"Now you're just being a bitch."

"Maybe, maybe not. It took me a long time to realize the problem wasn't Miss Kitty." She pauses to crumble a bit of cheese between her fingers. "Or you," she sighs.

Keeping her eyes on the cheese, she says, "The day Phil pronounced you dead, Celeste was supposed to be napping. Phil heard her giggling, so he went into the room to…to…to *redirect* her. She was sitting up in bed, laughing and clapping as Miss Kitty danced over her head. Phil swore the toy was possessed—and you'd given it to her. But it wasn't a spell you'd cast or a devil you'd summoned." She looks up. "It was Celeste. She's like you."

I slowly smooth Miss Kitty's fur and work hard to keep my tone neutral. "I'm sure Phil beat the devil out of her."

Maggie sighs. "He didn't have to. Kids don't remember."

"The hell they don't."

She shakes her head and brushes cheese crumbs from her fingertips. "Celeste doesn't remember you or Miss Kitty flying or the imaginary friends she used to talk to. Trust me. A mother knows."

"Uh-huh. Well, if you know so much, why come to me?"

She enunciates like each word is fire on her tongue. "You see what *is*."

I lean forward. "The news said Celeste was kidnapped, but there was no ransom demand. Do you think she ran away?"

Maggie sighs. "You tell me. I want the truth, whatever it is."

I sit back. "I can tell if she's alive or not, but if somebody's got her, I can't whisk her back home. If she doesn't want to be found, she won't be. I can't actually *do* anything."

Maggie slams her hand on the table. The knife on the

cutting board jumps. "All I'm asking is for you to do for your niece what you do for strangers." She opens her purse. "Is it money? How much?"

"How dare—"

She waves a pocketbook at me. "Why, Janet? Why do you have to make everything so bloody hard?"

"Put your money away."

"I'm the one risking the most here!"

I raise my voice. "Put it away! You have no idea what's at stake, Maggie."

"My daughter! My daughter is at stake!"

I breathe in basil, mint, and lavender and count to ten.

Is it enough? I wonder. Is she ready to pick a card and let me read the future she already knows?

I say, "The police? FBI? What do they think?"

She tosses her pocketbook back into her purse and dabs her eyes with a tissue. "They're split. Some think she left on her own; others think she was taken. Her browser history was wiped, but her cell phone and wallet were on her dresser. Nothing suspicious in her text messages. They think—" She looks into her lap and whispers, "They think it might have been someone from the church."

I touch my sister's hand. "You may learn things you'd rather not."

"But at least I'll know."

"And Phil?"

"Fuck Phil."

"Yeah, you said that." I turn Miss Kitty and look her dead in her marble glass eyes. I give Maggie one last out. "In the end, there's no guarantee you'll get her back. Still want to do this?"

"I have to."

Maggie's card is on the table.

Showtime.

I take a deep breath. "Okay. I'll do it."

"Oh, thank God, Ki—I mean, Janet. Thank you."

I gather my will and set a shield around us. I don't want any stray *something* getting in the way of what I'm about to do. Maggie's blind but not dumb.

I cradle Miss Kitty and think of the young girl who cherished her and the young woman she's become. I think of my sister and what I need to say. I close my eyes, find the soul thread I'm looking for, and *tug*.

"Uuuugggghhhh," I moan.

"What?" Maggie leans in.

My hands start to shake. The memorized words trip off my tongue. "Celeste! By Michael, the Archangel, and all saints past and present—"

"Do you see her? Is she all right?"

I'm not even through the first part.

"Shhhh!" I say without opening my eyes. "Be still. The connection's faint."

"That's good, right? That means she's—"

My eyes pop open. "It doesn't mean anything."

"You talk with the dead—"

"And sometimes the unborn, sometimes the never-born, and occasionally the still living. Hell, trees and butterflies and fishes—even rocks. Look, Celeste and I have an unusual connection. Over the years, I've been able to sense her, but right now there's something in the way. I need to center and try again."

I wiggle in my seat, clear my throat, and close my eyes. "Celeste! I call upon—"

"What? What's in the way?"

I fling open my eyes. We're never getting through this, and this is the easy part.

"You! You're in the way." I jump up, walk to the rosemary pot, and break off a sprig. I wave it over Maggie's head and around her shoulders, muttering under my breath. Gran sits in her rocker and yawns like it's all too much for words.

But clients are clients.

"Here," I say, thrusting the rosemary at Maggie. "Hold this."

"Why?"

"Just do it. Your negativity is harshing the vibe."

"I'm not holding a frigging twig. This is ridiculous," she says.

"You came to me, remember? And how is this more ridiculous than Phil's Power Hour of Prayer?"

"It just is."

"Take it."

Maggie sets her jaw.

"Take it or I break out the crystals and tarot cards!"

"Fine. I'll hold it. Sheesh."

"And shut up!"

"Okay."

"I mean it. No talking."

Maggie pretends to zip her lip.

I give her the hairy eyeball for a few beats, then sit back down. I need to turn this train down the right track, but Maggie won't be easily led.

Sisters are the worst.

I tuck Miss Kitty under my chin and take a deep cleansing breath.

"Let's both close our eyes and concentrate on Celeste."

Maggie nods and bows her head.

I reset the shield and begin again.

"Celeste! It is I, Auntie Kiki, who summons."

I sneaky-peek with one eye.

Maggie's eyes are still closed.

Good.

My voice drops an octave, chugging down the track.

"Celeste! Bone of my bone, blood of my blood! By the four corners and two poles, by lightning and wind, summer and spring!"

My hands shake first, then my whole body. The bench starts to rattle; the knitting basket tumbles across the floor as air rushes down the chimney. The train's at full speed.

My voice raises to a shriek. "I call to you through time and space! Reveal, reveal, reveal!"

I gasp and go stiff as a board.

Miss Kitty tumbles to the floor.

I open my eyes.

Maggie's eyes are round. She's breathing like the last mile of a marathon. "Did you find her?"

I nod. "You don't have to look anymore."

"What?"

"She's gone from you, Mags. She's at peace."

"How do you know?"

I look past Maggie's shoulder to the figure in the hall.

Maggie crumbles. "She's here, isn't she? She's standing

right behind me. I can feel her. Oh, Celeste, baby, I'm sorry, so sorry. What happened?"

I shake my head. "It doesn't matter. None of it matters now."

"Tell me."

The figure in the hall nods and sweeps her fingers at me.

She wants me to tell her mother.

I roll my neck, easing the tension. Although I've rehearsed what to say, it still sticks in my throat.

"Celeste snuck out of the house around 2 a.m. She didn't take her phone because Phil put a tracking app on it. She didn't take her wallet because she had no money to spend."

Maggie leans forward. "What was she wearing?"

"What?" I blink. The narrative's broken. "Why?"

"I need to know if you're telling the truth. What. Was. She. Wearing!"

When I look down the hallway, I can just make Celeste out if I squint. She points to her pants, then her shirt, and holds up her shoes. I say, "Gray fleece pajama pants with black cats on them, a black t-shirt, pink and grey Vans, no socks." She holds up her wrist. "Oh, and a leather bracelet, with, um, dancing alpacas on it." She shakes her head. "Or maybe llamas." She nods. "Yeah, llamas. I get those two mixed up."

"OhGodohGod, it's her. It's really her. We kept the Vans out of the news reports. I never told anyone about the bracelet. She'd come home with it just the day before." Maggie hiccups and pulls another tissue from her purse. "I thought some boy had given it to her. Told her to take it off before her father saw it."

I open my mouth but bite my tongue. Some things are better left unsaid.

I tug on my sister's soul thread, sending waves of calm and tranquility. I hope she'll skip this next part, that she'll just accept Celeste isn't coming back and leave. But I know my sister. She's going to want to follow her daughter's story to the bitter end.

Maggie drops the rosemary sprig and blows her nose. Her lip is bleeding again, but she ignores it. "Tell me," she says. "Everything."

I catch the eye of the shadow in the hallway and raise a brow.

She nods.

I know this part, too.

"Celeste was walking along River Road when a white panel van pulled past her and stopped."

"White van?" Maggie looks at the ceiling. "White— Tom? Tom Marco's plumbing truck! Oh my God, TOM? I'll kill that son of a bitch."

I latch onto Maggie's arm to keep her seated. I screw my eyes tight and pinch the bridge of my nose, but I don't know what to say. Tom's not part of the story.

I look down the hall. The shadow is still there. Celeste shakes her head. Nobody, she mouths. It was nobody.

By the fireplace behind Maggie, Gran rocks faster.

I say, "No, it's not Tom. It was nobody—nobody she or anyone knows."

"But—"

I hold up a finger, shushing Maggie before she can

speak. It's clear only Celeste can tell the story.

"Give me a second," I say.

I open my mind and invite Celeste in.

Things get wavy as I feel a *push*. There's a snap of electricity that travels from my toes up my spine and lodges in my chest. My heartbeat—*Celeste's heartbeat*—thunders in my veins as adrenaline squish-squish-squishes. Her thoughts are my thoughts—her feelings, my feelings.

Blood calls to blood. We are—as ever—connected.

And then from my mouth, her voice: *"Mom?"*

"Celeste! Is it you?" Maggie grips my arm, her knuckles white.

Pain shoots to my head. This time when I moan, it's real.

"Talk to me, Celeste! Momma's here!"

Celeste says, *"I didn't run when the van pulled over or when he asked me where the nearest gas station was or if River Road meets I-15. By the time I knew to run, it was too late. I woke in the back of the van, blindfolded and gagged."*

Maggie doesn't breathe.

"Momma? He hurt me, Mom. Bad. He called them games, but he always won. He's done this before, many times. I disappointed him. I died too fast."

Like coffin nails on a chalkboard, sound explodes from Maggie's chest, a volcano wail of a mother's soul shredding. Her pain hits me like a blast furnace, spinning my delicate connection out of control.

"Tell me, baby. Tell me so I can find this monster and make him pay!"

I shield hard and search for Celeste. She speaks.

"You can't. He's smart. He never hunts in the same place

twice."

"What does he look like? There's got to be something you can tell us."

"There's nothing. He took my eyes, first thing. He wanted to be the last thing I saw, but I don't remember anything except red. The taste, the sound, the smell of red."

From my mouth, Celeste's voice is flat and hollow, isolated from the pain and horror.

Bodies feel.

Spirits think.

Maggie rocks like a mother with a fussy toddler. "Celeste, honey, where are you?" She calls out to the kitchen. "I need to bring you home so you can rest in peace."

When Celeste paints me a picture of endless desert, I flinch.

A raging bonfire.

Ashes shifted.

Chemicals.

More ashes.

Black liquid swirling down gas station toilets and rest area porta-potties, dumped into irrigation ditches and ponds; Celeste is everywhere and nowhere.

Are you trying to kill her? I mentally shout. *I'm not telling her that. No mother deserves that.*

Celeste breaks our connection and leaves it up to me.

I clear my throat. "Celeste says there's no body to bring home. He scattered her ashes."

"Ashes? Where?"

"I'm not sure. The image is, um, dark. In water, I think."

"Oh, God!"

"It's peaceful. I mean, she's at peace. She's good."

"Good? My baby is alone!"

"I don't think she's alone."

Maggie pauses. "You mean Gran's with her? How can that be? Gran was...Gran was—"

"Like me."

"Exactly."

I say, "Of course Gran's with her. Gran's always been with her. Where else would Gran be?"

Behind Maggie's back, Gran rolls her eyes and picks Miss Kitty up from under the table, making her dance three feet off the floor. I give Gran the evil eye until she sets Miss Kitty down. In a huff, Gran passes through Maggie and heads down the hall to Celeste.

Maggie rubs her arms and says, "Is Celeste still here? I felt something cold pass by."

I peek down the hall.

Celeste is gone.

"No," I say. "She's moved on."

"With Gran?"

There's a thump and muffled giggles coming from Gran's old room, my guest room now.

"Yeah. I think Celeste was just waiting to talk with you."

"What happens now?"

I shrug. "She'll transition to a new existence. I can tell you she's joyous and excited at all that's to come. It's not how you wanted it, but trust me, we all go through it. We all leave the nest. Celeste is just transitioning a little sooner than expected."

71

Maggie abruptly stands. "You don't seem upset."

"It's not news to me."

"You knew?"

"Bits."

Maggie's eyes narrow. "You saw Celeste."

I shrug.

"When?"

I sigh. This part's tricky. I meet Maggie's eyes.

"A few days ago."

Maggie curls around the gut punch I've delivered and sinks back down on the bench. "Days. And you didn't call? We're sisters!"

I tell the truth. "You weren't ready to believe."

Her hand flies to her mouth. "Oh, God. Phil. What do I tell Phil?"

"Fuck Phil, remember? He's the whole reason it's come to this."

Maggie shoves her purse over her shoulder. "You can't blame him."

"Watch me."

She glances at the kitchen clock. "It's almost three. I've got to run." She stands and gathers her purse and tissues. "We're on again at five. Damn it! What am I going to tell the press?"

"Nothing. Celeste will just be a missing girl whose family refuses to engage with them—that's boring. They'll move on to juicer clickbait fast. Promise."

"And Phil's Power Hour of Prayer?"

I stand and square my shoulders. "Again, tell them nothing. Prayers harm no one. We could all use good thoughts and energy sent our way, living or dead."

She slides on her sunglasses. "I can't believe my baby's gone."

When Maggie sniffs, she spies Miss Kitty under her bench. She starts to bend, but I'm faster.

"Miss Kitty stays with me."

Maggie opens her mouth to protest, but I cut her off.

"I think we're done," I say and move toward the front door.

Maggie blows her nose and follows.

As she crosses the threshold, her little beasties wrap their claws around her arms, legs, and spine. One sits on her head like a party hat and whispers in her ear. She draws herself up.

"I don't believe you. You're just like Gran—a fake, a phony, and a fraud who leads people away from the truth."

I sigh. It's her voice, but the beastie's words. "Wow. A fake, phony, and a fraud. That's a lot of Fs. You're pretty fond of that sound today."

Maggie scowls. The beastie on her head sticks out its tongue. Gran leans over my shoulder, threatening it with a rolling pin. It cowers, its fear goosing Maggie into action. She doesn't know why, but she raises her hood and hides it.

Like that's going to help.

Her beasties are so ridiculous, I grin.

But Maggie doesn't see Gran or the beasties.

She snaps, "It's all a joke to you, isn't it? What kind of person tells someone that her daughter is dead? *Tortured* and dead! A sociopath, that's who. You never loved us. You can't love anything."

"Whatever, Maggie. Remember, you came to me."

"Phil's right. Celeste *was* better off without you. *I'm* better without you."

"Okay."

"You think you know things, so know this," she sniffs. "This was a mistake. You won't see me again."

"Kinda what I'm counting on," I say and shut the door.

Gran watches through the peephole until Maggie's car is out of sight.

"You're sure we'll never see her again?"

Gran nods.

"From your lips to God's ears," I say.

Behind me, applause breaks out.

I turn.

Celeste grins and takes a bite of freshly peeled apple. "Oscar-worthy, Auntie Kiki. That was awesome."

Lehua Parker writes speculative fiction for kids and adults, often set in her native Hawaii. As an author, editor, and educator trained in literary criticism and advocate of indigenous cultural narratives, Lehua is a frequent presenter at conferences, symposiums, and schools. Her hands-on workshops and presentations for kids and adults are offered through the Lehua Writing Academy. Connect with her at www.LehuaParker.com.

FOR SCRYING OUT LOUD

CARYN LARRINAGA

Here's the crappy thing about scrying: the mirror doesn't always tell you what you want to know. It only shows you what you need to see.

I don't know. Maybe that's a good thing. What I want to know is usually stuff like, "When will I meet my soulmate?" and "How much money should I save before quitting to open my own salon?" Sometimes, those are the deepest needs we have, I guess. But my point is, don't expect the mirror to cooperate every time you want something.

And don't be surprised if it shows you something you didn't want to see—even when you didn't ask it a question.

Most of the time though, my mirror and I were in agreement about what my scrying should show me, especially the mirror at my station at work. Those days, I just needed to see something to make my clients happy, something that would get them feeling giddy enough to leave me a big fat tip.

"Oooh," I told a bridesmaid who came in for an updo one day. "I see a handsome guy in your future. I'll be doing your hair for *your* wedding next."

My customer smirked. "That's pretty vague. I thought you were supposed to be this super-psychic hairdresser."

I got her type in my chair a lot. The loudmouthed skeptics were the ones who, deep down, really wanted to believe. But the more life let them down, the louder their pessimism got. There were few things more satisfying than knocking the skepticism out of somebody with a solid reading, so after checking over my shoulder to be sure my boss wasn't watching, I set down my curling iron, rested my hands on my customer's shoulders, and focused all my energy on the mirror.

Reflected in front of me was a red-haired twenty-something girl in a black salon cape. She sat in front of a short woman with an aquiline nose and—if I do say so myself—totally on-point glam makeup. I unfocused my eyes, looking past the truth of the moment into whatever the mirror might be willing to show me.

A calm washed over me. Goosebumps broke out along my arms, but it was a pleasant sensation, like when a friend gives you the chills by dripping an imaginary egg down the back of your scalp.

After a moment, our reflections swirled like an incoming fog. The image soon cleared, and instead of the monochromatic salon in which I stood, I saw a group of young, well-dressed merrymakers toasting a red-haired bride and her groom. I focused on the couple, trying to lock the details in my memory before the vision faded.

"You look pretty much the same as you do right now, so I'd say… this is within the next couple of years," I said as our reflections returned to normal. "Your husband has a burly beard and a fade, and flared gauges in his ears."

The client in the chair next to mine gasped and rested her hand on her chest. "Oh my God, Sidney—that's Bobby! You know, Misty's cousin? He'll be at the wedding! I always thought you two would be good together."

"The dude's hot." I wiggled my eyebrows. "If you don't want him, I'll take him."

An hour later, I pocketed a hefty tip and waved the happy bridesmaids out of the salon. As I turned around to get my station ready for my next client, my boss marched up to me, arms folded and eyes narrowed.

"Nekane, did you log that tip?" Benny demanded. "Or did you think I wouldn't notice you slipping it into your smock?"

I pasted a fake smile onto my face. "I was just on my way to key it in."

"Don't bother. I saw you doing that thing again. I told you to keep your black magic out of my salon."

Years of dealing with Benny's nonsense had allowed me to perfect the art of the eyeroll, but I had to balance that expertise with the need to keep a roof over my head and the desire to be my own boss someday. I forced my pupils to stay locked on his mustachioed face and calmly explained for the fiftieth time, "I'm just scrying, Benny. It's no different than you praying to your god for guidance."

"It's witchcraft." He scrunched up his nose in disgust,

clearly uncomfortable even saying the word. "I've put up with it for way too long. And the Bible is clear: 'Thou shalt not suffer a witch to live.'"

"Huh. And here I thought your motto was, 'Thou shalt not suffer a stylist to make a living.'"

Two pink spots appeared on his cheeks. "I pay fair wages."

"Right. Taking tips out of our checks is totally fair."

"Well, you're free to find something else." He pointed to the door. "Take your witchcraft and get out. You're fired."

Just like that, my dream of opening my own salon poofed out of existence.

I could have fought it, but he had me dead to rights for not reporting my cash tips. Taking time off while I hunted for a new job wasn't an option, and when I asked my mirror to show me the path forward, I saw myself behind the wheel of my car. Never one to ignore a clear vision, I filled out an online form, printed a decal for my windshield, hung a Royal Pine air freshener from my mirror, and bought some barf bags for the back seat.

Bada-bing, bada-boom. So long, Benny. Hello, gig life.

My first night driving rideshare started off at the airport, where a family of four tested the limits of my Versa's trunk space. From there, passenger after passenger led me on a tour of the city, and within a few hours, I'd seen four new neighborhoods I didn't even know existed.

I drove with my windows down, reveling in the warm summer air and the short bursts of socializing that came with every ride—quick low-stakes conversations with people I would probably never see again. I had to resist giving everyone who climbed into my back seat unsolicited advice about styling their hair, but apart from that, I thought I was doing a phenomenal job. The tips were steady, and I imagined saving up enough money to open my salon across the street from Benny's so I could drive him right out of business.

A spiteful smile curled the edges of my lips, but the pinging of my phone interrupted the fantasy. Another ride called my name. Plotting my revenge would have to wait.

The app took me downtown to the club district, a place I hadn't been since the wilder days of my youth. It was after midnight, but the street hummed with energy. The bassy music pouring out of the open doors reverberated through my windows and up my arms, and it took all my willpower to resist popping into a club for a few vodka tonics and some dancing. I reminded myself that it wasn't good enough to scrape by doing this. I had to hustle—really push myself—if I ever wanted to open that salon.

A tiny icon on my phone's screen guided me to the pickup point. There, a willow-thin girl in a shimmering gold dress swayed on the sidewalk.

I rolled down my window and read the name from my phone. "Victoria?"

"Yeah. Nekane?" she asked hesitantly, mispronouncing my name like *knee cane.*

"*Neck-ah-nay,*" I corrected. "Hop on in."

She slid into the back seat. Her smokey eyeliner had smeared into "it's been a long night" territory, and her thick, dark hair was matted to her forehead with sweat, like she'd been dancing on the surface of the sun. Her cheeks ballooned, and she burped. She murmured an apology and tilted her head back against the seat.

I glanced at the destination that popped onto my phone and, to be on the safe side, handed the girl a barf bag. "You live up by the cemetery, huh? That's a cool area."

Her hand flopped to the side, dropping the bag onto the upholstery. "I don't live here. It's a"—another belch, impressively large for her tiny frame—"rental."

"Oh, what are you in town for?"

A dainty snore was my only answer.

She dozed lightly as I drove us through the hills to the city's cemetery. I drank in the sight of the beautiful historic homes, most of them lovingly restored and painted in cheerful colors. I would have happily traded my apartment for any of them.

Victoria's destination, though... not so much.

The house faced the cemetery, and it looked like it had been abandoned for decades. Broken windows gleamed like teeth in the moonlight, and tall weeds reached right up to touch the peeling paint on the door. I assumed the Addam's Family decided it was too run-down for their tastes and decamped for something a little classier.

I glanced at the rearview mirror, about to ask Victoria if she was really staying in this dump. As my eyes flicked upward, a shiver ran down my arms.

The mirror didn't show me the girl as she'd looked when she left the club. She still wore the gold dress, but her once-cute face was slick with blood. Chunks of gore—from what, I couldn't say—were scattered across her cheeks and hair, and her glassy eyes bulged out of their sockets.

A shriek exploded out of my mouth as I jerked my head away from the mirror to check on her.

She wasn't behind me.

My car's door hung open, and Victoria stumbled up the walk toward the house.

I checked my mirror again, but the vision faded. I saw only my own worried face in front of an empty back seat.

"Crap," I muttered.

I didn't love the idea of chasing after a drunken stranger, but what else could I do? My visions had never been wrong before. All I knew was that if I didn't do something, the image of her bloodied face would haunt me every single time I looked in the mirror for the rest of my life.

I didn't really have a firm plan in mind as I hurried up the walk behind her. I thought I might try to convince her to get back in the car and then drive her somewhere safe until morning. Maybe I could give her a change of clothes and burn the dress she wore now. If she couldn't look the way I'd seen her in the mirror, that would outsmart fate, right?

Or—and the thought drew me to a sudden halt just before I caught up to her—what if I got into a head-on collision after talking her back into my car, and the little bits of skin and muscle that were sprinkled all over her face in my vision actually belonged to me?

What if she only died if I interfered?

The feeling of being followed must have penetrated through her drunken haze, because as I stood there trying to decide if doing something was worse than not doing anything at all, she spun around to face me.

"Are you some kind of creep?" she slurred.

"No. You... uh... you forgot...." My mind blanked for a moment, and then my hand found its way into the pocket of my jeans to retrieve a quarter. "This! You forgot your change."

"Change?" Her brow furrowed.

I winced, sure she was about to realize she paid through the app and never gave me any cash. Then, her expression cleared, and she held out an unsteady hand. I dropped the quarter into it, grazing her warm skin with my fingertips as I pulled away.

"Thanks." She turned toward the door and dug around in her purse.

I still hadn't decided on a course of action, so I hovered beside her awkwardly, hoping she wouldn't question my presence before I figured out my next move. I needed another sign, something to point me in the right direction.

With a deep sigh, she let her purse swing back down from her shoulder and pounded on the door. The half-rotted wood shuddered and groaned beneath her fist, and a minute later, a face peeked out at us through one of the cracked glass panels flanking the entrance.

"What is it?" a shrill voice called.

"Let me in," Victoria shouted more loudly than was necessary. "I lost my key."

The door opened. I reflexively recoiled away from the man who greeted us, immediately ashamed of the feeling of disgust that welled up inside of me. At the same time, I wished he had stayed at the window where the lines in the glass had partially masked his face.

He was excessively gaunt, as though the thinnest

membrane of skin had been pulled over a skeleton. Wisps of hair, as fine as spiderwebs, clung to his spotted scalp. The fingers that curled around the door were unnaturally long and thin, and his back curved into a hunch so severely that his chin was closer to the ground than his shoulders were. As he stared at us, a stench like rancid chicken wafted out the door and slapped me in the face.

When he spoke, his sharp voice scraped down my eardrums. "That's an extra fee."

"Is this your landlord?" I asked Victoria.

"Host. Just for the night." Her mouth opened in a wide yawn, and she rubbed her eyes with her hands. "Later."

She pushed past him and headed up a crumbling stair-case that was missing its banister.

I peered in at the rest of the foyer. An enormous antique mirror, edges dark with age, hung crookedly opposite the stairs. The weeds from the front garden had made their way inside, and water stains dripped down the walls from the ceiling. I couldn't imagine how it had gotten approved by any rental company. Didn't those websites do inspections or something?

The host watched Victoria as she climbed the stairs. His breathing was heavy and labored, each breath rasping through his lungs like shears against a sharpening stone. A thin line of saliva dribbled down his chin.

"Hey," I told him. "She's a person, not a piece of meat."

His head swiveled on his neck at an unnatural angle, and his cold eyes locked onto mine. I took an involuntary step backwards. What was this guy's deal?

At the top of the stairs, Victoria stumbled. One foot

slipped off the lip of the landing above, and for a moment, she looked like she might tumble backward.

My body shot into motion before my brain had even finished giving it the signal to move. I shoved the strange man aside and raced up the stairs, hands outstretched in case Victoria fell. But my heroics were unnecessary; she caught herself on the wall and shuffled onward.

I glanced behind myself, feeling self-conscious about my superfluous charge up the stairs. Victoria's host was reflected in the large ornamental mirror, and I gasped at the sight of him.

Patches of rotting skin covered a grinning skull, molars visible through gaps in his cheeks. Tiny spiders lazed sluggishly on his hairless head, and pupilless white eyes stared back at me. A tingle skittered across the back of my neck.

I blinked, and the reflection once more showed the oddly gaunt man who had greeted us at the door. His eyes narrowed into thin slits, and his pupils tracked me as I followed Victoria around the upstairs corner.

She was shouldering open a bedroom door when I caught up with her. She grunted and sighed then motioned for me to give it a try. The knob was stubborn, but I managed to heave the door open.

Her rented room was simply furnished. A small overnight bag sat open on a twin bed, and she dumped it out onto the stained comforter. With no warning, she pulled her sequined dress up over her shoulders and dropped it onto the floor.

I turned my back to her, heat flooding my cheeks, and studied the peeling wallpaper above the door. After silently counting to sixty, I chanced a peek back over my shoulder. Victoria had collapsed onto the bed, dressed now in a pair of polka-dot pajama bottoms and matching tank top, and heavy snores drifted across the room.

A deep sigh escaped me. I quickly gathered up her dress, needing to be sure she wouldn't ever put it on again and become the dead version of herself I'd seen in the mirror. Then, I rolled her into the recovery position, tucked the blanket around her body, and left.

To my great relief, her creepy host was nowhere to be seen. I hustled down the stairs and out the door, eager to get back on the road. There had to be a dumpster fire somewhere I could chuck the dress into for extra safety; I'd keep an eye out while I got back to work.

I slipped behind the wheel of my Versa and tossed the dress on the passenger seat. Out of habit, I checked my mirrors before starting the car.

The reflection in the rearview mirror made my heart stop.

Thick, crimson blood covered my face. Pink chunks of something—skin, I decided—peppered my hair. My mouth hung slack, and my eyes, normally bright and excited, were dull.

Lifeless.

Goosebumps marched resolutely up and down my arms, but this wasn't pleasant at all. None of my unsolicited visions that night had been. I squeezed my eyes shut, needing to block out the terrifying future the mirror presented me.

"Please," I whispered. "I don't want to die."

When I finally looked again, my face had returned to normal—contoured cheeks, bright eyeshadow, braided hair. My eyes slid off my own reflection, however, and widened in horror at what lurked behind me.

White, pupilless eyes watched at me from the back seat.

His thin fingers were around my throat before I could react. I clawed at them, fingernails scraping against bare bone, and desperately tried to suck in air. My legs thrashed, feet kicking, and one of my Toms connected with my steering wheel. The roadrunner-like *Meep!* of the horn did nothing to save me. I stuffed my left hand into the space between the door and my seat. When my fingers found the seat recline lever, I yanked it upward and leaned backward as hard as I could. I heard the crunch of bone as my headrest connected with his face.

His fingers loosened from around my neck. I ducked out from beneath him, kicked my door open, and stumbled across the street toward the cemetery.

A shrill, high cackle split the night air. "You'll regret that, girl. You're never safe from a ghoul in a graveyard."

Ghoul? My mind raced. The word rang a faint bell from childhood stories, but I didn't think they actually existed. A quick glance over my shoulder, however, confirmed that the thing shambling after me was all too real.

I ducked beneath the long, metal arm that kept cars out of the cemetery after dark and looked desperately for anywhere to hide. Could I cower behind a tombstone? Climb one of the towering pine trees? Barricade myself in a mausoleum?

That last idea felt the most secure; I liked the thought of thick marble walls between me and this undead monster. I ran up the hill toward the mausoleum and pulled on the rectangular handles.

They didn't budge.

The building was locked up tight.

The ghoul cackled behind me. I turned around and tried to flatten myself against the doors as the creature edged closer. His white eyes glowed in the moonlight, and he bared his teeth in a manic grin.

"What do you want from me?" I screamed. "Just leave me alone!"

"You should have kept your big nose out of my business. I was looking forward to devouring that girl tonight, but she doesn't know what I am. She doesn't threaten my future."

"Your future?" I stared at him. What kind of future could a creature like this have?

"Yes," he hissed. "I've come too far to let you shut me down now. Do you know how much work it was to set up the rental listing? I can't go back to scraps in the graveyard now that fresh meat comes to my door every day."

A pang of sympathy struck my heart. I knew what it was like to have your dream—the thing you had been toiling toward for years—yanked out from beneath your feet. To have someone heartlessly come along and try to crush your entrepreneurial spirit.

But then, my dream didn't involve luring tourists to a ramshackle old house so I could eat them. And if I didn't figure out a way to save myself, my dream and my life would disappear down the ghoul's gullet.

"I won't tell anyone," I lied. "Let me go, and I'll forget you even exist."

His head swiveled on his neck again, and his milky

eyes considered my proposal. "No," he said at last. "I can't take that chance."

He lunged at me.

I rolled away, feeling his hot breath on my neck. The stink of rotting flesh forced its way into my nostrils. I coughed as I ran, trying to clear my lungs of the stench, and frantically scanned the cemetery for any escape. The ghoul was between me and the street, and row after row of tombstones offered me no refuge. But in the back, where the tall chain-link fences that marked the edges of the graveyard met at a corner, I could see a low building. I couldn't tell what it was, but it was the only chance I had.

The ghoul lumbered after me as I hurried toward the dark shape. He ran like a dog with a limp, one forearm touching the ground between each stride. The wild gleam in his eyes sent a thrill of fear up my spine.

He didn't look nearly as exhausted as I felt.

I would never outrun him.

The moon shone down on me like a spotlight. As I drew closer to the building, I realized it was a small tool shed. And—miracle of miracles—the door was open. I dove through the narrow opening and tried to yank the metal door closed behind me. My muscles and my mouth screamed in unison with the effort, but no matter how hard I pulled, it didn't move.

It was stuck.

The ghoul's ragged breaths sounded from just outside the open door. I shrank back into a dark corner of the shed. My hands groped for anything I might use to defend myself, but in my heart, I knew there was no hope left.

Any second now, that thing was going to burst into this tiny space, white eyes aglow with ravenous intentions.

It was over.

I was going to die.

As I'd predicted, the ghoul slunk into the building with me. The cramped space filled with his stench—rotten garbage and decaying meat. I held my breath and closed my eyes, wanting to minimize his impact on my senses before he took my life.

His breath, hot and moist, pressed against my cheeks.

My arms dropped to my sides, no longer hunting for some kind of salvation. As my right hand swung downward, it grazed something cool and hard.

I didn't know what it was. I didn't care. Without opening my eyes, I grabbed it with both hands and thrust it in front of my body.

Something warm and wet splashed onto my face. The ghoul's rasping stopped. His humid breath evaporated, and I dared to peek one eye open.

My hands were wrapped around the handles of a pair of closed hedge clippers, the business end of which was lodged, hinge deep, in the ghoul's throat. I leaned two inches to the side and could just make out the pointed tip of the clippers sticking out of the back of his neck.

His mouth hung open, and his white eyes were wide with desperation. They met mine, and he tried to pull away from me. Before he could slip off into the night, I yanked the handles apart with every ounce of my remaining strength.

With a sickening squelch, his head detached from his body.

"Whoops," I said. "A little too much off the top?"

The hedge clippers clattered onto the shed's concrete floor. I left them there, along with the ghoul's twitching corpse, and headed down the hill toward my car. Out of habit, my eyes slid onto the rearview mirror as I got behind the wheel.

Thick, crimson blood covered my face. White chunks of something—the ghoul's rotted skin, I thought—peppered my hair. My lips were pursed in a grim line, and my eyes, though exhausted, glimmered with life.

I pulled away from the curb and headed home for a shower and a rest. Not too long, though. The mirror might be showing me the present, but I had my eyes on the future.

Caryn Larrinaga is a Basque-American mystery, horror, and urban fantasy author from Salt Lake City, Utah. Watching scary movies through split fingers terrified Caryn as a child, and those nightmares inspire her to write now. Visit www.carynlarrinaga.com for free short stories and true tales of haunted places.

RIP TO RESET

SARIAH HOROWITZ

Marie walked to the redline train stop. Her black dress contrasted against the cold grey of the concrete, and blazing September sunlight felt completely out of place weather for a funeral. Perhaps the universe couldn't be bothered to mourn a teenager. His family had seemed so calm. Didn't they care? Mark was gone, and no one seemed to notice.

The light rail train screeched to a halt. She stepped on and made her way to the back of the last car. The robotic female voice announced the next station. Marie braced herself as the car jerked forward, shaking back and forth as it sped along the tracks. This rocking allowed her to review the last few days.

It was all so sudden. Mark had been her best friend since they were little kids—since they were in diapers, as her parents called it—and had been inseparable until now. Mark was near perfection; dark hair, bright brown eyes, kind, and understanding. Marie assumed that when they reached high school, they would be dating, attend the same college, then marriage, and spend the rest of their lives together.

But then that Nancy Hanks ruined all of it.

Marie, along with Nancy and Zoey, two classroom friends she'd made, had started the magic society at school to avoid going home right away. It was fun, but Marie couldn't stand not having Mark there with her. So, she invited him to join. Whenever he was with her, life was close to perfect.

Then, everything went wrong. Nancy and Mark started getting close. Too close. They began talking to each other outside the club. Marie had even seen them holding hands as they walked to the Corner Deli Cafe across the street from their high school. She knew she was supposed to feel happy for them, but all she felt was anger and betrayal.

He was with Nancy when the crash happened. Instead of driving Marie home, like he always did, he took Nancy to the aquarium. Why couldn't Nancy have died? Why couldn't she be gone and Mark still be alive? It wasn't fair. She didn't even get a chance to say goodbye to Mark before he left. She wanted to cry, but no tears came.

A woman in a dark red business suit sat across from Marie on the train. Short black hair framed her pale face and mismatched pale-grey and brown eyes. Instead of doing the polite thing and avoiding eye contact, the woman stared right at her.

"What?" Marie finally snapped.

"Any regrets?" The woman's eyes seemed to glitter with untold secrets.

"Huh?"

"Regrets." the woman enunciated the word. "Wish you could change events? Fate even?"

Marie cleared her throat. "No. No one can."

"If you say so." The woman reached into her breast pocket and held out a business card. "In case you find one."

Marie's hand took the card before she realized she had reached out. The woman in red rose and went to the doors, walking smoothly while the other passengers wobbled as the train slowed down. In a moment, she was gone through the doors. Marie looked down at the card. It felt like thick papyrus paper, thick enough for printing but brittle, and threatened to rip if held the wrong way. Red and black printed letters read 'Madam Fury Wish Card.'

"Weird," Marie muttered. Then, she realized she'd missed her stop.

Later in her room, she inspected the card more closely. Under the name, 'Madam Fury' tiny lettering explained what this card was supposed to do. Marie squinted, reading the words aloud to the empty room.

"Congratulations. Three wishes are in your grasp. Right wrongs, get wealthy, anything can happen. The first wish is free, with no risks. Bring this card to our shop to redeem for more wishes."

Turning the card over, Marie saw three lemon shapes. The top one was green while the others were shaded red. Instructions over the green lemon shape stated. 'For your free wish, remove and speak.'

This had to be some kind of joke, right? Marie bit her lip as she flipped the card back and forth between the promises. Right wrongs. A thought came to her mind.

Maybe she could bring Mark back to life. Put their lives back on track. Back together. But that was impossible. Then again, if this was a dud, nothing would change.

She found a slight lip at the edge of the green lemon and pulled it off. The green peeled away to show an eyeball with what looked like a cat pupil staring back at her. Feeling rather stupid for talking to a drawing of an eyeball she stated: "I wish Mark Spencer was still alive."

Nothing happened. Then, the drawing seemed to blink and then close, the lid showing a number one on it. Marie blinked, rubbing her eyes to make sure, but the one was still there.

The next morning, she woke up and reached to check off the date on her calendar. But something was off. The date before was not marked off. In fact, they were not blocked off all the way back to last week, Wednesday the 13th—, the day before Mark died. This couldn't be right. Assuming she'd just forgotten to mark them, she rolled out of bed just as her phone went off. Looking at the screen, her eyes widened at Mark's name and number shining back at her. After a third ring, she answered.

"Are you coming to school today?" Mark's cheerful voice came through the speaker.

"Mark?" she said. "Is that you?"

"'Course it is." his voice laughed. "Hurry or I'm leaving you."

A few moments later, Marie sat in the passenger seat of Mark's car like she always had. She smiled as they drove talking about different topics as they always had. She kept checking her phone for the date. The date didn't change:

Wednesday the 13th. Mark would still have his accident tomorrow. She'd have to find a way to stop it. She looked at Mark. Maybe she didn't have to worry about it. If the universe changed this, maybe it changed more things. Time would tell.

They arrived at the school, already filling up with cars and students. Everything was just as it was before. Nancy and Zoey waved hello to them as they passed in the halls. The teachers were annoying as always with their mountains of homework. Realizing she'd have to do the same homework from a week over again made Marie groan, but she didn't care. Mark was alive.

At lunch, she slipped down the back steps with the rest of the kids to head for the deli. As she came out of the doors, she stopped. Mark and Nancy were already outside walking towards the Corner Deli Cafe, hand in hand. Anger ran through Marie. Stupid. She'd only brought Mark back. She didn't fix the real problem.

Later, Marie caught up with Nancy at the top of the east side stairs on their way to the club meeting.

Marie got right to the point. "I want you to stay away from Mark."

"What has Mark got to do with you?" Nancy said.

"Everything."

"Don't be immature. What makes you the one to dictate our lives?"

"Something bad is going to happen to Mark if you go out with him."

Nancy looked at her, her expression impossible to read. "Mark asked me to go to the aquarium tomorrow. I'm not canceling because you like him too. If Mark chose me, then

I can't change that. I don't want to hurt you, but that's how life is." Nancy turned.

Selfish, terrible, horrible bitch. She didn't care about Mark at all. She was going to take Mark away from her again.

Marie's hands were on the other girl's back before realizing what she was doing. Nancy didn't have time to make a squeak as she tumbled down the steps. Marie stared down at the crumpled form of her former friend, her mind trying to calculate what had just happened. The realization hit her. Someone could find the body at any moment. Running away from the stairs, she headed for the atrium staircase.

Everything was falling apart again. Her hands shook. She had to fix this. She pulled out the card. The back of the card gave an address in downtown Salt Lake City. Marie went straight there, doing her best not to worry about the disheveled men hanging out on the curbs and the leather-and-spike-clad groupies blowing scented smoke rings outside rundown shop doors. The shop in question was housed in one of the historic stone buildings, curtains and displays of cards in the windows making it feel like the site belonged in a stereotype setting in a movie. Rechecking the name of the place to be 'Furies: Fortunes and Curios,' she pushed the door open.

A strong wave of incense hit her as soon as she entered the dark interior. Rows of face playing cards with multiple symbols and images were set on the walls behind plastic on every available wall like a cigarette cabinet at a gas station. Their gazes seemed to follow Marie as she made her way to the counter.

An old-fashioned bell sat on the grimy counter beside an out-of-place modern cash register. The sound ripped through the silence with an unexpected deep gong-like sound. Marie again looked around the shop. She'd never realized there were so many different designs for face cards. The closest to her look almost lifelike. The faces and hair looked like photographs placed on elaborately drawn costumes.

"Looking for something?" A smooth voice came from behind her.

Marie jumped, spun around, and found herself looking up at the woman in red. Only this woman was different from the one Marie had met before. Instead of short black hair, this one's hair was pulled back in a long brown pony-tail. She also had mismatched eyes, green along with the pale-grey. She wore the same outfit, except for a name tag stating 'Cinthia' pinned to her lapel.

"I, ah," Marie stammered. "I need more wishes."

The woman nodded, walking behind the counter. "You still have the card, don't you?"

"Yes." Marie pulled it out. "But I don't know how to activate the rest of the wishes."

"It's quite simple," Cinthia said. "Wishes like that need energy to fulfill. One free one is good, but after that, they need more nourishment."

"Such as?" Marie frowned. How do you feed a card?

"Blood is the easiest to do." Cinthia inspected her own exceptionally long nails. "A drop or two after removing the lid should give it enough energy to fulfill your wish."

"If this actually works, then why are there only three slots?" Marie asked.

"It's in your best interest." Cinthia's expression became serious. "Each wish you make drains a little piece of your own life. You won't feel a thing, fortunately, but the more you give the card, the more it is tied to your soul."

"Soul?"

"Exactly." Cinthia held out the card. "These cards are hard to make. A lot of coaxing fate is necessary to give its blessing to each one. Fate doesn't like being manipulated unless it feels like you are taking it seriously. Once you pay with your own blood, guard your card with your life. If your card is damaged," Cinthia cracked a crone-like smile, "it gets angry and will take what it thinks it deserves."

Marie waited for any hint of a joke, but the other woman only watched her with hungry eyes.

"I'll remember that." Marie took her card and backed up slowly towards the door.

"I hope your next wishes are worth it."

Back in her room, Marie looked at the card. Everything in her mind told her this wasn't a good idea. But then, what was there? She'd killed a person, and if she wasn't careful, they'd find out she'd done it. Simple. Marie just had to wish for Nancy to come back, and everything would be all right.

Marie didn't move. But if she brought Nancy back, then everything wouldn't change. She could see Nancy's smug face and the way her straight long brown hair flicked as she'd turned away. Resentment bubbled inside of her. Bringing Mark back hadn't changed a thing. He still had chosen Nancy over her. This wish had to change things for the better.

This wasn't for her. It was for Mark. She had to save

him. Help others, wasn't that what good people did? She mulled over every word in her mind until she got her wish down perfectly.

"This isn't for me," she said aloud. "This is for Mark."

Ripping off the cover of another cat-looking eye, she pricked the side of her finger with a pin and let a drop of blood pool on the card.

"I wish Nancy Hanks never existed."

The next morning, she checked her phone. It was still Wednesday the 13th. This time, she was waiting as Mark's car pulled up to pick her up. He seemed a bit tired this morning. Marie checked her phone contacts but couldn't find Nancy's number among them. Taking this as a sign, she hummed a bit as she placed her phone in her bag.

"Marie," Mark said. "Do you ever get a weird feeling?"

"Like what?"

"Like, you've already done something before."

"You must have had too much chocolate last night before bed again." Marie laughed. "Chocolate gives you bad dreams, they say."

Mark gave her an odd look but didn't push the topic.

It was almost exactly the same day. Same classes, same assignments, but no Nancy. No one seemed to realize there was a student missing. All traces of her were gone. Marie was able to walk with Mark to the deli and spent the entire day with him. Except for Zoey trailing behind them, it was close to perfect. The magic meeting was perfect too. No Nancy to get in the way of Marie's demonstrations of a new trick.

The next day started perfectly as well. Still no trace of Nancy. Zoey basically acted invisible as she tagged along.

Marie never realized how quiet the blond was before this. Mark and Marie were basically alone. Marie even asked him to go to the deli for lunch, to which he agreed. Everything was back on track.

On the way to the club meeting that afternoon, she realized the door was closed. Peeking inside in case the room had been taken over by another club or teacher, she gasped. In the back of the classroom, she saw Mark and Zoey. Zoey looked on the brink of tears, and Mark had his arm around her.

That witch. Trying to get close to Mark. Using his kind heart to get closer to him. Marie leaned against the hallway wall, familiar anger churning in her body. Mark was so easily swayed. Having another girl there was going to distract him too easily. She should have gotten rid of both girls at the same time. It wasn't Mark's fault the girls wanted him. He was so open and kind. Of course, Zoey would want him.

Marie had to eliminate all rivals.

Back home, she could barely keep her hands still enough to get two drops of blood to finish the ritual. The blood disappeared into the thirsty papyrus. Now that all her wishes were over, fear hit her like a dart. The card. She had to protect the card. Looking around her room, she couldn't find a location that seemed safe enough. Her mom did a cleaning raid in her room and might throw it out by accident, but if she kept the card on her person, nothing bad would happen to it. Taking a plastic card cover from her brother's collection of trading cards, she slid the card inside and fashioned a lanyard so she could keep it under her clothes. There. She sighed. Now she knew where the card was at all times.

Wednesday the 13th dawned again clear and beautiful. Marie practically sang as she waited for Mark. He pulled up but was strangely silent as she climbed in. She prattled along and didn't realize they weren't driving to school until he made the turn into The Avenues.

"Where are we going?" she asked.

"I felt like ditching today." Mark kept watching the road. "Sitting through chapter five would drive me nuts."

"Yeah, I know, it sucks." Marie said. "Mr. Sikes is way too into the fates."

The car climbed up The Avenues streets before opening up into the winding canyon road. Mark kept driving until they reached a wide empty bend in the road. He parked along the steel barrier that lined the bend to keep cars from plummeting into the ravine below. They stepped out and walked along the rim. The warm fall day was accented by a cold breeze whispering through the canyon.

Mark finally stopped, turning to face Marie.

"What did you do with Nancy and Zoey?"

Marie stared blankly at him. "Who?"

"Don't lie to me," Mark said. "I know you did something."

"I've never heard of those girls in my life," Marie said. "Mark, are you feeling all right?"

"You've done something. I thought it was just déjà vu at first, but something is definitely wrong."

"Nothing's wrong." Marie snapped. "If you're going to act like a baby, I'm going home."

"Chapter five," Mark said. "You said that chapter sucked, but we were going to start that section today."

"I read ahead." Marie's heart began speeding up.

"You hate reading," Mark said. "You don't study unless you have too. I know you."

"Know?" Marie spun around. "Took me for granted, more like. If you did know me, then you'd realized I feel for you more deeply than those other girls ever would."

"So, you do remember them."

"Of course, I do. How you remember them is the real mystery."

"I can't explain that. But after Zoey came up to me and asked if I remembered Nancy, that no one else could remember, I began to realize my weird feeling was that I'd already relived today. And when I checked my phone this morning, Zoey was gone from my contacts. What did you do to them?"

"I erased them." Marie grinned. "They're gone, and no one knows. Amazing, isn't it? I don't have to explain a thing. And it's much cleaner than killing them."

Mark's eyes widened. "Marie, did you kill me?"

"No, I brought you back," Marie stepped forward. "Nancy killed you. She killed you in a car accident, but I brought you back. That was the very first wish. I couldn't believe you were dead, and I wanted you back. Saving your life was the first wish I ever made." She reached for him but he backed away from her.

"Then why did you kill Nancy and Zoey? You should have left fate alone."

Rage boiled inside Marie. He was still thinking about those other girls. After everything she'd done for him, he wasn't thinking about her. The miracle that he was back to life wasn't enough to make an impression? This is how he treated her love?

She lunged for him, shoving him towards the cliff, scratching and pushing.

"Ingrate!" she shouted and slashed at his eyes. "I bring you back to life, and you reject me again."

One of Mark's hands reached out and grabbed her, his fingers snagging on the front of her shirt. A crunching sound made her freeze. His fist was around her card, crumpling it in his grip. She pushed him away, and he lost his balance and grabbed the barrier. She ran a few feet away and pulled the card out of the plastic. It was crumpled, but the damage didn't seem bad. Maybe she could glue or tape it. A breeze swept in, lifting the card out of her hand.

"No!" She tore at the air, desperate to catch the card. She lunged, snatching the card out of the air. Relief turned to horror as she opened her hand and found only a crushed piece of papyrus. The rest had scattered in the wind.

Pain shot through her hands. She looked down at her trembling fingers. Tendrils of green and red came out from under her fingernails. They thickened into ribbons sliding around her fingers and crawling down her fingers and up her arm. Heat seared into her skin. She screamed, but no sound came from her throat.

A shout made her look up, and she saw Mark running towards her. She reached for him, but by then, she was completely covered in the tendrils. The last thing she saw was Mark's horrified face and his hand reaching for her.

The burning sensation continued. Colors and pain clouded all her senses. All air was pushed out of her body, and then the rest of her felt compressed. Finally, the color cleared away from her eyes and she stared out unto the world. Unable to move, she watched helplessly as a woman picked her up. Unable to move her eyes, Marie got a glimpse of blond curls before a pale-grey eye took up her view, inspecting Marie's face. The red-clad woman shook her head before sliding Marie's card on the wall with the others.

Sariah Horowitz is a member of the League of Utah Writers. She's been previously published in the Utah Horror Writers' *Peaks of Madness* anthology, as well as anthologies through the League of Utah Writers. Follow her at facebook.com/authorsariahhorowitz

FRANKENBEAR

C.H. LINDSAY

In autumn's chill
the witches watch
for teddy bears
in graveyards dark.

Where smallish tots
leave favored toys
in severed parts
and mangled limbs.

Beneath full moon
the witches chant
for graveyard bears
to coalesce.

With faded yarn
they stitch them up.
A spark of life
from sun's first ray

gives monsters life
for Hallow's Eve
to haunt the dreams
of treat-filled young.

C. H. Lindsay is an award-winning poet & writer,
booklover, and housewife—not necessarily in that order.
She spent thirty years as an event planner, helping
organize and run science fiction, fantasy, and horror
conventions, and a decade acting in community theatre.
Now she prefers to stay at home with her family and write
poems, short stories, and novels. This is her twelfth
anthology. She's a member of SFWA, HWA, SFPA, and
LUW. Mostly blind, she lives in Utah with her "seeing-eye
husband," son, and a cat who thinks she's another child.

THE FINAL SPELL

ELIZABETH SUGGS

My reflection showed not only my pale face but also his and those bleeding eyes. He had pleaded with me. Begged me to stay my hand, but I couldn't. Not that night. There was a full moon that night. Power coursed through my veins in just the way it coursed out of his cuts. I drank from his power, and he weakened. As long as I shut my heart out, his pain wouldn't affect me.

Every night, I remembered his face, and anytime guilt tickled my senses, I shoved it away, back into the darkness. I had needed his power more than him, so why did his red eyes bother me? Why wasn't I like the other witches? The ones who could forget.

The spell had worked too well. Everyone saw what I was capable of, so they gave me more. More victims. More chances to show my ability. I was to be next in line for the president's chair, if I worked things just right. It was the ultimate goal for anyone, so why wasn't I happy?

To dampen my mood further, my twenty-fifth birthday

kept coming up, and more importantly, so did his horrible eyes. My birthday would mean my last victim. The final test. My final show of power. Tonight, a full moon would emerge. Power would pump through me to either save or destroy me.

I picked up my foundation, gently easing it over my cheeks and face, hiding the blotches where I'd cried. No one needed to know. Not tonight. Once blended, I added blush and stepped from the bathroom.

Twenty-five. A birthday seldom celebrated in my community but this was the night of my reckoning.

I slipped into a black dress and matching black hat. The hat weighed heavy on my head. I tended to avoid the traditional attire, but tonight, everyone would be there with their black hats and black dresses and suits. They'd have a black cat for me, if I succeeded. If I didn't, well, I'd keep the cat in death.

When the clock struck ten, I went to the Wasatch forest, the most sacred forest in Utah. Everyone was already waiting, many of them with their own snacks and drinks. One even had the gall to bring a black birthday cake, as if I could stomach it. In the center of the crowd was a stranger. A man. What stopped me in my tracks wasn't that he was unconscious and tied up, rather, it was his marked similarity to my first victim. The only difference was that the first one had stared at me, watching me in my most fiendish act. I could have awakened this new man, but I dreaded those tears. I dreaded the whimpers.

I walked over to him, listening to his heavy breathing. He was safer unconscious, unperturbed by my actions.

I shut out my heart and summoned the whispers from

my ancestors. If I did it right, he could be the last one I ever killed. I could live my entire life, using magic the way I wanted, but only if I did it right.

I expelled the words to siphon the blood out his heart, and at first, it worked. At first, he gurgled and choked. At first, elation warped my bones and pumped my heart, taking me into a trance, but then he woke. Then, his red eyes stared at me. He struggled against his restraints, calling out to me, begging for release. But I couldn't release him. If I did, the power would implode, bursting me from the inside. Didn't he understand? It was either me or him.

He started to beg. Why did they always beg? I tried to shut him out. I tried to push out his pleas, but they crawled beneath my skin, pumping around my heart. His soul dripped into me, clogging his siphoned blood, clogging my speech.

I stopped speaking, the words of many tongues bulging in my throat, forcing me to cough up his blood. I had failed, and everyone around me knew it too, despite how they cried and shouted for me to start up the spell again. They reassured me it would work; the devil wouldn't let one of his chosen fall away so easily. But their calls were hollow; we all knew it. The spell was reversing, muting my speech and any attempts at another spell. I was choking up his blood, and when that drained from me, mine, too, would escape.

I should have been bothered, yet I kept smiling because my victim was silent. In fact, his red eyes were almost peaceful, the opposite of what had happened to my first.

I dropped to the ground, crawling over to him. I lay my head in his lap, feeling his cooling warmth. He had been a stranger during life, but maybe now, we'd be close in death.

My stomach rumbled, warning of what was to come. I wouldn't get the same peace on my face. There'd be nothing left of me, and maybe that was okay.

Sharp cramps punctured my root chakra, like a thousand knives in my womanhood. I think I cried out, but a pop broke my eardrums, silencing the world. Momentarily, I drifted in darkness, alone, and then I wasn't alone. His hands wrapped around and held me close, telling me I'd never be alone again.

Elizabeth Suggs is co-owner of the indie publisher Collective Tales Publishing, owner of Editing Mee, and is the author of several stories, two of which were in a podcast and poetry journal. She is the president of two writing groups, one being part of the LUW. She's a book reviewer and popular bookstagramer. When she's not writing or reading, she's playing video/board games or making cookies. You can find her on Instagram and FB: @elizabethsuggsauthor or Twitter: @elizabethasuggs or one her websites: www.editingmee.com and www.collectivedarkness.com

THE MOTH

ROBERT BAGNALL

And at that moment, the Prince saw the dragon.

He saw its ruby red eyes and darting tongue and the snorts of smoke from its nostrils. And he felt his limbs turn to stone.

Literally turn to stone.

Everything below his neck was now the grey of granite, the weave of his cloak merely scratch marks.

He turned his face to the statue of the princess and saw that she had become flesh. He was caught between terror at the approaching monster and sheer wonderment at her release.

He felt his neck grow cold, his tongue thick.

"Why?" he asked groggily.

But even as he said it, he knew the answer.

Doctor Kilty paused, searching the horseshoe of faces in front of her, as if letting an echo fade.

"Come on, people. Let's offer criticism without being critical. The assignment was to write your own fairytale. Did Gypsy succeed?"

Foot scraping.

"Anybody?"

From the corner, I raised a hand. There was some snickering, and I caught the word 'cripple'.

"I didn't see any foreshadowing."

I kept my gaze on Gypsy. She had turned her work over and was absent-mindedly doodling, but I saw her darting gaze challenge me through the curtain of black hair behind which she hid her eyes.

"Well, we ought to somehow know that Oberon can turn the prince into stone in advance. Otherwise, it just comes out of nowhere."

I had more to say, to casually drop in Deus ex Machina, but Doctor Kilty had pulled up. Her fingers went for her collar as if gasping for air. We all stiffened—was this what a heart attack looked like?—everybody except Gypsy. She just carried on sketching.

Doctor Kilty had gone pale.

And then Gypsy stopped and looked across at me.

"I think that's enough for today," Doctor Kilty managed, catching a breath, eyes on the wall clock.

After she had been helped away, brushing off the clucking of girls, I saw, abandoned, what Gypsy had been sketching. A moth, in miniscule detail, albeit incomplete. The outline of two wings: one reaching forward, one paddle-like behind; the body: thorax and abdomen. Deft flicks of the pencil suggesting the facets of a compound eye. Antennae, each with wisps of hair.

Benzedrine thin, she had been dropped into our class as if from Mars rather than Ogden, Utah, where she said she came from, halfway through a semester, chewing gum and studying us from behind the redoubt of her fringe. Somebody said she was an exchange student from a wandering Dada theatre company. She always wore black but on her it was somehow more colorful than all our denim and hoodies combined.

I recognized her accent, but in every other way, she was from no place I had even been or could ever imagine. When they asked her name, she said 'Gypsy', because she used to collect moths, with no sense of the outré or the theatrical. Wordlessly, she challenged us to find it off the wall. I don't think she ever told us her real name.

The rest of the class had departed; it was my fate to forever walk in other people's wakes. I propped a crutch and snatched the drawing up and loosely rolled in into a pocket. If she didn't want it…

———

THE NEXT TIME I saw her, she was delivering flyers, a military-style knapsack swinging at her hip. She'd hop up the steps of the brownstones and slip a card through each mailslot, skitter back through gates.

"Hey, you want me to do the other side?"

She shook her head almost imperceptibly as she brushed past me.

"I can take some if you like."

But she was onto the next house.

I limped up a path to where one of her cards stuck out of a sprung letterbox. On it, in bold black print, were five words.

WE KNOW WHERE YOU LIVE

Just those five words, bold and black on a plain white card. It made no sense.

"What's it advertising?"

I wondered whether I should mention stealing her drawing. But if she left it behind it wasn't stealing…

"Isn't advertising anything."

For once, my withered limbs had no problem in keeping up with her as she went from door to door.

"Is this some kind of art project? Like Dada or something?"

"Like Dada or what?" Words shot back at me, returns to server that I couldn't catch to my tentative forays, like checking for depth whilst crossing unfamiliar waters.

I laughed, unsure, tongue-tied, and she made to walk away. The next set of houses was a way off. They had traditional mailboxes on poles out front. I wouldn't be able to keep up with her nor catch her on the next drag. I had to do something if I were to have just a few minutes in her orbit.

"I think you're just like me. Damaged."

She stopped and turned. I quaked slightly, uncertain at what her face would tell me. There was a sneer in there—it wouldn't be Gypsy without a sneer—but something else as well. A quizzical quality, like she'd just seen me for the first time. Like she was studying me.

———

AFTERWARDS, in bed, I asked her why she sketched moths.

"They're my familiars," she said simply. "You know what a familiar is?"

I shook my head.

"I'll sketch you," she offered.

She pulled her shirt back on, missing out buttons, before draping herself sideways in an ancient recliner. Finding pencil and paper from my desk, she began to sketch me. In order to stay still, I concentrated on her legs swinging over the duct-taped arm, straight and slender, fragility and strength combined.

I suddenly wanted her gone. Suddenly, those legs, so perfect, felt like they were mocking my twisted and disobedient limbs.

I made to rise.

But my limbs felt as if they were glued to the bed. As if they were made of stone. I tried to move, but I couldn't. Confusion was replaced by fear, my mind no longer speaking in any language that my body could comprehend.

I think I made some sort of gurgling noise as I tried harder to move, not caring if my effort showed.

But Gypsy just carried on drawing, quickly, efficiently, carefully, and yet without a care in the world.

My chest constricted, tightened, like metal straps being ratcheted. I had to really pull to breathe. But if all my effort, all my energy, was focused on merely breathing, then what had I left?

And then she breezily dressed, as I gurgled and gasped, and was gone. I didn't even see her go. My eyes were closed, all energy focused on trying to draw in air, no concern remaining for my spastic body.

My greying gaze settled on the drawing that she had left abandoned on the carpet. A moth; perfectly executed.

Each eye with its countless facets, each leg dotted with hairs. The ridged abdomen. Pencil on paper, monochrome and two-dimensional, but with such a sense of vibrancy, of life. It even left you with a sense of the dust on its wings.

As my vision grew narrow and dim, I knew. I knew the truth.

The moth may only have been scrapes of graphite on paper.

But I was the one who had been collected.

Robert Bagnall was born in Bedford, England, in 1970 and now lives in Devon, between Dartmoor and the English Channel. He is the author of the science fiction thriller *2084 – the Meschera Bandwidth*, and the anthology *24 0s & a 2*, which collects two dozen of his thirty-plus published stories. He can be contacted via his blog at meschera.blogspot.co.uk.

FATA MORGANA

DANIEL R. ROBICHAUD

"Tourist?" the woman asked when Bill pulled out his credit card to pay for the red T-shirt sporting "Salt Lake City" atop Wasatch mountain artwork.

She had a smoky voice, something immediately engaging. Bill glanced her way with interest as his credit card's information passed through the wild world of electronic billing. The speaker wore dark, sensible clothes that still managed to show off her plentiful curves. Although the black fabric mask she wore covered her face from nose to chin, what he saw convinced him she was gorgeous. He gauged her as in the ballpark of forty, but those eyes were downright enchanting.

"Of the airport," Bill said. He was surprised when she spoke up. Weren't there more handsome guys than him, a forty-pound overweight middle management career track guy with mud brown hair and pasty complexion? Her eyes and interest remained fixed on him, however. Lonely, he supposed, which was something with which he could empathize. As he received his card back, signed the screen, and thanked the salesperson, he said, "I end up traveling a bunch for work. I got the idea I might pick up a shirt whenever my plane lands me somewhere new. Silly, huh?"

"I suppose," she said, and Bill saw she was waiting to trade cash for the opportunity to drink a bottle of Crystal Geyser Spring Water.

He could have headed back to his seat and waited for his next plane to venture up to the gate, but it was so depressing right now. All this coronavirus stuff left the airports like ghost towns. Not even a view of the snow-capped mountains could erase just how lonely the airport was. How lonely everything was since Carol…

"I'm local, myself," the woman explained. "Taking the opportunity to head to Las Vegas on the cheap. I figure I'll make a little fortune this trip. Just a little one."

Bill realized that while he had backed off from the register with plastic bag in hand and roller board next to him, he was still standing in place like an idiot and maybe even staring at the way those pants showed off the round-ness of her ass. *God, what a prick I am,* he thought and looked back up in time to meet her eyes as she turned away from the desk. Maybe she thought he was waiting for her instead of standing like a moron. That would be nice.

"You sound confident," he said. "Have you got some kind of a system to beat the House?"

"I do," she said. "All it takes is a little energy, and things go my way. Care to donate?"

"Sure," he said with a laugh. "I'm all about positivity.

It's great. But I hope you won't be too disappointed when the odds don't fall your way."

"Odds don't fall," she said. "They get pushed." She glanced around as though ready to leave but stopped herself. "Where's your gate?"

He rattled off the number, and she said, "It's right by mine. Is this Fata Morgana?"

"Fata whatnow?"

"Fate," she said with a throaty chuckle. "That's *me* being silly. Showing off the benefits of a classical education."

"Oh, of course." He laughed, not because he got the joke but because he wanted to be polite. No, what he really wanted to do was convince her to stick around. They headed off toward his gate, chatting along the way. She had been born in the area but took every opportunity to venture abroad. She was not worried about the virus and was looking forward to getting away from all the depressing news to lose herself in slots and whatnot. She did a terrific job of feigning interest in his answers to questions like, "What do you do?", since middle management in the oil and gas industry and flying to and from Houston was not terribly exciting.

When she asked, "How long have you been married?" he froze. A glance down told him he did not put the ring on today. "The tan line gives it away." She was looking?

"I was married for sixteen years," he admitted.

"Divorce?"

"I'm a widower."

"Sorry," she said. Her eyes flashed more than mere compassion. Was there hunger in them? Since he was untethered, was she hoping for a little connection? That might be nice.

Bill's mouth moved because the silence was too much. Her eyes were too intense. "It was long, and it was terrible, and I was so relieved when she finally—"

He stopped speaking. "I'm sorry. That was not what... I must sound like a... Yeah. Time to shut up, Bill." He mimed locking his mouth up and chucking the key. She mimed catching it.

"Don't apologize," she said. "I have one of those faces. You can't see the whole thing right now, but I have one of those faces that people just open up to."

"You do," he said. "But I..." He shrugged. "I didn't intend to sound like a prick."

"You've been alone for a while." She nodded, and that was right. He had been so lonely since Carol passed. The job was no substitute for her companionship, but he threw himself into it regardless. "And you just need someone to talk to. Someone to talk to you. Someone to wink, maybe." Her left eye did just that, and it was a lovely, flirty gesture. "Someone to help you forget for a while, am I right?"

"Dear God, yes."

"How long until your flight?"

"Hour and a half?"

"Mine's in about an hour. So, plenty of time to forget."

Forty minutes later, he was exhausted from talking about anything and everything that wasn't his dead wife. Her eyes never stopped flashing. They held his gaze, patient and flirty, and he was getting a hard-on just from talking. When her plane was called, she leaned over to squeeze his groin, and he just about exploded. "Farewell," she said.

"Bye," he replied.

Wherever her gate was, it was nowhere near his. She strode down the hall full of purpose.

As the headiness of human contact wore off, Bill realized his arms were heavy. And his legs, too. He felt like a lump in the chair, a weary vessel waiting for someone to dump a pot full of coffee into him. When his piss-swollen bladder demanded it would no longer tolerate sitting in one uncomfortable chair a minute longer, he managed to shove upright. His back ached. His knees cracked like gunshots with every step to the nearby Men's.

The reflection in the restroom mirror gaped in horror, but *it* was the source of that sensation. Where did all those liver spots on his cheeks and forehead come from? And why was the hair on his head so thin? What had happened to his neck to make it look like a turkey wattle? He looked ten years past his real age of forty-five, looked like his own father in his dying days. He felt older still, drained, empty, and utterly *miserable*.

Did that woman somehow do this? How? He did not know. If so, how?

His bladder demanded attention. As he tottered to the urinal, fumbling himself into position just in time to void his bladder's contents into the basin, he realized he did not even know her name. Upon completion of his messy business, he stepped back to pass his hand in front of the sensor. The flush water swirled his highlighter-yellow piss down the drain.

Then, he heard the last call for his flight, and he hurried as fast as his prematurely old man's legs would carry him.

Daniel R. Robichaud lives and writes in East Texas. Some of his short fiction has been collected in *Hauntings & Happenstances*, *Gathered Flowers, Stones, and Bones*, and *They Shot Zombies, Didn't They?* Recent fiction appearances include *The Other Side: A Horror Anthology, Infernal Clock: Inferno, Cryptid Chronicles*, and *parABnormal* magazine. Keep up with his weekly film and fiction reviews at the ConsideringStories website.

ASPENS

EDWARD MATTHEWS

I stared blankly at the two-lane Utah state road stretching ahead of us, so straight I barely needed to nudge the wheel, and listened to Steven drone on. This was my idea, I thought. I had to live with it.

I was born in Utah. I had lived here all of my life, but like many people, I had never really explored my native land. Steven had lived here only a few years, and it seemed that he knew everything about the valley. Really about the whole state. He had been to places I had never even heard of. Then, over dinner one night in early Spring, he mentioned how crazy it was that there were so many festivals and celebrations in the valley. I had never thought about it before, never really paid attention to that kind of stuff. But he kept going on about the Peach Festival and Swiss Days and the Alpenhorn Fest. His litany of crazy gatherings only made me more acutely aware of how little I knew about the world going on right around me. I was not okay with this. This was my state.

"Fine," I had exclaimed. "This will be Karrina and Steven's Year of Festivals."

And with that, the idea was born. We agreed that we would go to twenty-four festivals or celebrations in the next twelve months, and we hit the ground running. We had gone to the Peach Days festival (how could we miss the one that had started the whole conversation), the Pride Festival, and the Utah Arts Festival. We even found an obscure belly dancing festival and had marked our calendar for a scarecrow festival later this month. We were well on track, having made twelve festivals by mid-October. Now, we were on the road to the Aspen Festival, a lucky find Steven made in his latest internet search. I had no idea why they would have a festival for aspens, the only thing that seemed more common than pine trees here, but it was the Year of Festivals, so why not?

Now, on the road to a little town that neither of us had ever heard of in the middle of the state, Steven was looking up everything he could about aspens.

"Karrina," he said excitedly, "These things are so cool. I totally get why they have their own festival. They're amazing. The species we have here are called the quaking aspen. How cool is that?"

This is one thing I loved about him. He could get so excited about such random things. We had only been together about a year, but I had really fallen for him. And I liked to tell myself that I had become accustomed to listening to his excited monologues about things no one else would have thought twice about, but in truth I really enjoyed them.

"Did you know that whole forests of aspens can be one

living organism? Just one tree can send out a forest of trees around it. But it's one living thing. They're all connected. That's amazing!"

It went on like that for the next twenty minutes with Steven reading every fun fact he encountered about aspens until he lost internet connection. We had officially entered the middle of nowhere.

"It should be a few miles up ahead. The town's called Populus Haven. Man, Utah has some strange names for cities."

I looked sideways at him. I knew he was joking, but he knew it bothered me when he made fun of Utah. I don't know why I had such a protective streak, but I suppose it came from this being the only place I had really ever know. I knew the place had its quirks, but I loved my state. He did not get to make fun of it. Steven grinned back at me.

We drove the next forty minutes in silence, turning off of the lonely state highway to an even lonelier dirt road after seeing a sign pointing us toward our destination. The road was quickly engulfed on either side by thick rows of aspens. Passing into the forest, I smiled at the way their white bark and golden leaves passed by like a beautiful kaleidoscope. It was a hypnotic blend of white, black, yellow, and gold. It felt like I could have stayed on that road forever, watching the pattern swirling past me. I knew it could not be true, but I thought I could almost hear the rustling of the leaves, like a great applause from nature. But this would have been impossible over the noise of the car on a dirt road. This must have been my imagination. Too soon, we saw a dilapidated sign for Populus

Haven proclaiming it to be "a place so nice, you may decide to stay!"

At first, I wasn't sure if we had actually entered the town. There were a couple of houses along the side of the road and a small red building with a post office sign fading above the door. But there was nothing that would have made me believe we were in a city deserving of its own name, much less one able to hold an annual festival of any kind. But it was the right place.

"Look," Steven said pointing to a handwritten sign with the words "Aspen Festival" written on it, circled by poorly drawn yellow leaves. "Looks like this is it."

We followed a series of similar signs to a small park. The area seemed to be cut out of the forest, a grassy expanse encircled on all sides by a white and golden wall. The festival, like the town, could hardly have earned its title. There were fewer than a dozen other people there, not counting us and the people tending the booths. And the number of booths was nothing to talk about either, just a few food carts with nothing but carnival fare, a couple of craft tables with local trinkets, some displays of bad art, and one booth with local honey and another with home-made bread. There couldn't have been more than eight or nine in total. But what caught my eye was that the people "manning" them were all women, and they were all dressed the same. They all wore white dresses with black spots and streaks with simple gold wreaths of leaves crowning their heads.

"They're aspens," I proclaimed to Steven. I loved this. All of the women were dressed like trees for the festival. Okay, I decided. We can stay. This was the kitschiest festival we had seen, and I wanted to experience it in all of its amazing silliness. We drove all this way, and they had gone to all the effort to dress like trees. The least we could do was eat their funnel cakes, buy some of their honey, and enjoy whatever else they might have planned for this festival. It was probably the biggest event that this middle-of-nowhere town had all year. I remembered the sound of the soft Fall wind rustling the leaves as we dove into the festival.

Steven was enjoying this as much as me. He grabbed my hand and pulled me to the first food cart he found. After sampling a corndog and trying to look interested in some of the worst local art that we had the pleasure of seeing in our tour of festivals, we made our way to the handmade jewelry stand. We were greeted by a young blonde girl wearing the compulsory aspen garb. "Hi and welcome. I'm Sophyia," she said with a smile so broad that it could have seemed forced, but she wore it with casual genuineness. Her bright mood was infectious. I felt happier just being near her. She spoke to us like we were family or old friends, grabbing my hand and telling me that I had to see the things she had made for the festival. She showed us all of her wares—necklaces, bracelets, toe rings—almost insisting that I try on every piece. Eventually, Steven grew bored with the display of female bonding and wandered to the next booth to talk with them about cultivating local honey.

"Girl time," Sophyia said, grinning when Steven left. "Try this one now," she said producing a lovely necklace of red and yellow and orange glass beads held together by a delicate spiderweb of gold filament. It looked impossibly fragile but easily withstood Sophyia's excited hands as she put it around my neck. "I made this one to honor the Fall," she said. "It is the One Life, each piece held together by the tangle."

"It's beautiful," I said.

I expected a polite "thank you" or an offer to lower the price "just for you." But I did not expect her to say what she said next.

"Listen to the sound." I looked at her, unsure if I had heard her correctly. Was she saying that the necklace was making a sound? "Listen to the sound," she repeated. "Listen to what is around you. I know you heard it. I saw you when you came in. I saw you hearing it, but you did not listen. Listen to it." I paused and cocked my head sideways in an exaggerated display of listening. I played along. Or I thought I was playing along. But I did hear it. I heard the rustling that I had heard on the road. I heard the sound of the leaves that welcomed us to the festival. I heard the sound of a hundred thousand leaves clapping. The leaves of the aspen are shaped in a way to protect the tree. They are special. And now, the aspens were moving. The aspens were quaking.

Steven reappeared suddenly, pulling my mind back from the trees. The sound faded. It was not gone but in the background. Sophyia sold me the necklace. Fifteen dollars seemed a steal for the Honor of Fall or, what did she call it? The One Life.

Steven and I set out again. He pulled me along from cart to cart. Steven loved engaging with the women at each of them. This is something he had done at all the festivals. He was a lovely, social man. This took the pressure off of me. I had never been as outgoing, and now it was even harder. I was distracted. My mind was in the trees. The rustling of the leaves, the quaking, became a backdrop to the day. Once I heard it, it was hard to not hear. This was the soundtrack to festival number thirteen.

As the day wore on, most of the few other festival-goers disappeared, heading to their cars for the trek home. There were only a small handful of us left. As Steven and I were talking about leaving, thinking of the lonely road back to civilization, Sophyia ran up to us and again grabbed my hand.

"You have to come to the after-party," she said. "There's a bonfire. It's amazing. You have to come. Just follow that path. Go about a quarter mile and you will find it. You just have to come." She pointed to a break in the aspen wall about a hundred yards west of the festival site. And with that, she was gone, running back to her trinket-lined booth, pulling her wares in, and pulling the front down to secure her livelihood. I could see the excitement on her face. This after-party must be something.

"Come on, this will be fun," I said forgetting about the drive ahead of us and pulling Steven toward the path. He pulled back at first, just a bit, but gave in. I listened to his excited monologues, and he allowed my exuberant whims. That was the unspoken deal. This is why we worked. So he followed me down the trail. Hand in hand, we darted through the stand of aspens, passing through an ocean of white trees coiffed with golden tresses, leaves rustling, cheering us on down the path.

We emerged into a glade lit by a bonfire in the middle. Yellow-orange light illuminated the faces around the fire. I recognized the women from the festival and at least three of the couples who had been wandering the booths earlier. The women from the honey stand and one of the carnival food carts approached me, reached out, and placed a wreath of golden leaves on my head. It wasn't a wreath. It was a crown. A halo. A warrior's helmet and a wedding veil. I felt its warmth encircling may head. How could dead leaves be warm? My whole body felt warm. They handed me a cup. I drank. It was cool. I could feel it tracing a path to the center of my body, the coolness sliding through the warmth to my middle. I felt the ground beneath me. The dirt. I felt the air around me. I felt the sun, though I could not see it through the trees, and could tell that it was fading behind the distant mountains. I knew it would be gone soon and I would be hungry. I heard the rustling, but it was a whisper. It was more than a sound. It was a word. It grew louder. Over and over. Pando. Pando. Pando. The women in the circle were chanting.

U'ta dola etu Pando U'ta dola etu Pando U'ta dola etu Pando

A hand held mine firm and led me to the circle around the bonfire. I was invited in and embraced. I was warm and safe. I found myself saying the words.

U'ta dola etu Pando U'ta dola etu Pando U'ta dola etu Pando

But Steven, where was he? It was his hand I was holding. I looked to one side and the other. I was holding Sophyia on my left, the woman from the bread booth on my right. Around the circle were all of the women from the booths and the few guests who were left as dusk was coming. Not all of the guests. The women. But where was Steven?

U'ta dola etu Pando U'ta dola etu Pando U'ta dola etu Pando

The rustling of the leaves grew louder, at first like paper being crumpled. Then, a growing chorus of whispering voices. It was something I had heard so many times walking in the woods, hiking on a trail, but not like I heard it now. It was a shuddering, the gentle quaking of everything around me. Growing and growing. Something moved just out of sight, a hulking form gliding by. Just a dark mountain moving impossibly through the forest. Something that size surely would have been knocking over trees as it went, but it moved like it was moving between them or through them or with them, somehow passing along the perimeter of our glade without disturbing a branch or a leaf. I could not make out what it was.

U'ta dola etu Pando U'ta dola etu Pando U'ta dola etu Pando

My eyes strained against the darkness beyond the aspens, trying to make out what the thing was. It felt me searching for it. It knew. The monstrous form slowed. I could feel it look back at me, and for a brief moment, I saw its face. It turned toward me from behind the veil of trees, and I saw it. It let me see it and I understood. It held me for just a moment in the embrace of its gaze and began to move again.

When it moved again, the forest came alive. But it was the forest. It was all one. We were all one with it. The trembling trees became a symphony, shaking with the sound of an inferno. Golden leaves rained all around me. It struck me that there should be something sad about this. The Fall was on us. But it was not sad. It was a ritual offering to honor Pando and to protect the One Life. I was now part of that life. I was part of the One Life. I screamed in glee, my sound mixing with the cascade of the forest and the chanting of my new sisters.

U'ta dola etu Pando U'ta dola etu Pando U'ta dola etu Pando

Then, a thought broke through the glee. The men. There were no men at the festival other than those in the couples winding through the booths. None of the locals who were there were men. None of those around the bonfire were men. Where were the men? Not the men. My man. He had a name. Steven. Where was Steven? He should join me. We will all be one together.

Looking around, outside of the circle, I saw them. The men. Steven. Three others who had been there at the booths. They were on the ground at the edge of the glade. They were on the ground, covered in roots and leaves, branches winding in serpentine coils around their bodies like great constrictors holding them down. Steven's eyes caught mine, wide and frightened. But why was he scared? I smiled at him. Just listen to the rustling, I thought. Listen to the orchestra of the trees. Listen to the One Life. Listen to Pando. You will see his face. You will be okay. It is nothing to be afraid of.

U'ta dola etu Pando U'ta dola etu Pando U'ta dola etu Pando

The hulking shape moved again at the edge of the glade. The trees again reacted. The shuddering. The quaking. The rain of gold. The chanting grew louder. Steven's wide eyes held mine, and my mind wandered briefly to a first kiss, laughter, touch, times together. But the building reverie was interrupted as a great form broke from between the trees. But not *between* the trees. I would have imagined the trees rending and shattering as it crashed through the white wall, but this is not what happened at all. The trees lurched forward in a mass, merging as the form took shape. Brilliant white skin streaked and speckled with black. Shimmering gold hanging from its head, draping its form. Gold raining all around it, like sparkling suns highlighting paper white skin. Holes that must have been eyes rested below the golden crown. A beard of yellow vines below that revealed a hole opening as if to speak. The sound that came out was the rustling of all of the leaves of a forest, the middle of a forest fire, a gale. I was transfixed.

U'ta dola etu Pando U'ta dola etu Pando U'ta dola etu Pando

I looked again at Steven. Surely, he would understand now. The men were still held firm by white wooden arms on the forest floor. But as Pando spoke, they began to shudder and convulse. They arched against their restraints, and their restraints pulled back against them. There was no way that the flesh could win this war. I heard their bodies pop and rend. The white ropes tightened, and the din of Pando's voice was broken by sounds of horror and pain as the men were pulled under. I looked into Steven's wide eyes again as a scream caught in his throat. He did not understand. He would feed Pando. He would be part of the One Life. We would all be together. He would live forever in the white skin and the golden crown. He would fall to the earth as a golden leaf. He would understand all of this soon. I watched as Steven was swallowed by the earth, pulled down by loving fingers. I first saw his middle disappear. Then his head. I was glad that his fear was gone. And last went his feet. I laughed at the sight of his feet sticking straight up before being pulled into the earth.

I smile. He understands now. He is part of the One Life.

Holding hands in the circle, we continue to chant together, and I feel Pando's embrace. The crown on my head, the fire we have gathered around, the circle we have formed. I am being held by the forest and surrounded by my family. My sisters. My home. We are wreathed in white and crowned in gold. We are all part of the One Life.

Edward Matthews lives in Salt Lake City with his wife, two children, and his aging but still noisy hound dog. He spends his days in the mundane world of a government cog. But when night falls he retreats to his loft to scratch the itch of the dark things that inhabit his brain. This is his third offering to the collection of Utah horror.

FLY BY NIGHT

MICKIE BOLLING-BURKE

She ran down the long hall screaming and then flew down the central staircase to the heavy wooden door at the bottom. Grimacing as it shrieked open, she fled into the night. She ran through trees, branches slapping her. She ran along dirt paths, roots tripping her. She ran in the moonlight until the skittering clouds brought the dark. She ran in the dark until she could run no more.

At the edge of town, she slowed. Smoothing her hair, straightening her skirts, she walked the streets, looking at the shops, looking at the people. No one looked back at her. Of course they didn't. No one looks at ghosts. She saw their gaze always where she had been, never where she presently was. If the business lights had been dimmer, she might have been noticed. Might have because she was pale and misty; her whiteness hid her in the lights.

Caught up in the bustle, she danced from shop to shop, gazing long and hard at the jumbles of dresses and shoes, jewelry and hats, all so colorful, so shiny and new. It had been a lifetime since she'd had a night on the town. She watched customers enter shops and, anxious to enter a trendy boutique, worked up her daring to slip in behind a black-root blonde. Surely, she wouldn't be noticed here.

She followed the blonde closely, wandering through the aisles, fingering dresses on the mannequins, examining dresses on the racks, muttering over each one. Bored with the choices, she picked the blonde woman's purse and went through the wallet. *Gerte.* What a thick, unattractive name. That explained the black roots. Gerte chose three house dresses and disappeared into a fitting room.

Refusing to be caught dead in a house dress, her attention was caught by a slim, laughing brunette examining party dresses. That was more like it. She followed that customer into the fitting room with anticipation. She examined each dress as it was modeled, and her heart chose the ruby red with the swirling skirts. She loved swirling skirts. She stood behind the brunette and stepped forward so she could see herself in the dress reflected in the mirror.

She drank in the dress—it was perfect. She would shine on the dance floor in that ruby red dancing dress. And what a perfect color for her. She looked up to see the roses the dress would put in her cheeks. And froze. That pasty white reflection couldn't be her. Nobody could be that white and live. Oh, right. They couldn't. She knew she was pale, but did she really have to be so ungodly white?

Bitter, she stepped back and watched the happy brunette twirl in ruby red delight. When the dress was chosen and hung on the hanger, she stared at it. The customer turned away, readying to leave. With the brand new ruby red swirling-skirted dress. Her dress. She reached up and tore it, ripping it from shoulder to waist. And laughed when the customer cried.

Leaving the boutique, the pub across the way caught her attention, and she watched the door. When a tall, lean, black-haired man entered, she followed and took a seat at the bar next to him. Attractive face, easy smile, nice hands. She always noticed men's hands, maybe because they were so nice to hold.

He ordered a beer and let it sit in front of him while he read his paper. She enjoyed an occasional beer and thought one would be lovely now. She leaned in towards the glass and inhaled. Nothing. Puzzled, she leaned closer. No scent at all. She stuck her finger in and touched it to her tongue —no taste. She knocked the glass off the bar and laughed when the beer drenched the man's trousers. Let's see that easy smile now.

She saw the pattern, but desperate to ignore it, she followed a smiling couple into the restaurant next door. Soothed by the soft piano playing in the center of the room, she sat at their table and looked around happily. Everyone was so pretty, all dressed up in their finest. She turned her attention to the couple she shared the table with and listened to them discuss the menu. An anniversary. That should call for lovely champagne and a first-rate meal. She licked her lips in anticipation.

While the couple was enjoying the dance floor, their meal was served. This suited her; she'd eat her fill before they returned. In the dim light, no one would notice cutlery and food moving. She buttered a roll, poured dressing on a salad, and took a bite. Sawdust. Frowning, she tried the champagne. Sawdust again. Tears of rage blurred her vision. The happy couple came back, and she threw the food in their laps and the champagne over their heads. Let's see a happy anniversary now.

She ran out of the restaurant and sank onto a bench on the sidewalk. Had she ever shopped for party dresses or drank beer at a bar or sat at a table in an expensive restaurant? Had anyone ever laughed at her words? Had anyone ever looked at her expectantly? Not remembering made her sad; not being part of the fun made her mad. She had ripped the dress, spilled the drinks, and ruined the meals. Her heart gladdened at the misery and chaos.

She wandered through more stores, throwing purchases out of carts and tripping shoppers. She pinched a baby and laughed aloud when it cried. Until the baby pointed at her. Her laughter choked. If the baby could see her, could its parents see her?

She needed to be careful. What if someone recognized her? Sent her back? She had left her house because she didn't want to be there anymore. She didn't want to live in a haunted house. They were dark, ugly, frightening places. She didn't remember how she had come to be in that house; she didn't remember how she had come to be a ghost. She only knew she'd been one in that house as long as she could remember. When she closed her eyes, she saw a Ouija board, but didn't know what it meant.

The passersby began to thin as people wound down their evening. The street became quiet, and businesses closed as people called goodnight and headed home. Home. She wished she had one. Why should they get to go home when she couldn't? It's not as if she chose to be a ghost. It's not as if she chose to live in a nasty, filthy, old house.

———

"Lisa. Lisa! Get up now."

"Mmmm... I'm awake."

"Get UP, Lisa. I'm going now, so you're responsible for yourself."

"Is breakfast ready?"

"Breakfast is over. You'll make your own."

"Hell, Ma, you can't even make something for me to eat?"

"Hell, Lisa, you can't even get up when I make something for you to eat? Stop being rude. Goodbye."

Lisa watched her mother leave the bedroom and sneered. Her mother was a horrid cook anyway. It was just easier to eat her cooking than make something. She got out of bed and sat down again, head pounding. She'd slept. Must be those weird nightmares making her so tired. She'd take an aspirin with her coffee then go lie on the couch, just until she could pull herself together and face the day.

She woke when her parents came home.

"Lisa. Tell me you didn't just lie on that couch all day."

"Well, okay Ma, I didn't just lie on that couch all day."

Her father stood in front of the couch. "Don't talk to your mother that way. Apologize and go up to your room and get dressed like a civilized woman."

Lisa huffed up the stairs.

"Tell me again why we let her stay here. She's old

enough to have her own place, and I want to know why she doesn't."

Lisa's father smiled. "Because you didn't want an empty house. Changed your mind, Linda?"

"But she's so different, Dennis. She's not the girl we raised. She's become nasty, lazy…" Linda frowned. "Let's just leave it for now. I'll start supper."

After dinner, they sat in the living room watching television. Dennis interrupted them to share a story in the newspaper. "Vandals ran through Kanab businesses last night, terrorizing customers and damaging merchandise."

Lisa frowned. She'd had a dream about some shop, a dress or something…she couldn't remember…but it made her uneasy. Unable to get it out of her thoughts, she went to her bedroom.

Lisa was a thirty-something who lived with her parents. She paid her way, but it was still cheaper than having her own place, so she could save money. And have some companionship. It had worked, for a while. They'd gotten along, and things had been fine. But since a co-worker had taken to hounding Lisa about it, mocking her, the situation made her desperately unhappy with her whole failed, miserable life.

Grateful she had found a way to cope, she lit her candles, turned off the lights, and sat on the floor in the middle of her room. She'd come across an old Book of Spells, but it was too hard to navigate. Luckily, she'd later found a pamphlet that promised a better life and got her nightly ritual from it. She was meant to also honour the moon, to connect to spirits, but she sneered. The only spirit worth connecting to was the warm, bright sun. There was no comfort in a cold, dead moon. She had drawn a circle on the floor and covered it with her rug. Her parents would have called it witchcraft and begged the local priest to exorcise her. She sniffed. It was merely her safe place, where she could forget her problems and call down the gods of calmness and light. She closed her eyes, slowed her breath.

"Quiet is the night, quiet is my mind, calmness is the reward, calmness is what I find.

"The gods of light are with me, the gods of light protect me, the gods of light carry me far away from here."

Extinguishing the candles, she lay down on her bed. She imagined herself floating up and out of her body, leaving her pain and misery behind.

———

SHE RAN down the long hall screaming and then flew down the central staircase to the heavy wooden door at the bottom. Grimacing as it shrieked open, she ran into the night. Hearing running behind her she turned wildly, looking for a hiding place.

"Stop her! Don't let her get away again!"

"Give me your flashlight. She can't get far. Spread out and find her."

"I've lost her..."

The voices slowly moved out of earshot. She didn't know who they were or what they wanted, but she was grateful they hadn't caught her. Nowhere else to go, she drifted slowly into town. Tonight, she chose the movie theater. At least she could sit unobserved and unterrified.

Unable to concentrate on the screen—she didn't like horror films anyway—her thoughts chased each other. What was happening to her?

Fidgeting in her seat caused the man in front to turn around to shush her. Shush her be damned. It didn't matter to her that he actually didn't see her and was confused and uneasy. She kicked his chair, dumped his popcorn, and slapped his date on the back of the head, causing said date to slap him back, call him clumsy and hurtful, and storm out of the theater. He trailed behind, apologizing, while the rest of the audience yelled at him.

A smile of anticipation brightening her face, she followed them. Maybe she hadn't had quite enough town last night.

———

LISA OPENED ONE EYE, groaned, and shoved a pillow over her face. She had a bigger headache today than yesterday, and the light was going to split her head wide open. She consoled herself with the thought of a lovely, lazy day in bed. Or on the couch if the parents weren't around to bite at her. She reached for the door handle and then remembered.

"Lisa, I want you to take your father's dry cleaning to the shop tomorrow."

"Ma, I'm on vacation so I can go back to that horrid job next week."

"I don't ask you to do a lot around here, but this one errand would make my life easier. I'm not on a luxury vacation like you. I have a time clock to punch."

"Well, what about Dad then? They're his clothes; he can take them in."

Linda stared at her daughter. "Never mind. I'll see to it. Very sorry to have bothered you."

Linda slammed out of the living room. Lisa gritted her teeth and followed. "Give me the clothes. I'll take 'em in."

"No, no, I'm ever so sorry to have bothered Madam."

Lisa sighed. "I'm sorry. I didn't realize how mean I sounded. I'm just tired. Please."

Linda studied her. "Thanks. It would help a lot. They're in the closet in the back hall."

This morning, Lisa wished she hadn't agreed. But she'd die before she had to hear her parents go on about it, so she shrugged her coat on, threw the dry cleaning in the back seat, and promised herself a coffee in town.

She passed the lane to the old Hatch mansion, and a chill ran down her neck. She laughed uneasily. "Goose walked over my grave." She turned on the radio for company but couldn't get past the loneliness of that long, shadowed, tree-covered lane. She hadn't been to that house in years, but its image stood clear in her mind. What could possess them to live in such isolation, on such spectral grounds? No one would hear any screams for help. Why had she thought of screams? She pushed the accelerator down and turned the radio up.

She dropped off the dry cleaning and went to find the promised coffee. She drove by the theater and thought she might take in the matinee. "But I don't like horror, and that one in particular is too bloody." She smiled…then stopped. She hadn't seen the display. She backed up, read the marquee, and her stomach dropped. "How did I know that?" Wait. She'd had a dream about that theater last night... She tried to bring the dream back, to remember more. There was a man... He'd said—

Lisa forgot about her coffee and went home, speeding past the Hatch mansion lane. That night, she didn't want to hear Dad read from the paper again, so she made her goodnights early.

Again, she called down the spirits of calmness and light. Again, she lay on her bed and imagined herself floating up and out of her body, desperate to leave her problems, her life, behind. "A new me. That's what I need."

———

SHE RAN down the long hall screaming and flew down the central staircase to the heavy wooden door at the bottom. It wouldn't open. Hearing voices, she frantically looked around for escape. Seeing another hall next to the staircase, she ran, no longer screaming, not wanting to be found, to the door at the end. She reached it, desperately turned the knob, and burst into a kitchen. She found a door to the outside, but neither would this one open. In her terror, she beat at it, cursing, but it held her prisoner. She turned to the beckoning windows that wouldn't open when she tugged at the sashes and smashed at the glass.

"Oh...it worked..."

A male voice. In the kitchen with her. Screaming, she clawed at the wood door and then threw herself against it again and again.

"Hey, stop, don't..."

Was it talking to her? She tried to hide. She tried to run.

"Lady, stop! Nobody's gonna hurt you."

She clutched her arms around herself, her breath hitching.

"That's better. Geez, we didn't mean for THIS to happen."

She slowly turned to find three teenage boys staring at her from the other side of the kitchen table.

"You…can see me?"

"Well…yeah…we called you."

"Why can *you* see me when others can't?"

The boys looked at each other. "I don't know. Wait—what? *Who* can't see you?"

"No one can see me."

"Who is no one? What are you talking about?"

"I've been in town. No one could see me. I'm a ghost. So why can *you* see me when they couldn't?"

"Huh. I guess probably because you're here, where you came through, so you have some power? Or something."

"Well, who are you, and how did you 'call' me?"

"I'm Mark. That's Lenny and Alan, and we use this place as our headquarters because old man Hatch died a long time ago and nobody comes here anymore. We're interested in the paranormal. We investigate that stuff. Like this house. It's supposed to be really haunted. We started using this house so we could document all the ghosts that come around here."

"And that wasn't scary enough? You had to pull me into it?"

"Well, we didn't specifically call *you*. We were just calling any spirit that was around," Lenny explained.

"How was I 'around?'"

"You must'a been around just on your own. We could-n'ta called you otherwise," Mark said.

"Why can't I get out now? I got out of the house before. Why am I stopped now?"

"We put three nails over all the exits—even the windows! That keeps you from getting out," Lenny said.

"Yeah, you put 'em in upside down triangles. Cool, huh?" Mark laughed.

The table flew across the floor and slammed into the wall as she pushed it aside to get at Mark. She slapped him, her handprint stark on his face. The boys stared at her, white-faced, mouths hanging open.

"Well, don't just stand there staring at me, get me back. Now."

The boys eyed each other and stared at her again.

"Holy crap." Mark shuffled his feet. "Well, see, we… Well, we don't know how to do that. It seems that you aren't really…"

Alan stepped forward. "You aren't really a ghost. You couldn'ta slapped Mark if you were. It looks like you somehow must'a left your body on your own, and we just managed to call you."

She regarded the boys one at a time. They dropped their eyes. The silence stretched.

"I'm…*not*…a ghost?"

The boys all let their breath out and grinned. "No, you're just, uh…on an adventure."

"Yeah, we didn't kill you. We just called you."

More silence. Grins faded.

"You're idiots. You're insane idiots."

"But we're not. There's laws we can't break. You did leave your body. Maybe you were bored and looking for something to do."

"BORED?"

"I don't know! Please stop yelling. All I know is you hadda've helped us. Lady, I'm sorry, I don't know. Somehow, you left your body on your own. You wanted to leave."

Images flashed in front of her—in the circle, imagining herself floating up and out of her body, chanting 'gods of night carry me far away from here,' wanting to be somewhere else, wanting a new life. Her lousy damned ritual that was supposed to make her miserable life better. Lisa sagged against the kitchen table, eyes closed. But that didn't stop her memories. She straightened up. "So. How did it work?"

"We set up a Ouija board and called to the spirits."

"Show me how you 'called to the spirits' with your little Ouija board. I don't want to spend any more time in this damned haunted house than I have to. I don't want to meet any ghosts. And you shouldn't be here either. It's dangerous to mess around with this. Who are you? Alan? Get a hammer and get those nails down. All of them. Mark, help him. You, go get that Ouija board." Lisa looked at the boys who were looking at her. "Go!"

Lenny returned first and held the board out to her.

"Don't give it to *me*. Do what you normally do."

Lenny gestured to the living room. "We normally go in there."

"Then GO in there. Do I have to walk you through every step? Honest to hell, I couldn't fall in with any of those intelligent teenagers people like to brag about. I get the three stooges." She shoved him through the door and followed behind. "Call the others."

She stood in the dark, shabby living room; the once elegant gold brocade wallpaper now patterned in green and yellow fungus, the gay flowered furniture now dirty and tattered, the fabric flowing to the ground in ragged streams. The air was fetid, and her lungs protested having to breathe it.

The boys stood in the middle of the room. "We don't... I can't...um..."

"You can't REMEMBER? You've done this often enough," Lisa screamed.

"Well, ah, not...really." Lenny mumbled. "We actually just started. We only had like two times."

"Two times?"

"We had to work out what to do."

Stumbling into the furniture and each other, arguing about places and phrases, they finally set the Ouija board on the table in front of the massive, filthy fireplace. As the boys tried to work out how to send her back, the planchette moved.

"Quit moving it, Lenny."

"I'm not doing it! Why would I make it say we're all dead?"

"Not funny, jerk."

The planchette flew into the air, spun around, and faced each boy, while the four watched, immobilized. The planchette swooped and dove at the boys; the Ouija board flew across the room at Lisa and she ran, breaking their paralysis. A huge wind roared out of the fireplace, slamming the living room doors shut in their faces.

"Leaving? Before we've even been introduced?" The voice was soft and furry, like phlegm caught in a throat. Low laughter built to ear-shattering decibels. It circled around them, driving them back into the middle of the room where they clung together.

"Now then. Playmates?" No one answered. "Oh, come then. You called me. Now play with me." Silence. "Because I will play with you."

The planchette sailed across the room from the mantel where it had settled and drove deep into Lenny's throat, blood spurting from the hole. Lenny choked a cry, grabbed at Alan, and slid to the ground. The planchette turned and smashed into the fireplace, shatters falling to the floor. Alan screamed and tried to wipe away Lenny's blood. Mark clutched his own throat, shuddering at Lenny's body. Lisa stood in shock, her screams matching Alan's.

A tall figure, vaguely human, materialized in front of them. Wispy gray, resembling a cobweb, its only color was pale blue eyes. Lisa was mesmerized by those eyes. The irises were slits, like goat's eyes. Or the Devil's.

"I'll not ask again." It pointed at her. "You will answer me."

"They're just kids. You didn't have to kill him," she whispered. She swallowed hard. "What do you want?"

"You go first. What do *you* want?"

"We don't want anything. You came to us."

"No. You called me. And I want to know what you want now that you have me."

"Well, I didn't call you. I just want—" She shut her

mouth. She didn't want this thing to know she was out of her body. She didn't want this thing knowing her body was empty and defenseless. She didn't want this thing to know anything about her.

"Oh, you don't want to go home just yet. Think of all the fun to be had."

She froze. She clawed her cheeks. Her mouth opened and shut. The specter laughed.

"How...do you know?"

"How do I know what?" It stepped behind the boys. "How to catch a ghost? How to find an empty body that nobody is using?" It came up behind her and whispered moistly in her ear. "How to get you back into yours?"

She shrieked and turned. "How do you know? How do you know?"

"I told you—you called me. Your little friends here have been broadcasting their call to all and sundry. I apparently am the first to answer. Well, the first that meant to answer. You, technically, are the first, but you're an accident, so it's my show now. And what I want is your body. Let's go."

"No!"

It shoved her forward. "You will come with me now, Lisa."

The specter gripped her by her neck and pulled her to the door. She tried to fight, but her mind wouldn't work. Evil knew her name.

With a gesture, the specter slammed open the front door of the mansion and dragged her down the driveway. The night air revived her, and she struggled in its grasp. It circled its grip around her, binding her arms to her sides.

At the driveway's end, it turned left, and its long steps had them at the crossroads in seconds.

Holding tight to Lisa's neck, the specter stood the two of them in the center of the crossroads, facing the moon hanging low in the sky. "Hecate, God of Witchcraft, Ruler of Witches, I ask that you hear my prayer. I ask that you grant my wish.

"God of the moon, God of the night, I call you here to show your might.

"I bring your prize, I bring your answer, I beg that you will grant the transfer."

The moon disappeared behind the clouds, night sounds filled the air, and a wind circled them. Lisa felt the earth turn under her feet and saw the trees whirl over her head. A single ray of moon pierced the darkness. The air grew heavy and pushed her to her knees.

"You have done well, shadow. You brought me the transgressor. Release her. I will deal with her now."

The specter's hand slid from the back of Lisa's neck to the front and cupped her cheek. As it stared into her eyes, it laughed. Its laughter was silenced as it was knocked through the air, hitting a tree, and sliding to the ground. It scrambled to stand, to escape the growling and snapping that surrounded it.

"You presume, shadow. Touch her again without my say, and my hounds will have you."

Arms free, Lisa stood and spun around. "Who is that? Where are you?"

"It is not for you to see me. It is not for you to ask questions. You broke my laws, and I am here to judge you."

"Laws? What laws did I break? Who are you?" Lightning hit the ground beside her, and she fell back to her knees.

"I grow weary of you. You dabble in my magic as if it is a game. Now you will pay."

"I didn't dabble in your anything! Turn that light off so I can see." She stood, shielding her eyes with her hand.

Hecate's laugh rang out like bells on a winter morning, freezing Lisa's soul. "Turn off the moon, wretched girl? You are far more insolent and ignorant than I heeded." Hecate raised her arm, and Lisa flew into the night sky and hung there. "Look deep into my beautiful moon and tell me again to shut it off."

Lisa twisted her head back and forth, kicked her legs, and flailed her arms, trying to avoid the light.

"I said look."

Lisa's ears ran blood from the power of Hecate's command. Head stilled, she stared, unblinking, into the brilliant light. Her eyes opened wide to draw it in. Her mouth opened wide to drink it in. The moonlight surrounded Lisa, engulfing her, growing brighter and whiter, burning her in it. The scream in her throat tore out with agonizing clarity. At its brightest and whitest, the light dropped Lisa to the ground and returned to the moon.

The crossroads once again were dark and silent. Hecate appeared in their center and regarded the specter. "Well done."

"Thank you, Madam. But is it well enough done?"

"You have your body. Be in it before the cock crows or it is lost to you."

The specter bowed before her.

"Leave now. But note well—meddle in my magic, and my hellhounds will feast on you."

"It is noted."

Hecate whistled once; she and the hounds faded into the night.

The specter picked up Lisa's body and walked down the road to its new home. The night was still black when it slinked up the stairs. Working silently, the specter folded back the rug and gently placed the body in the middle of the circle. Lighting the candles around the room, it stood over the body, took seven deep breaths, and then enveloped the body in its gray mist.

"This body, this home, I seek to own. This body, this home, is mine alone.

"This body, this home, I will have and will cherish. This body, this home, I will live in 'til I perish.

"I claim this body in Hecate's great name."

Nothing happened; the specter was still shut out. It peered at the sky. No sunrise—safe there. It breathed deeply to calm its racing thoughts. It brought its hands together, palm to palm, and chanted silently again. Damnation! Still shut out. How much time was left? What was it missing?

It smiled. Breathing again seven times, it saluted the moon. "Thank you for this gift, thank you for this favor. I promise to care for this body and be a credit to you, Hecate. Thanks be to you." Its world tilted; its vision went black. When it opened its eyes again, the sun was shining brightly through the window.

With a joyful salute to the now invisible moon, the

resurrected Lisa laughed, threw on her robe and danced down the stairs to join her family.

Mickie lives in the Southwest, where she spends her nights writing stories of horror and suspense inspired by her beloved rescue cats, Pal and Lassie. She spends her days sleeping with her fists clenched because Shirley Jackson taught her that not everything that wants to hold her hand is a friend. You can find her on Twitter @MBollingBurke.

CADMIUM BLUE

JEFF DOSSER

Cadmium blue. Emily Ray lowered her binoculars and studied the children. The girl's aura was a brilliant cadmium blue.

The leather of Emily Ray's utility belt creaked as she glanced over her cruiser's back seat and checked the empty Cedarview streets.

Satisfied, she lifted her binoculars and studied the children once again. They sat beneath a rusted 'Bus Stop' sign. The boy was nothing special, virtually no aura at all, but the girl...

Dropping her police cruiser into gear, Emily Ray pulled up to the bus stop and stepped out of her car.

In the bleak February wind, the children snuggled beneath the protection of a stained Hulk blanket. Two sets of bright blue eyes and a few blonde tangles poked from above Hulk's torso.

"Oh, you dear children. Where did you come from?" Emily Ray's eyes drifted to the Waffle House a half-block up the road and then to the empty carwash across the street. "Is your momma or daddy about?

Only a headshake from the smaller of the two gave any indication they'd heard.

Emily Ray stepped around her car and leaned against the passenger door. She studied them a moment then smoothed down a torn piece of the reflective Sheriff's Department decal plastered to the door.

"Ya'll don't talk much do ya?" Emily Ray said.

The children considered each other before the older of the two let his end of the blanket drop and revealed the dirt-smudged face of a boy no older than twelve.

"W-w-we are...we are not s-supposed to talk to s-strangers." He spoke at a halting, stuttered pace that made his words seem too big for his mouth. Once he'd had his say, he raised the blanket and once again peered over the top.

In that brief instant, Emily Ray recognized something different in the boy's features.

"Have your parents told you about the police?"

Both nodded.

"And are the police good guys or bad guys?"

There was a time when the question was a no brainer. Nowadays, it seemed almost a tossup.

"The good guys!" the smaller one blurted. Her young voice was as sharp and clear as the bright winter air.

"That's right, we're the good guys." Emily Ray squared her shoulders and smiled. "I'll bet you two are cold. Am I right?"

Another shared glance and a nod from both.

"Would either of you like a muffin?"

Their eyes widened.

"Hungry huh?"

Fast, wide-eyed nods from the girl and a narrowed, suspicious gaze from the boy.

Emily opened the cruiser's door and leaned in to retrieve a rumpled paper sack from the back seat. She crinkled it open and took out a blueberry muffin.

"I'm sorry I don't have more." She handed it to the boy.

The blanket dropped into their laps as he peeled away the wrapper, pulled off a piece, and handed it to his sister. Though their faces differed, their blue eyes and blonde hair virtually guaranteed they were related.

The girl, maybe seven, was towheaded just like her brother, her long curls crushed beneath a stocking cap. Her thin face stuck out from a down jacket easily three sizes too large. Borrowed from her brother, Emily Ray guessed. The boy, his clothes just as dirty, wore two layers of sweaters over a pair of holed jeans.

As they devoured the snack, Emily Ray studied the empty streets.

"Well, I can't leave you two out here on your own." She looked at the children and smiled. "Now can I?"

The boy rose from the bench, muffin crumbs plastered to his chin. As he spoke, he said each word with purpose.

"I am...I am her b-b-brother," he pointed a finger at the girl, "and *I* am the one t-taking ...taking care of her."

The boy's thick, studied words and peculiar features suddenly clicked. He was retarded.

"Aww, look at you out here," Emily Ray said. "A little retarded boy taking care of his sister."

His face darkened as color bloomed in his cheeks "I

am…I am a D-D-Down syndrome p-person," he said. "I am…I am *n-not* retarded."

Emily Ray took a step back, smiling.

"Oh, my." She looked to the girl and winked. "I apologize Mr…." She straightened and placed a finger aside her chin. "You know, we haven't been properly introduced. I'm Deputy Emily Ray of the Cedarview County Sheriff's Department." She looked at the girl. "But you can call me Miss Emily." She offered her hand to the boy. "And what's your name?"

He looked to his sister and then to Emily Ray's outstretched hand. His grip was soft and moist.

"I am…I am Hans G-G-Gunderson, and this is my little s-sister, G-G-Greta."

She gave Hans's hand another shake then crouched down beside the girl.

"Hi, Greta. I'm Miss Emily." She offered her hand. "Do you know where your parents are?"

"They left us and ran away to do drugs, okay." Greta lifted her blanket so only her eyes peered out.

Hans shoulder bumped his sister, his brows knit into a rebuke. "You're not supposed to s-s-say." He looked to Emily Ray then quickly away.

"That's all right," Emily Ray said. "I guessed as much."

When she took the girl's hand, Emily Ray's eyes widened. "Goodness, gracious, you're cold as a popsicle." She took Greta's other hand and pressed them in her palms. "Aren't you two freezing?" She looked to the boy. "It's thirty-eight degrees out; you've got to be cold."

"I'll tell you what," Emily Ray said. The children shared

a look as she rose and opened the cruiser's back door. "My police car's nice and warm, and besides..." She shrugged. "I can't leave you out here all alone, not without your mom and dad. If I did, I'd get into all sorts of trouble with the sheriff." She looked to them shaking her head. "You wouldn't want me to get into trouble, now would you?"

The girl skootched to the edge of the bench with the blanket bunched in her lap. The boy's eyes narrowed.

"Did I mention I have lunch?" Emily Ray said. She looked to Hans. "Does a hamburger sound good? Maybe with jack cheese and onions?"

"I...I don't l-like onions," Hans said.

"Okay, nix the onions."

And with no more trouble than that, Emily Ray bundled the children into her back seat and slid behind the wheel. With a satisfied sigh, she lifted the mic from the dash.

"Robert one-oh-two, show me ninety-seven on that check the well-being call."

"Ten-four, Robert one-oh-two," the dispatcher's voice crackled over the speakers. "Time now, thirteen-forty-two hours."

Emily Ray set the mic in its cradle then slung an arm over the front seat so she could see the children. "I'm gonna run into the diner real quick, and then it's off to lunch." She smiled. "So, stay right here, 'kay?"

Emily Ray pulled up to the Waffle House, took her keys from the ignition, and locked the doors. She strode up to the front door and stepped into a warm rush of breakfast-scented air.

"Hey, Gail." Emily Ray waved to a waitress at the far end of the counter. "How's it goin'?"

"Emily, how are you?" A stout woman with jet-black hair and a sleeve of tattoos slapped a dishtowel over her shoulder and stepped around the counter. She pulled Emily Ray into a hug.

"Girl, I ain't seen you in a month ah Sundays," Gail said. She leaned past Emily Ray and looked into the streets. "You here about them kids?"

"Yup, we got your call." Emily Ray turned and looked towards the parking lot. Only the cruiser's hood and front tire were visible from the window. "Two kids, right? A boy and a girl?" She turned and followed the waitress's gaze. "Did they say anything before they left?"

"Not much." Gail produced an order pad from her apron, flipped it open, and began to read. "Hans and Greta Gunderson." She stuffed the pad in her apron. "Seven and twelve years old."

She shrugged. "That's all I got." She leaned against the counter and sighed. "It was pretty busy, and the next time I looked up, they were gone."

From her breast pocket, Emily Ray produced her own notepad and jotted down the names.

"Can you describe em'?"

Gail's eyes drifted skyward in thought. "Blonde, both of 'em. Towheaded, you know?" She met Emily's eyes. "The boy was maybe five foot tall, heavy. The girl …" She shrugged. "I don't know…forty, maybe fifty pounds… skinny. Didn't look like they'd had a good meal in days." She paused a second in thought. "Oh, an' the boy's special needs. Down syndrome, I think."

"Uh-huh." Emily nodded, scratching on the pad. "Anything else?"

"Yeah." Gail leaned against the counter and frowned. "I think they're abandoned, runaways maybe." She crossed her arms and sighed. "I noticed 'em starin' in the front windows around ten or ten-thirty, right before the lunch rush. They came in and sat down at the bar. The boy wanted to know how much they could get for fifty-seven cents." She shook her head. "Sad really. I gave 'em some eggs and pie but couldn't get much out of 'em. Just that they'd been staying at the Holiday Express up on Highway 9."

Emily gnawed her lip as she imagined the rundown motel at the edge of town. The Holiday Express was known for two things—one-night stands and meth.

"Any mention of parents?" Emily Ray asked.

Gail frowned. "Nope."

Emily Ray closed her notepad and stepped to the counter. "Thanks, Gail, you've been a huge help." She eyed a stack of donuts beneath a glass cake cover. "How about a couple of donuts for the road?"

Emily Ray slid into her cruiser and turned around. "Well, I see you guys met Gail." She removed the donuts, wrapped each in a napkin, and handed them back.

"She was nice," the girl said.

"Mmm-hmm," the boy agreed, his mouth filled with donut.

Picking up the mic, Emily Ray dropped the cruiser into gear and headed down the road. "Okay, now be quiet, then it's off to lunch." She met their eyes and smiled.

Emily Ray keyed the talk button, "Robert one-oh-two."

"Robert one-oh-two, go ahead," the dispatcher returned.

"Robert one-oh-two, show me ten-eight off this call. Negative contact, break."

"One-oh-two," the dispatcher acknowledged. "Go ahead."

"Show me ten-forty-six at my residence," Emily Ray said.

"Ten-four." The dispatcher's voice was mellow and slow. A jazz voice, Emily Ray thought. "Are you sure, you don't wanna drop by dispatch?" the voice asked. "We've been ordering low-fat meals and walking on our lunch hour. Natalie's already lost five pounds, and I've lost two."

"No thanks, Tina," Emily Ray said.

In the rearview mirror, she spotted Greta poking Hans in the ribs, eliciting a yelp. Emily Ray scowled and held a finger to her lips. "I'd love to, but I'm swamped. Maybe next week."

A chuckle came over the speakers. "Okay, Robert one-oh-two. Ten-four. But watch out for those home-cooked meals. They'll catch up to you one of these days."

Emily Ray lived deep in the woods at the edge of Lake Thunderbird Falls state park. After pulling out of Cedarview, they took Highway 9 to the north gate park entrance and bounded along the rutted gravel track, leaving behind a cloud of gray dust to mark their passage.

"Forgive the mess," Emily Ray said as she helped the children from the car and escorted them onto the front porch. "But I wasn't expecting guests."

The door opened onto a dim open space with a Navajo-patterned couch and a rough-wood coffee table. The kitchen was situated against the back wall with an assort-ment of overhanging copper pots above tan marble coun-tertops and gleaming stainless-steel appliances. But what caught the children's eyes and froze them in place were the paintings.

Above the stone fireplace hung a squared canvas eight feet tall. On it was painted a brilliant, sunset-colored rose. The flower's pink and purple-shadowed petals stood out in almost 3-D clarity atop a green stalk that breathed with life. Despite the room's shadows, a dozen similar paintings lit the space to brilliance with their joyous and bright colors.

With the children left gawking on her couch, Emily Ray flitted to the coffee table and scooped up an empty plate and a half-filled glass before rushing into the kitchen.

"We're gonna have so much fun," she said. "You just wait an' see."

With a clatter of pans and several dives into the pantry, the smell of frying burgers and battered fries soon filled the air. In minutes, she'd set an open-faced bun with a cheese-topped patty, a pile of fries, and a scoop of choco-late pudding in front of each.

"All right, my dears." Emily grabbed the remote and flicked the TV to Nickelodeon. "While you two eat, I'll get everything ready."

Though they eyed the food hungrily, neither ate. The girl looked from her plate to the boy, who looked, in turn to Emily Ray.

"What's wrong?" she asked. "I thought you were hungry."

"W-w-we don't have any m-money," Hans said.

"Don't worry about that." Emily Ray waved a hand and chuckled. "You and your sister are now wards of the state."

The children exchanged a confused look.

"That means you're *my* responsibility until we find your parents."

They still looked uncertain.

Emily Ray laughed. "It also means your burgers are free. So go ahead…eat all you want."

It was all the encouragement they needed. As they ate, Emily Ray pulled out her phone and tapped across the screen. Satisfied with what she saw, she dropped into a chair, crossed her legs, and watched them eat.

"Do you know," Emily Ray uncrossed her legs and reversed them, "that I've rarely seen such a beautiful aura."

The boy tucked the last bit of burger between his lips, a sheen of grease on his chin. The girl had only taken a couple of bites of burger, focusing her attention instead on the pudding and fries.

At Emily Ray's words, they looked up.

"W-w-what's an aura?" Hans asked.

Emily Ray's eyes narrowed as they flicked to the boy. Ignoring his question, she leaned closer to the girl. "Do you know what an aura is, sweetheart?"

Greta's curls, freed of the dirty cap, bounced when she shook her head.

"An aura's a person's spirit. Their soul." She leveled a finger at Greta. "I can *see* a person's spirit." She nodded as Greta's eyes widened. "I can see *your* spirit." She leaned back, once more crossing her legs.

"The Lord's blessed me with synesthesia. Have you ever heard that word?"

They shook their heads.

"It means I can see colors others can't." She waved a hand to the windows and the winter-grayed world beyond. "I see colors in the wind, in music." She smiled and met Greta's eye. "And sometimes in people too. Like *your* spirit, Little Miss, is cadmium blue. No doubt about it, a brilliant cadmium blue."

Greta squared her shoulders and looked to Hans.

"I'm cabinet blue," she said with a wide, gap-toothed grin.

"Cad...me...um, sweetheart," Emily Ray corrected. "Cadmium blue."

"W-what color am I?" Hans asked.

Emily's smile faded. "I'm sorry, little man." She reached out and patted Hans's knee. "You don't have an aura like real people." She pushed out her lower lip. "You're just a muddy ol' gray. Nothing special 'bout you at all." Her eyes drifted to the window. "Like a dreary February day."

The boy's face fell, and he looked to the floor.

"Oh, don't fret. It's some people's lot in life to be a burden to others." She patted him again. "It's not your fault. It's just the way the world is."

"Well, now. "Emily Ray pushed to her feet. "Enough sad talk. I've gotta get back to work, and of course the sheriff has rules against unsupervised children wandering the streets." She pursed her lips and, hands-on-knees, bent down to face them. "We can't have you roaming around all cold and hungry, now can we?"

"But." She clapped her hands. "Even though you've got to stay here, we'll have so much fun you won't even notice you're locked up."

She took Greta's hand and led her down the hall. Hans followed a pace behind. "I've never had two children with me." She looked back at Hans and smiled. "The sheriff's quite strict on how we house our little boys and girls." She met Hans's eye and winked. "So, we'll have to bend the rules just a little."

At the center of a short hall, a bedroom opened on one side and a bathroom on the other. At the end of the hall, a third door stood ajar.

"This will be *your* room, sweetheart." She laid a hand on Greta's shoulder and guided her in. "At least until we find your parents."

A twin bed with fluffy pastel pillows and a dancing kitten comforter sat beneath a set of sunflower-yellow curtains. On a bedside table beside a mini-fridge sat an Xbox controller and games and mounted on the wall was a 56" flatscreen.

"The toilet's in here." She opened a door beside the bed and revealed a sink, toilet, and fiberglass tub with smiley-face shower curtains.

"And a closet." She opened a second door, but it was empty. "Don't worry, I'll pick up some clothes, and tonight we'll get you all cleaned up." She closed the closet and met Greta's eyes. "Do you have a preference in PJs? Unicorn, princess, superhero?"

"Princess PJs, please."

Emily Ray smiled. "Princess PJs it is."

Emily Ray stepped to the room's mini-fridge, opened

the door, and frowned. Inside sat a half-empty Dr. Pepper, two bottles of water, and a jar of strawberry jam.

"I guess it's been a while since my last guest." She crouched in front of Greta. "But tonight, we'll make a list and fill this thing with anything you want."

"Anything?" Greta asked.

"That's right, sweetheart, anything at all. You just name it."

Hans stood at the doorway, loudly clearing his throat until Emily Ray turned her eyes on him.

"Yes," she said through gritted teeth, "what is it, Hans?"

"P-Papa, said we shouldn't eat too many s-sweets. It'll r-r-rot our teeth."

Emily Ray's eyelids fluttered, and she took a breath. "Well, this is a special case, don't you think?" She looked to Greta nodding. "Isn't that right?" When the girl mirrored her nod, she turned back to Hans.

"How about I get her a fancy new toothbrush and she can brush to her heart's content?"

Hans looked a little confused but nodded anyway. "I g-g-guess that'd be okay."

Emily Ray looked past him into the living room. "Finding a place for you might pose a challenge."

As they turned to go, Emily Ray held out a hand to stop Greta from leaving. "Not you, little angel, you've got to stay here."

Emily Ray poked her finger into a latch in the door's frame and pulled a pocket-door from the wall. The pocket door, a set of thin metal bars, slid to cover the doorway while at the same time allowing the bedroom door to be shut from outside. Emily Ray withdrew a key and locked the bars with a click.

Greta rushed to the opening and pressed her face against the bars.

"W-why… Why do you have bars on G-Greta's room?" Hans's brows furrowed as he looked from his sister to Emily Ray.

"That's because we're a bit like a jail," she said. "But a fun jail."

Emily Ray took Hans's hand and led him into the living room. When they stepped out of view, Greta shrieked and reached out for her brother. Hans rushed back and they hugged each other through the bars.

As they cried, Emily Ray checked her watch. "Okay, that's enough," she said.

When their wails only intensified, she pulled the baton from her patrol belt and clattered it across the bars. "I said, enough!" Her red face punctuated the ring of wood on steel, and the children looked up in surprise. Emily Ray's features softened.

"I said…" She tilted her head and forced a smile. "That is enough. There's no need for tears." She laid a hand on Hans's shoulder and drew him away.

"Don't worry," Emily Ray said to Hans's concerned look. "She'll get used to it soon enough. They always do."

"Bu…bu…but you can't l-leave her there." He turned and stared down the hall.

"If I were you." Emily Ray extended a bony finger. "I wouldn't worry about my sister." At the word 'sister,' she poked Hans in the chest. "I'd be worried about myself." She jabbed him again, and Hans's eyes widened.

"You and your sister." She poked Hans and backed him against the wall. "Are my responsibility." Jab. "And you will do exactly." Jab. "As I say."

Hans's eyes grew moist, and he rubbed at his chest. "Do you understand?"

He stared up with wide, frightened eyes.

"I *said*, do…you…understand?"

Hans nodded.

"And do you see those cameras?" Emily Ray pointed to one peering into the hallway from a spot on the wall. She pointed to a second, looking like a cue ball on a block. It sat beside a stack of books in the living room shelves. She pointed out a third floating cue ball in the kitchen atop the fridge.

"Besides those, there's a camera in your sister's room, my room, and outside."

She waited for Hans's eyes to complete their tour before going on.

"I can see and hear everything." She nodded towards the front door. "And when I leave in the morning, no one's coming in or out."

"You." She jabbed him again. "Will not touch my cameras, or I will be very, very upset. Do I make myself clear?"

He nodded.

"Good." Emily Ray stepped back and her features softened.

"I don't like being the bad guy," she cocked her head, "but sometimes I must. You understand?"

Hans nodded again.

"Good." Her face brightened and she opened her

palms. "See, we've come to an understanding already."

Brushing her hands on her thighs, Emily Ray looked around.

"Well, I supposed I'd better get back to work." She looked to Hans. "But what to do with you." She scrubbed her chin and examined the room.

"Do you know how to sweep? You do? And mop?" She smiled at his nod. "Excellent."

She led him to the pantry where a mop and broom hung beside a bucket of cleaning supplies and a vacuum cleaner.

"This should keep you busy until I get home." She looked at Hans and nodded. "And tonight, besides a list of goodies for your sister, I'll make a list of chores for you." She checked her watch. "After dinner, you and I will have an in-depth discussion about rules."

Tears sparkled in his eyes. "Bu…bu…bu…"

"Bu…bu…bu…what?" mocked Emily Ray. "Spit it out, for God's sake."

A tear drizzled down his cheek and patted on his shirt. "B-but I…I…I want g-goodies too?"

Emily Ray laughed. It was a hearty, full laugh.

"And why waste money on you?" She stepped to the door and smiled. "If I gave you something, you'd only forget it a few minutes later." She reached down and tucked him beneath the chin. "That's almost like throwing it away."

Emily Ray closed the door, and the deadbolt ground shut with a 'thunk.' Not sure of what to do, Hans rushed to the front window and drew back the curtains. They were blocked by black steel bars bolted to the wall. Beyond them, he watched Emily Ray pull out her cellphone before climbing into her cruiser. A second later and he heard her voice, tinny and clear, over the camera's speakers.

"Get away from that window and get to work," she said.

Hans looked around until his eyes landed on the bookshelf camera. The ball swiveled its electronic eye and glared.

"Come on, chop-chop," Emily Ray's disembodied voice said.

The car started and the scrunch of gravel dwindled as it pulled away.

"Get to work," Emily Ray said once more. "You don't have all day."

———

THAT NIGHT, Emily Ray returned with an extra-large dog crate, a padlock, and an armful of cushions for Hans's bed. She crafted a list of everything Greta wanted and a shorter list of chores to keep Hans busy while she was away.

Over the next several weeks, their lives ran to the relentless tick of Emily Ray's clock. At 5:50 A.M. they were awakened by the chuffing of Emily Ray's automatic coffee maker. At six, the grinding buzz of her alarm announced the beginning of another day.

She released Hans by seven and was out the door by seven-thirty. At noon, she returned for lunch, sometimes carrying a bag of burgers or box of pizza, but usually only a set of barked orders telling Hans what to make for lunch. By five, she returned and changed into jeans and a baggy shirt before allowing Greta out of her room. She and Emily Ray would play checkers or watch TV as Hans prepared their meal. At eight, Emily Ray put them back in their cages and disappeared into her backyard workshop. Greta could see the shop through her bedroom window, but the children never discovered what Emily Ray was doing.

In the moments between the coffee maker firing up and Emily Ray scuffing sleepily out her bedroom door, the children talked. Greta sat at the bars with her legs tucked beneath her. From his crate, Hans could hear her breathing. Just knowing she was there made him feel better.

"Rise and shine," Emily Ray called from the kitchen. She filled her mug and puttered into the living room. At the grumble of distant thunder, she pulled aside the shades and peeked outside.

"All right, outcha go." She unlocked Hans's crate and nodded towards the kitchen. "Breakfast isn't going to fix itself."

He scrambled eggs, fried bacon, and buttered toast as Emily Ray ducked into her bedroom to dress. When the high-pitched whine of Emily Ray's water pipes announced her entrance into the shower, Hans crept back to Greta's door. He knew from painful experience that they had until Emily Ray's hairdryer fired up to talk.

Crouching beside Greta's bars, he considered her as she waddled over and dropped down beside him. Hans worried at all the weight she'd gained since Emily Ray took them in and wondered if Papa would even recognize her.

"Hans." She slipped an arm through the bars and took his hand. "How much longer do we have to stay?"

Hans studied his sister's face and shook his head. Her once thin cheeks were plump and rosy, her fingers and arms round. On a steady diet of cake, pop, and pizza, her skin glistened with the effort of holding her all in.

"I d-d-don't know."

From behind Emily Ray's door came the sound of a dresser being closed, the squeak of a faucet, and the splash of water in the sink.

"M-Miss Emily is a good g-guy," Hans said. "We just have to…have to wait un…un…until she finds Papa."

Greta let go of his hand and stared at her fingers.

"Papa's never taken this long." She raised her eyes as a tear crept down her cheek. "What if something happened to him?" She leaned closer, her voice only a whisper. "Hans, I think Miss Emily…" Her eyes cut to Emily Ray's door and then back. "I think she's bad."

Hans's eyes narrowed.

"Bad? But she's a p-police." He shook his head; the concept of Emily Ray being bad was impossible to accept. "Miss Emily has a ….a badge an'…an'…an' a gun, an'…an'…an' she drives a police car and *everything*." He said this last word louder than the rest, and his eyes darted to Emily Ray's door.

"I know she *said* that," Greta whispered.

From Emily Ray's room, a blow-dryer hummed to life and propelled Hans to his feet.

"But, Hans. She lied."

That day, Hans thought hard on what Greta had said. He began as he always did, with the dishes. Next, he swept and mopped the kitchen and scrubbed the hallway bath until its fixtures gleamed. He tried recalling all the stories where good guys had gone bad. Then, he remembered Star Wars. Hadn't Anakin become Vader? Anakin had been good. Then, his mother died, and he'd been so angry. Hans wondered if something happened to make Emily Ray so angry too.

He mulled this over as one by one he dusted each of Emily Ray's paintings. There were fourteen in all, copies according to Emily Ray; all except the big one over the mantle. That painting was of a giant, pinkish-purple rose so wonderfully realistic that sometimes Hans thought he could smell it.

Of all her paintings, though, Hans liked Candice the best. Like all of Emily Ray's work, each was named after a missing child, and on each, she'd stuck a photo. Hans recognized the Candice flower from Papa's garden back home. It was a Tiger Lily with six orange petals against a vague background of woodsy green. Tiger Lily was a fun name, Hans thought, and he liked the way Candice smiled at him from her school picture at the corner of the frame. She had blue eyes and was missing her front teeth, just like Greta.

Emily Ray said that after helping children at work, she liked coming home and making paintings for all those who were lost. She told Hans she donated most of the money she made from her paintings to the Utah Society for Lost and Exploited Children. It sounded *very* important. She told him the painting above the fireplace would bring more than twenty-thousand dollars when it went to auction in the fall. Hans hadn't ever seen that much money, but it sounded like a lot. He figured Papa could put things back the way they were if he had money like that.

As he dusted, Hans studied the grinning photo at the bottom of each painting and wondered what they were like. Candice and Joseph, Allison and Crystal, Ethan with his crooked smile, and Olivia with her bright, dark eyes and head of black curls.

He was jolted from his thoughts by a crack of thunder and flicker of living room lights. When Greta cried out, despite Emily Ray's rule to never talk with his sister while she was away, Hans dropped his duster and raced into the hall. He found Greta crouched beside the bars crying.

"It's dark outside, Hans." She took his hand in hers. "What if there's a tornado?" Her eyes darted to the window. "There's tornadoes coming, Hans. I saw it last night on TV."

"D-don't worry," he reassured her. "Remember what... remember what Mama always says. You can't have r-r-rainbows without a st-storm."

They sat in silence as the sky darkened, and with a sudden, jagged crack, it opened up, and rain sheeted down.

"I don't like Miss Emily," Greta said. The pale light from her window sparkled on a tear caught on the roundness of her chin. "She's never letting us go."

Greta's words bound the warning in his heart with the conflict in his head. With a lightning-flash of clarity, Hans understood. Emily Ray had trapped them. He was the older brother. He was supposed to take care of Greta, but instead, he'd failed.

"I'm s-sorry, Greta." His eyes grew hot. "If I wasn't so st-st-stupid, stupid, stupid!"

With each accusation, Hans slammed his head against the bars.

"Hans quit! Stop! Stop!" She reached up and held him as tears streaked his cheeks.

"You're *not* stupid! You're *not!*"

Thunder boomed, and with a pop, the house sank into darkness. All the sounds Hans had overlooked—the hum of the Xbox, the electric click and gas hiss of the water heater, the refrigerator's purr. All of it was gone. What remained was the sound of their breathing and the steady exhalation of the storm.

Cowed by the silence, Greta whispered into Hans's ear, "You've got to get us out."

"But G-Greta? How? Emily Ray's w-w-watching." He turned and looked at the camera.

"She can't see us now," Greta said. "There's no power."

Hans studied the kitchen camera. Its red light was gone. "S-so, they don't w-w-work?"

Greta shook her head. "I don't think so."

Hans rocked back on his haunches and looked down the hall.

"W-what should we do?"

"Can you get outside?"

Hans shook his head. "N-n-no. Emily Ray t-t-takes the key to the front door and the backdoor's p-p-padlocked."

Greta rested with her chin on her knee and considered. Outside, the monsoon dwindled to a steady shower.

"What about the garage?" Greta asked. "Can you go through there?"

Hans hugged himself and rocked back and forth.

"Oh, n-n-no." He shook his head refusing to meet her eye. "I c-can't."

It was their first week when Emily Ray led him to the garage door. She'd pulled an odd yellow gun from behind her back and snapped off a black square at the end. Hans recognized it as one of the guns Emily Ray wore on her police belt.

"This is the only door outside that's not double-locked," she'd told him. "Do you know what happens if I find out you've opened it?"

Hans shook his head.

"This." Emily Ray pulled the trigger. The gun clattered like an alarm clock without a bell as tongues of lightning flickered across the end. When she slammed it into Hans's shoulder, every muscle ignited in pain. His jaw, his arm, his whole body locked as electric fire jittered through his limbs.

When he opened his eyes, he was lying on the floor with Emily Ray staring down. Her eyes were hard as glass. "If I find out you've opened that door, that's what will happen." She smiled. "But not to you." She pointed to Greta's room. "To your sister."

Hans shuddered at the memory.

"Whaddya mean you can't?" Greta asked.

"Emily Ray said if I open that d-d-door, she'll h-hurt you." Hans's heart thundered like the storm. "Greta." He squeezed her hand. "She'll hurt you b-b-bad."

Greta sighed and pressed against the bars. When she looked up, her face was set, her jaw tight.

"You've got to do it anyway." She took his hand, drew

it through the bars, and placed her cheek in his palm. "You've got to get us out, Hans." She looked up and met his eye. "We've got to find Papa."

Hans took a deep breath and nodded. "Okay, G-Greta. I'll try."

His legs were wobbly as he pushed to his feet.

"Wait a second," Greta said, "I've got something to help."

She raced to the toybox and threw back the lid. She scooped out toys by the armload and dumped them to the floor. With a "got it!" she rushed back to Hans. In one hand, she held a flashlight. Sponge Bob and Patrick were printed on the side. In the other, she held two walkie-talkies: one with an image of Princess Elsa and the other with Princess Anna.

She handed Hans the flashlight. When he flicked it on, it threw a dim yellow circle on the wall. She clicked on the Anna walkie and handed it through the bars. Hans frowned.

"Greta, we got the same toys from Santa l-last year." He shook his head and took the walkie. "These things are c-c-crap. Don't you remember?"

"I know." She dropped down beside him. "But it's all we've got."

With a staticky hiss, she clicked on her walkie. She smiled and spoke into the mic, "Ten-four, ten-four, can you hear me?"

With the flashlight in hand and the walkie in his pocket, Hans crept through the silence until he found himself standing at the garage door. He rubbed the spot where Emily Ray had tazed him and looked over his shoulder.

"Don't be scared," Greta called. "I'm with you."

Hans turned the deadbolt and opened the door. He stepped quickly into the garage and closed it behind him. It was warm and stuffy, but despite that, Hans trembled. As his eyes adjusted to the dark, the first thing he noticed was the smell of gasoline. Light seeped around cardboard blinds nailed over a pair of rectangular windows in the garage door and through a lace-curtained window at the back. Hans flipped on his flashlight and cast the beam across the floor.

The space was empty except for a scuffed dresser beside the back door. Two rows of shelves above it were lined with paint cans, spray cans, ceramic pots, and a red jug of gasoline. Hans jumped as the walkie chirped in his hand.

"What do you see?" Greta asked.

"It's a g-garage." He stepped across the concrete floor and cast the flashlight's beam onto the shelves and dresser. "But m-maybe there's t-t-tools we can use to g-get you out."

With a grinding squeal, Hans opened the first drawer. Inside were neatly folded stacks of old towels, rags, and a heap of ancient magazines. The second drawer was filled with old paintbrushes.

Hans keyed the walkie. "Greta, wha…what kind of tools should I be l-looking for?"

After a brief pause, she said. "I don't know. Something to break the lock or cut the bars. Like a saw or something."

The rain had let up, though the growl of thunder grew nearer.

"G-Greta," Hans said after a thorough examination, "There there's n-nothing we can use."

"Can you get to the shop?"

Hans made his way to the back door. He unlatched the eyehook, turned the lock on the doorknob, and pulled it open. Water drizzled from the gutters in a line along the garage's outer wall, and the air was charged with an energy that set the hair on Hans's arms standing on end. Beyond lay Emily Ray's shop.

It was an old building constructed of horizontal wood slats and ancient curled shingles. It had a white wood door with a window beside it. Though the rain had stopped, the clouds remained. They circled overhead like water in the drain. Hans thought the dark strands of clouds reaching towards the ground made them look like a giant, swirling octopus.

"Greta, I'm scared," Hans said over the walkie.

"I know," she said. "Me too."

He heard a shout and looked to his right. He spotted Greta's arm waving at him through the window.

"See," she called. "I'm with you."

Feeling less alone, Hans squared his shoulders and crossed the yard as fat, chilly raindrops patted onto his shirt, his arms, and his head. At the shop door, he paused. A latch secured it, clamped shut by a huge, rusty padlock. He checked around back, but there was no other entrance, and the windows were barred.

Hans cupped his hands and peered through the grime-fogged glass to the darkened space within.

"G-Greta." He turned to where she peered through the window. "It's l-l-locked."

"Maybe she hid a key," Greta called. "Remember how Grandma Tammy kept a key under the pot?"

Hans scoured the ground, searching a line of loose bricks which might have once bordered a garden. He checked beneath a cracked pot which was now a nursery for weeds, and there it was. Rushing back to the lock, he fitted in the key. With a click, the hasp sprang open, and Hans pulled it from the latch.

He looked to the window and waved. "I'm g-g-going inside."

Greta waved back. "Be careful."

Placing his fingertips on the paint-blistered door, Hans pushed, and the door creaked open. Light trickled through the doorway and revealed a smooth concrete floor and a stack of cardboard boxes beneath the window. A second window, on the far side of the room, cast a glow across a cluttered wooden desk. Atop it sat rows of glass jars, many stuffed to overflowing with dozens of wooden brushes. A handful of jars were filled with mysterious dark fluids.

A wooden swivel chair with a faded blue pillow seat was pushed in front of the desk, and beside it, a thick row of stacked canvases leaned against the wall. A pair of green propane tanks were set at their base to hold them in place.

"What do you see now?" Greta's voice hissed over the receiver.

"Sh-she has an art st-st-studio," Hans said." And lots… an' lots of p-p-painting stuff.

Hans's breath caught as a skitter of movement and a thump turned his eyes.

"G-G-Greta," he whispered into the walkie. "I th...th-think someone's here."

Slow as a minute hand, Hans guided the pale beam of his light across the brush stuffed jars, past a broken easel leaning against the wall, and past a huge iron cauldron perched atop cement blocks. The light fell, at last, upon the dark form standing in the corner. A chill shot up Hans's spine, and he clasped his hand over the light and dropped behind the desk.

He turned the walkie's volume to near zero then keyed the mic. "G-G-Greta." His mouth was dry, his heart pounding. "There's a w-w-witch."

Hans held the walkie to his ear. "Are you sure?" Greta asked.

Hans peeked over the desk and stared into the darkness. The witch stood in the corner, unmoving. She leaned against the cauldron with a conical witch's hat perched atop her head. She wore a long black cloak and had spindly, broomstick arms.

"Yes. I c-c-can hear her m-m-moving."

"What does it sound like?" Greta whispered.

Hans listened. Beneath the storm's scattered rumble and the patter of rain, there was a scratching noise. Almost familiar.

"It s-s-sounds like..." Hans lifted his head and peered over the desk. With a nervous chuckle, he stood. This sound was the same scuffing noise his hamsters Cuff and Link made inside their cages back home. When they had a home. Fear drained from Hans like water from a tub as he flicked on his light and marched it across the floor. The witch's cape became a faded green tarp, her spindly arms a push-broom and mop leaning against the wall. And her tall, conical hat? Three nested traffic cones sitting atop the shelf.

"It's okay," he said. "It's n-n-nothing."

Hans searched for a light switch but only found a pair of buttons near the door where a light switch should be. They clicked heavily when he pressed them, but nothing happened.

Next, he checked the boxes under the window. The top one was open and filled the air around with a smell like the jasmine vines from back home. Inside, he found several neatly stacked bars of soap. Each was wrapped with an image of a beautiful yellow rose and the name 'Candice' scrawled beneath. It was the same rose and Candice from Emily Ray's painting. The other boxes were sealed, but their outsides were stamped with the same yellow rose.

Hans began his search of the desk by pulling out the slim middle drawer in front. It was filled with razor blades, rulers, erasers, and a stack of blank pages.

Before he could open the next drawer, a howl arose in the distance. Hans turned and eyed the open door.

The yowling dwindled slowly, slowly, almost to the point he could no longer hear it over the rain. Then, it rose once again until its plaintive cry rang in his ears.

His walkie crackled as Greta's voice spilled over the airways, "It's a ... *staticky hiss...* alarm." More static followed.

"G-Greta? I c-can't hear you."

Hans rushed to the window. Day had become night beneath the canopy of clouds. Peering into the darkness, he spotted Greta's pale arm waving from the window.

"Hans, get out!" Her voice was tight with fear over the walkie's tiny speakers. "A tornado's coming."

Hans rushed to the door and tilted his head skyward. The air had grown cool and dark, and wispy fingers groped down from the clouds, but he saw no tornado. He returned to the desk and from the drawer lifted a leather-bound book. The leather was pale and fleshy with several folded pages stuffed in back. When he flipped open the cover, he saw a pencil drawing of a flower.

"I f-f-found her notebook," he said into the walkie, "but no t-t-tools."

He cast his light on the witch's cauldron, a large metal pot the size of a tub. It squatted atop four scorched cinder blocks with the handle of an old oar jutting over the lip and a tarnished ladle dangling from its side.

Stepping closer, Hans shown his light on a plastic tarp sitting beside the cauldron. The whole area had a cold, baconey smell that made his skin crawl. Hans nudged aside the tarp to reveal a toolbox beneath.

When he flipped open the lid, he found what he'd been searching for…tools. On top sat a saw unlike any he'd seen before. It had a black plastic grip and a wide silver blade. What made it unusual was the saw's wide, silvery body. Beneath this were a set of knives inside a stained leather case, three pairs of pliers, as well as an assortment of screwdrivers, and a hammer.

Hans examined the saw. It wasn't like the ones Papa kept in his shop for cutting steel. No, this saw had big teeth, not the small, fine ones needed to cut metal. He set it back in the box. The tool was meant to cut something softer than steel. It would never work on Greta's bars. Then, he lifted the hammer.

Now, this. The smooth wood grip and solid heft felt good in his hand. This he could use. Hans thought back to when Papa broke his fist punching the wall. He'd been drinking again with Carla. He did that a lot after Momma died. Hans couldn't remember what started the fight between him and Carla. Once they started drinking, they didn't need an excuse. He remembered yelling and a deep thud that rattled the walls. Papa's cries of pain soon followed, along with a trip to the ER. But it wasn't Papa's broken hand that caught in Hans's mind. It was the fist-sized hole he'd left in the wall. Hans stuffed the hammer in his back pocket, the handle leaning awkwardly from his pants as he looked back to the house. A hammer could make a hole in the wall. One big enough for Greta.

Outside, the tornado alarm rose and fell in waves.

"Greta, I f-f-found something."

Lightning splashed shadows across the walls.

"Hans, it's Miss Emily!" Greta's voice crackled over the speakers. "She's back!"

Hans spun with indecision, turning to the desk, the toolbox, the front door.

"G-Greta. W-w-what do I do?"

Hans heard it now, the distance scrunch of gravel. It grew closer with every breath.

"Grab what you can," she said, "and get out. Get out now!"

Hans stuffed the leather book in the back of his pants and pulled his shirt down to hide it. He was surprised at the baby-smooth softness as it pressed against his skin.

With the flashlight in one hand and walkie in the other, Hans set the workspace like he'd found it. He rolled the chair into place and covered up the toolbox. At the front door, he paused. The grassy lawn between the shop and house was gone, replaced by a shallow, rain-ringed pool.

"Hurry," Greta's shouted from her window. "She's almost here."

Hans latched the door then returned the key to its place beneath the pot. He splashed across the yard sending up horsetails of water as he went. When he reached the back door, he could hear Miss Emily's car. He stepped into the garage and closed the door behind him. With shaking hands, Hans lifted the hook, securing the back door and fitting it into its ring.

It was too late. Emily Ray was home. She pulled up to the garage door and stopped. Hans stood glued to the floor with his rain-soaked sneakers puddling beneath him.

As Emily Ray opened the car door and marched up to the garage, one thought echoed in Hans's mind: *She's gonna hurt Greta.*

The certainty of it filled him like a scream. The garage door rattled, and Hans felt his bladder let go. The heat of his terror pooled in his crotch and streamed down his leg.

But the garage door did not open. Instead, the footsteps marched to the porch. The returning shadow flitted across the line of light at the garage door's base before the car door opened and closed again. The engine revved as the driver backed down the drive and disappeared into the distance.

Hans dashed inside and slammed the door behind him. "G-Greta, are y-you okay?"

Greta hugged him through the bars, laughing and crying in shared relief.

"B-b-boy, that was a c-close one."

Greta smiled and ran her fingers through her hair. "It sure was."

Then her eyes widened. Hans heard it too. The crush of gravel and gritty skid of a car racing up the drive. Hans sprang to his feet as a car door slammed shut outside.

"She's back," Greta whispered.

Hans looked along the hall where his waterlogged footprints cut a trail of guilt across the floor.

"Hide this." Hans passed Greta the hammer, notebook, walkies, and light, and then stepped into the living room.

His heart clawed its way into his throat as the front door rattled. The deadbolt turned, and Emily Ray stepped in. She wore a rain-soaked slicker with the word POLICE in yellow letters across her chest. In her hands, Emily Ray held a toaster-sized cardboard box with the word FedEx printed on the side.

"It's here!" Emily Ray's face was alight as she raised the box over her head.

She stalked into the room, coming straight at Hans. He fell back against the wall as she slid to a halt before him. He flinched as she reached down to tousle his hair, then turning for the hall, she spread the good news to Greta. Hans looked to the front door where Emily Ray's damp passage had obliterated his tracks. Tears of relief crowded his eyes as all signs of his adventure were erased.

When Emily Ray strolled back into the living room, box in hand, she paused to flick the light switch toggles and then turned around and sighed.

"Well, the first thing to do is light some candles." She pulled the flashlight from her belt and flicked it on.

Hans lifted a hand against the glare as she pinned him in its glow.

"You disgusting thing."

She stepped closer and focused the beam on Hans's crotch. "Did you piss yourself?"

Hans's eyes dropped to the stain of his fear.

"There was a t-t-tornado." He looked up, squinting against the glare of Emily Ray's scorn.

"You may be okay living like an animal." She flicked off the light and headed for the kitchen. "But that's not how things are done. Not around here." She dug into a cabinet and pulled out a box of candles. "Now, go change your clothes then get to work mopping those floors. Someone has to make dinner."

Hans changed and then returned to the kitchen. He found Greta at the table while Emily Ray busied herself at the stove. Though the lights were out, the stove's blue flames danced cheerily.

"As I remember," Emily Ray bent over and looked to Greta with an elbow on the counter and her chin in her hand, "your favorite dinner is roast pork." She turned to the refrigerator and removed a cylinder wrapped in white paper and tied with a tan string. She set it on the counter. "Mashed potatoes." She opened a cabinet door and with a groan hefted a machine with an attached silver bowl. She set this on the counter as well, along with a five-pound bag of potatoes. "And peach cobbler." Emily Ray stretched on her tiptoes, and with a crystalline clatter, removed a glass pie pan from the pantry's top shelf.

"Did you get ice cream too?" Greta asked. "And bubble gum?"

Emily Ray leaned down to Greta's level, her hands on her knees. "Of course, little angel." Greta drew back as Emily Ray chucked her under the chin. "Strawberry ice cream and Double Bubble, right?"

Emily Ray unwrapped the pork then turned to the spice cabinet and sifted through the bottles.

"I've got everything your heart desires." She looked over her shoulder and smiled. "Tomorrow's a big day for you, kiddo." She turned back to Greta and wiped her hands on a towel then cocked her head. She frowned, pursing her lips as if talking to a toddler. "It'll be a hard day too, but we'll get through it together." She leaned over and patted Greta's hand.

Greta looked to her brother. "Does Hans get dessert too? You said it's *my* special day."

"Of course." Emily Ray smiled. "It is *your* day, honey. If you want to waste dessert on your brother, that's fine by me."

Hans's eyes drifted from Greta to Emily Ray.

"But until then." Her eyes darkened as he considered him. "I suggest he get back to work."

———

DINNER WAS SOON OVER, and Greta pushed back from her plate with a satisfied sigh. Despite—or perhaps because of —the day's events, she found herself more famished than ever. She'd been so hungry that after two helpings of pork, she'd still found room for cobbler and ice cream. It had been like that ever since they'd arrived. It seemed the more Emily Ray fed her, the hungrier she got.

With the table cleared and Hans at the sink doing dishes, Emily Ray, instead of inviting her into the living room for their pre-bedtime episodes of Andy Griffith and Perry Mason, pulled an amber bottle from the cabinet and set it on the table.

"I usually don't drink, especially in front of minors." She removed a glass from the shelves, and then with a rattle of ice from the fridge's dispenser, filled it to the brim. "But at this point, does it really matter?"

Emily Ray opened the bottle, filled her glass, and dropped into her chair. The ice made a glassy clink as she swirled it, her eyes never leaving Greta. She took a sip, and the questions began. Who were her friends at school? Who was her favorite teacher? Did she like sports?

It was strange, this new, interested Emily Ray. Gone was the Emily Ray Greta had known for the past several weeks. The predictable Emily Ray who woke at six, returned for lunch at noon, then came home at five for dinner. Rarely did she utter more than a few barked commands before waltzing out to the shop. The more this new Emily Ray drank, the chattier she became.

Hans set the last of the dishes in the rack and stood behind them drying his hands.

"I all d-d-done with the dishes."

Emily Ray rolled her eyes and rose from her chair, grasping the seat back unsteadily.

"This looks all right." Her eyes scanned the dishes stacked neatly on a towel. "Why don't you get into your crate and call it a night." She looked back at Greta. "Your sister and I are having such a nice conversation, I thought I'd let her stay up a bit longer."

With a look to his sister, Hans slunk into the living room with Emily Ray behind. After the metallic rattle of Hans's cage and the hard snick of the padlock, she returned and poured herself another drink. For a long while, Emily Ray stared into the distance. The clink of her ice as she raised and lowered the glass was the only sound.

"Did you know I once had a little girl?" Emily Ray dropped her eyes to Greta. She slurred like Papa did when he'd been drinking. "A perfect angel...juss...like...you."

She refilled her glass with ice and dropped into the chair. "You remind me of Jessica, ya know?" Emily Ray sighed. "All of you remind me of her, but you." She lifted a finger. "You most of all." Emily Ray cocked her head. "It's something in your aura. A certain..." she circled a hand in the air, "energy. That's...that's what it is. A certain energy."

Emily Ray leaned closer, took Greta's hands, and squeezed them between her gnarled, tree-branch knuckles. Emily Ray's breath was sour with liquor, and Greta turned away.

"It was your intensity that convinced me you were special." She looked over her shoulder towards the living room. "Convinced me it was worth taking your brother too."

"My Jessica was like that." Emily Ray rose and disappeared into the living room. She returned with the FedEx box in hand.

She opened the box and removed a clear plastic container shaped much like a jelly jar. The jar's label was a stylized paintbrush and the words *Shine Paints:*

Cadmium Blue beneath. Emily Ray opened the jar and tilted it so Greta could see the clumped blue powder within.

"This is the color of your aura," Emily Ray said. "Or at least it will be." She screwed on the lid and returned the jar to its box. "It may not look like much, but once I've added your essence, poof." She splayed her fingers in a fan. "Magic."

Greta cut her eyes to the darkened kitchen window and its reflection of Hans inside his crate. He looked at her and shook his head.

"Your daughter's name was Jessica?" Greta asked.

Emily Ray lifted her head. "Oh, aren't you sweet. Yes, Jessica. Would you like to see her?" Emily Ray held up a finger, "I'll be right back." She rose and disappeared down the hall and into her bedroom.

"Hans," Greta whispered. "What should I do?"

"J-just keep her t-t-talking," he said. "An' try to think of s-s-something."

Emily Ray returned with her wallet in one hand and a duffle bag slung over her shoulder. She set the bag on the counter and flipped open her wallet. Emily Ray's eyes grew damp as she removed a two-inch by three-inch photo and slid it across the table.

The girl in the picture was no older than Greta. She stood before the traditional, blue-smudged school picture background wearing a dated green jumper and an enormous red bow. She stood with her arms crossed and a confident lift of her chin. The gleam in her eye made Greta think they might be friends.

The candle cast flickering shadows across Emily Ray as

she sat with her elbows on the table. She stared into nothing as Greta studied the image.

"What..." Greta began in a whisper. "What happened to her?"

Emily Ray didn't move. Greta looked to Hans's reflection and snapped her gum nervously.

"What happened to her?" Greta asked again.

Emily Ray blinked and looked around like a woman waking from a dream. "What happened?" A sad smile played across Emily Ray's lips. "Bad people took her." The line along her jaw tightened. "And did terrible things." Her eyes softened, and she looked to Greta with a smile.

"But she's in a better place, a wondrous place." She took the picture and studied it before hugging it to her breast. "A place where she can play and be free. Where she'll never be hurt ever, ever again." She patted Greta's arm and smiled.

"You two will be the best of friends." Her eyes misted. "I can tell."

She leaned back in her seat. "And I wanted to show you how much good we're going to do."

Leaning back in her chair, Emily Ray reached out and snagged the bag's strap and pulled it from the counter. It hit the floor with a heavy thud. Emily Ray hoisted it onto the table and zipped it open. The bag was filled with money.

The bills were stacked and bound at their centers with yellow and white paper straps. Though there were a handful of $20 stacks, most were $100 bundles with $10,000 in blue ink written on their label.

"Christmas was always Jessica's favorite." Emily Ray

pulled out three blocks—two $100s and a $20—and dropped them to the table. "So, I keep all the proceeds from my sales until then. I make an anonymous Christmas day donation." She leaned over and nudged Greta in the ribs. "But everyone knows it's me."

She picked up the bills and stuffed them into the bag.

"How's you get so much money?" Greta's eyes followed the cash as Emily Ray stuffed it into the bag.

Emily Ray lifted her glass and took another sip.

"Mostly from signed limited editions of my work." With the hand holding the glass, she pointed. "See Joseph over there?"

Greta followed Emily Ray's finger to the painting of a pinwheel-shaped flower with purplish-red petals fading to a soft orange center.

"Joseph sold at auction for only $8,200." She took another sip. "And I cooked up a hundred bars of soap." She raised a finger. "I sell em' for $100 a bar now, but back then, I could only get $40. So that's another $4,000. But signed prints." She puffed a raspberry through her lips and shook her head. "Five-hundred signed prints will go for six…seven-hundred apiece." She waved a hand at the painting. "And Joseph was my first. The price only went up after that."

"A hundred dollars for a bar of soap?" Greta couldn't believe it. "Why would someone pay so much?"

"They're desperate and in need of healing." Emily Ray reached out and patted Greta's hand. "The reason they pay is because the soap's special. And the *soap's* special because *you're* special." She leaned closer, the shadowed profile of her jutting chin and long nose formed a crescent on the wall. "You see, my soap washes away sin."

Emily Ray leaned back, and her eyes drifted away. "Washes away sin," she whispered. She sat like that for a long while before announcing, "I need to visit the lady's room."

With the photo in hand, Emily Ray rose from her seat.

Greta looked to Hans then back to Emily Ray as a plan formed in her mind.

"Hans has to go too," Greta said.

Emily Ray clung unsteadily to the back of her chair.

"Now?"

"I might h-have another ac-ac-accident," Hans's voice drifted from the crate.

Emily Ray rolled her eyes before digging into her purse and retrieving her keys. "All right, follow me." She led Greta into the living room and unlocked Hans's crate.

"Take him to the hall bath." Her eyes narrowed beneath her bushy brows. "And remember, all the doors are locked."

With a final glance over her shoulder, Emily Ray weaved down the hall and slammed her bedroom door.

"I d-don't have to go."

"I know," Greta said. "I've got a plan." She pulled the gum from her mouth and rolled it into a tube. She shoved it down the hole designed for the padlock's shackle. In the candlelight, Greta prayed Emily Ray wouldn't notice.

"Okay, get in," Greta said. "This needs to look real."

Hans stared at the lock. "B-but Greta. I d-d-don't under—"

She cut him off by grabbing his arm and pressing him

towards the crate. "Hans, we don't have time." Emily Ray's bedroom door rattled open, and Hans hurried in.

"Good night, Hans," Greta said. "See ya in the morning.

Emily Ray strode up behind them and peered over Greta's shoulder. Greta looked back and smiled before bending down and squishing the shackle into the lock. The gum proved stiffer than she thought, and Greta pressed her fingers hard against the metal hump of the lock. It stuck but didn't catch.

In the candlelight flicker, Emily Ray bent to examine Greta's work, nodded in satisfaction, then laid a hand on the girl's shoulder.

"All right, young lady, bedtime. We've got a long, hard day ahead of us, and we'll need our sleep."

Greta changed into PJs and let Emily Ray tuck her in. As always, she kissed her on the forehead and laid a hand atop the kiss. "Sweet dreams," she said, and then she was gone.

The house lay in eager silence as the remnants of the storm tapped on the gutters outside. A rattle from Hans's cage had Greta sitting up in bed. She heard the creak of his passage as he slipped along the hall.

"G-Greta? W-w-wake up."

She slipped from the sheets and joined him at the bars.

"We c-c-can't use the hammer. It'll w-wake her up."

"I know." Greta held out the notebook with its soft leather cover. "Maybe we'll find something in here."

She retrieved the flashlight and played it across Hans's lap. Besides the book, he had Emily Ray's purse as well.

"Where'd you get that?" Greta tilted her head to get a better look. "Did you find her keys?"

Hans shook his head. "I haven't l-l-looked. And I got it from the kitchen." He turned and pointed over his shoulder. "She left it on the table."

Greta gripped the bars as Hans shone the light inside the purse. He removed a plastic bag holding a glass bottle, Emily Ray's brown leather wallet, a small floral purse with a silver clasp, and a half-empty pack of Double-Mint gum. He yanked the purse open and looked inside.

"N-No keys." Hans set the purse down.

Greta searched the wallet while Hans took the floral purse. Other than a few $20 bills, there was nothing.

Greta looked up from Emily Ray's wallet as Hans examined the plastic bag.

Red lettering on the bag's outside read:

Cedarview County Sheriff's Department
EVIDENCE

Beneath were several lines of neatly labeled categories such as 'Case No:, Suspect ID:, and others. Each line was filled with a scrawl of neatly penned letters and numbers that made no sense.

The bag had been sliced open at the top, and inside was a jar the size of Mama's nail polish bottles only a little taller. It had a black top and was filled with clear liquid.

"What is it?" Greta asked.

Hans unscrewed the cap and sniffed.

"It doesn't s-s-smell like any...anything." He held it out to Greta. She lowered her nose and shrugged.

"What's it say on the side?" she asked.

Hans replaced the cap and turned the bottle in his hand.

"G-g-gamma…hy-hydrox…hydroxy." He shook his head.

"You try, G-Greta. It's a really b-b-big word."

She eyed the label and sounded it out: "gamma… hydroxy…buty…rate. Gamma hydroxybutyrate." She shrugged. "It must have ta do with police stuff."

Hans set the purse aside and picked up the notebook. When he did, the stack of papers in back slipped out and dropped in his lap.

They were crisp with age and crackled as he unfolded them. The first three pages were stapled together, and the broad text at the top read: How to Skin a Hog. Among the black text and rust-colored fingerprints on the paper was a photo. It showed a fat black hog dangling upside down from a hook. Vertical lines, spaced every few inches, had been sliced along the length of the animal's body. In the photo, a man laid a knife into the flesh as he made another cut. The next page held an image of a pair of pliers clamped to the animal's skin. A strip of flesh was ripped halfway down the body and revealed the thick, white layers of fat below.

Greta turned away and laid a hand over the page.

"Hans, I don't want to see it. It's terrible."

She watched out of the corner of her eye as he examined the last page then folded the document and laid it on the ground.

"What's next?" She asked.

The next three pages and the two stapled together after

them all had to do with making soap and rendering bacon for fat. They showed, in upsetting detail, how to cut the fat away and prepare a hog for rendering. Hans laid these papers atop the first.

"I don't s-see how this helps," Hans said.

At Greta's suggestion, they went on. The last page held several handwritten paragraphs Greta found hard to understand. Most dealt with mixing things together to make oil paint. The notes spoke of linseed oil and alkyd resin and several other things Greta had never heard of.

Near the bottom, several swatches of paint had been dabbed on the paper. Each had notes such as: Pthalo Green + Cadmium Yellow Light 3 to 1. Beside it was a green dab of color.

Setting the final sheet down, Hans turned the leather book in his lap and then ran a hand over the cover. He met Greta's eyes and sighed. "M-Maybe we'll find something h-here."

The first page was crowded with pencil drawings of flowers. They jostled for space in a myriad of designs, some complete, some no more than shadowy lines. The next page held only three penciled flowers. Greta recognized them as versions from the first page. Each showed the same flower but at differing angles. At the bottom of the page was scrawled the name *Jayden*.

"Hey, I recognize that," Hans said. "It's the painting in the bathroom."

The next page was an almost perfect pencil representation of the yellow, daisy-like painting hanging in Emily Ray's hall bath. 'Jayden—Black Eyed Susan in Summer,' was scrawled at the top.

The following pages were the same. They began with a sheet of doodles, followed by a more detailed study. The final page held a sketch recognizable from the collection of Emily Ray's work.

"Hans, was there anything in Miss Emily's shop like what we saw in those pictures?"

She pointed to the terrible pages from the back of the book.

Hans's shoulders rose and fell in a sigh. "Well." He cocked his head. "Sh-sh-she has a b-big pot like in the picture where they're m-m-making soap." He twisted his lips. "And I remember seeing a h-hook in the ceiling above it." Then, he remembered the toolbox. "Oh, and knives and p-p-pliers in…inside a toolbox." He lifted his eyes and met his sister's gaze. "Why?"

Greta shrugged. "I have a feeling, Hans. A really bad feeling."

Hans turned to the next page of drawings. 'Blue Butterfly Pea,' was written at the top. The final page held a drawing of a beautiful and unfamiliar flower. Beneath was written the name:

Greta.

She felt a chill slide down her back.

"That's your…" Hans eyed the page closely then set it down. "Greta. That's… That's your name."

When he looked up, his eyes were wide. "I don't… I don't…" Hans looked down and swallowed. When he looked up, he took her hand. "I don't think Emily Ray, is a g-g-good guy."

"Hans. What do we do?"

He ran his fingers through his hair and looked around.

When his eyes fell on the plastic evidence bag, he picked it up.

"What if this is p-p-poison?" He reached inside and pulled out the bottle. "M-Maybe we can... We can pour it in her c-c-coffee when she goes to take a shower."

Greta looked to the purse and then back to the kitchen. "Hans, go get two empty glasses."

While he was gone, Greta went to her mini-fridge and removed a bottle of water. When Hans returned, she poured the poison into an empty glass and then poured water in the other until the two glasses held the same amount of liquid. Greta emptied the rest of the water bottle into the sink before pouring in the poison. She handed the glass with water to Hans.

"Pour this back into Emily Ray's bottle," she said.

"W-What about that?" He pointed to the poison. "Where ya gonna hide it?"

Greta walked to her bed and shoved the bottle beneath. When she returned, her eyes fell on Emily Ray's purse and the book.

We need to put everything back the way it was." She turned towards the window then back to Hans. "Including her book."

He nodded, gathering up the papers and shoving them in the back. As he did, the sheet of paint formulas slipped from his hands and drifted to the floor. When he picked it up, Greta's breath caught.

"Hans, look!"

He eyed the page and frowned. "It's the s-same as before."

"No, turn it over."

What he saw on the other side made his eyebrows rise. Just below the bold red letters MISSING, a picture took up half the page. It was a photo from when Hans took fifth place at the Special Olympics weightlifting competition. He stood in his black singlet with a medal dangling from his neck. Greta stood with her arms wrapped around his waist, and one of Hans's arms draped over her shoulder. They looked to the camera with wide, goofy grins.

Beside the photo were their names and physical descriptions. Below that, it read:

IF YOU HAVE ANY INFORMATION REGARDING THESE CHILDREN, PLEASE CONTACT:
ONNI GUNDERSON AT (555)919-7488
OR THE
CEDARVIEW COUNTY SHERIFF'S DEPT
AT (555)876-1910

Greta's stomach backflipped after reading the flier.

"Papa's been looking," she said.

Hans lifted the flier, and his eyes flowed across the page. As he read, color blossomed in his cheeks.

"She d-d-did lie. She did!"

He said the last word so loud, Greta grabbed the bars and peered down the hall. Hans panted, clenching and unclenching his fists. Greta felt it too. The sickly flip in her stomach at the realization that Emily Ray had fooled them the whole time.

She reached through the bars and took her brother's hand. "Go put everything away, then get back in your crate." At her touch, Hans calmed. He met her eyes and nodded. "Okay, G-Greta." He looked back to Emily Ray's door. "Okay."

———

DESPITE HER FEAR, Greta fell asleep soon after Hans returned and crawled into his cage. She was awakened moments later by the house coming suddenly back to life. Virtually every light winked on, and the sound of a TV screamed from Emily Ray's bedroom. Greta looked at the DVD player flashing on her shelf. It was 5:09 a.m.

The TV noise vanished, and a split second later, Emily Ray's door banged open. Greta stepped to the bars and peered down the hall. She spotted Emily Ray leaning against the door jamb with a hand pressed to her head.

"Jesus Christ, what time is it?" Emily Ray said.

She lumbered into the kitchen, and a rattle of drawers and the splash of water followed. Soon, a hiss of steam announced the coffee maker was running. Then, as she'd done every day since Greta's arrival, Emily Ray strolled along the hallway and rapped at the bars.

"Come on over," she said. "One last check."

Greta kicked away her covers. There was no use pretending to sleep. Emily Ray would not be denied her morning routine. At the bars, Greta stuck out her arm and let Emily Ray pinch up a thick knot of flesh. She nodded and let Greta go.

"Good enough," Emily Ray mumbled on her way back to the kitchen.

A cabinet door opened and closed, followed by the sound of coffee being poured. Then, there was silence.

Greta rubbed at the pinch's rising bruise and waited. When Emily Ray took her shower, Hans would pour in the poison.

Then, Emily Ray's gruff exclamation caught Greta's attention. "What the hell?" Emily Ray said. "Why are the shop lights on?"

Greta rushed to the window and peered out. Sure enough, the shop lights were on.

Emily Ray rushed to her bedroom and emerged moments later wearing scuffed leather boots beneath her yellow dressing gown. In one hand, she held a flashlight, and in the other, a gun. She clicked on her light and looked to Greta.

"I'll be right back."

When the garage door closed, Greta rushed to her window.

"Hans, get ready. This is our chance."

Light from the open back door played across the yard, followed by the illuminating circle of Emily Ray's flashlight. As she paced across the yard and opened the shop door, Greta dug beneath the bed and took out the poison. Hans was waiting at the bars.

By the time Emily Ray returned, Hans was back in his crate and the empty poison container hidden beneath Greta's bed.

Emily Ray closed the garage door and stood before Hans's crate. Greta could see her shadow on the hall floor. With a snort, Emily Ray turned and marched into the hall. To Greta's surprise, she stopped and unlocked her door.

"Go ahead and get dressed." Emily Ray said. "This morning, I've got a special treat."

As Greta dressed, the normal sounds of morning activity drifted into the hallway: the clatter of pans and rattle of plates, Emily Ray's husky morning cough, the sound of a chair being pulled out from the table, and a jingle of keys.

Then, there was silence.

For long minutes, Greta waited. She crept to the hallway and peered into the living room and the kitchen beyond. There was no sign of Emily Ray. When she caught Hans's eye, he only shrugged. Greta returned to the bedroom and slid the hammer into the back of her pants.

"G-Greta," Hans whispered at last. "I think w-w-we should check."

"Okay," she whispered back. "But be careful."

A moment later and Hans was back.

"I think it worked," he said. "She's ly...l-lying on the coffee table," he said. "And n-n-not moving."

Greta followed Hans to the kitchen where Emily Ray was slumped over the table. Her head was down on one arm and the other jutted out before her.

"D-D-Do you th-think it worked?"

Greta's body tingled, and her arms and legs felt like jelly. They stepped to the edge of the kitchen's flowered linoleum, and still Emily Ray hadn't moved.

"L-Look in her other hand." Hans pointed to the table. "Her phone."

All they had to do was get the phone and call Papa.

"I'll g-g-get the phone, then we'll r-run out the back."

Hans took a step and Greta halted him with a touch.

"Be careful, Hans."

He smiled. "I w-w-will."

Step by reluctant step, her brother slunk to Emily Ray's side. With a final look back, he bent over her shoulder and reached for the phone.

Greta's breath caught as Emily Ray's outstretched hand curled into a fist. It balled like a question mark at the end of her bony arm.

Through her terror, Greta's warning was only a breathy whisper. "Hans!"

When he turned, Emily Ray sat up and cocked her question mark fist. When Hans turned back, Emily Ray's punch caught him in the nose. Blood spattered across his shirt, and he stumbled back with a yelp.

Before he could react, Emily Ray grabbed a pan from the stove and, with a clang, brought it down on Hans's head. He crumpled to the floor and lay still.

"You fools think you can win?" Emily Ray's chair clattered to the floor as she shoved it out of the way and closed in on Greta.

Her slap caught Greta on the cheek and slammed her against the wall. As she sagged to the floor, Emily Ray snatched her by the hair and hoisted Greta to her feet. In an instant, her face was shoved against the wall and a handcuff was clicked onto one wrist.

"Come on, you." Fire shot through Greta's wrist as Emily Ray yanked her down the hall and dragged her from the house. She kicked open the shop door and jerked Greta inside.

The room was exactly as Hans described it, except the lights were on and blue flames jetted from four green bottles set beneath the cast-iron pot. A column of steam rose from the cauldron and roiled across the ceiling as

Emily Ray shoved Greta to the floor.

"You just had to make trouble, didn't you?" Emily Ray snapped the other cuff onto Greta's wrist and then turned to rummage in her desk. She returned with a length of rope which she looped around the handcuff chain and tossed over the hook in the ceiling. Hoisting the rope so that Greta was forced onto her tiptoes, Emily Ray looped the rope's other end around the desk's leg then stretched a plastic tarp beneath Greta's feet.

"I'm trying to help you, Greta." Emily Ray lifted her hands in a palms-up shrug. "Don't you see?"

Emily Ray took a shaky breath and ran her fingers through her unkempt hair.

"I'm going to go get your brother." She examined Greta's restraints then let her eyes follow the rope to the hook then down to the desk. "If you make more trouble, I'm taking it out on him." Greta tried turning away, but Emily Ray pincered her cheeks between her thumb and palm. She forced Greta's eyes to hers. "You understand?"

"You're… You're a witch!" Greta cried. "Why can't you leave us alone?"

Emily Ray turned. "Leave you alone?" She stepped closer and stroked Greta's cheek. The numb fire of the slap had receded, and Greta blanched at her touch.

"I'll make you immortal." She lifted her arms to the sky. "I'll reveal your aura to the world."

"You mean you're going to kill us!" Greta shrieked.

"That's right!" Emily Ray jabbed a finger at the pot. "And when I'm done, I'll stick you in that pot and turn you into soap." She reached up and patted Greta's cheek. "And parts of *you*, little angel, I'll turn into *paint*." Emily

Ray clasped her hands over her breast and closed her eyes.

"Let your light shine before men," she said, "that they may see your good works and glorify your Father who is in heaven."

She opened her eyes and smiled. "And your light is so very, very bright."

After Emily Ray left, Greta narrowed her hands and sagged at her knees, letting the weight of her body drag against the cuffs. The steel bit deep into her skin, and soon blood dribbled down her forearm and soaked into her gown. Greta grunted with effort as the pain in her wrists gave way to an icy numbness.

At the sound of a slamming door, Greta straightened. She smoothed the blood beneath the cuffs and her skin then threw all her weight into it. She felt a wrist slip halfway out before Emily Ray's panting grunts had Greta looking towards the door.

The first she saw of Emily Ray was her rear-end as she backed through the shop door. She paused a moment, breathing heavily, then bent down and dragged Hans in. One of his shoes was missing, and a sock dangled off his foot. His arms trailed out behind him, and his shirt was bunched around his chest.

He was dead! A jolt of terror skittered across Greta's heart. Then, she saw the round, whiteness of his belly rise and fall in a breath. Hans was handcuffed and bloodied, but he was alive.

"Boy, and I thought *you* were heavy." Emily Ray reached to the back of her desk and uncapped a half-empty water bottle. "On the plus side." She took a gulp and then tipped the bottle towards Hans. "He's gonna have lots of fat."

Greta's eyes never left her brother. A crimson-streaked skid of mud and grass had been dragged with him across the floor, and a dark red puddle expanded beneath his head.

"Now, my dear." Emily Ray reached into her pocket and removed a vial filled with brown liquid. It was the bottle from the evidence bag.

"If you'd used only a few drops, you might have gotten away with it." She turned the bottle and watched the bubble inside. "But dumping the whole thing in my coffee..." Her tongue darted in and out and she made a sour face. "That I could taste."

Emily Ray stepped up to Greta and grabbed her by the jaw. "But I'll admit. It *was* a good plan." Her fingers pressed like a vise and forced apart Greta's teeth.

"Now, just a little taste for you and a little for your brother, and it will be all over."

As Emily Ray forced open Greta's mouth and tilted the vial over her lips, a voice arose above the horror.

"L-L-Let m-me win..." Hans's voice was faint and slow.

Emily Ray let go and turned. Behind them, Hans knelt on the floor with his forehead on the concrete and his hands cuffed behind him. Lifting his head, he stumbled to his feet. He wobbled unsteadily as a stream of bloody sputum dangled from his face and drizzled to the floor.

"Let you win?" Emily Ray laughed. She looked to Greta and hiked a thumb at Hans. "Who does he think he is?"

Greta recognized the Special Olympics motto, and with each uttered word, Hans wobbled a bit less, stood a bit taller.

"Let...me...win!" he called again. He was bent almost double, wobbling unsteadily as he raised his eyes and glared.

"But... if I c-cannot win..."

Emily Ray turned from Greta and removed a knife from the toolbox. She turned towards Hans.

"Then let me b-b-be br-brave in the attempt."

Greta let her legs go limp and dropped against her bonds. Pain spiked in her wrist, but her hand slipped free. She felt the pinpricks of circulation come alive in her fingers as Emily Ray gripped her blade and dropped into a crouch.

Hans lowered his head and charged.

Emily Ray stood silent as Hans closed the gap.

He didn't stand a chance, and Greta knew it. Emily Ray was bigger. Emily Ray was stronger. But no one hurt her brother. She pulled the hammer from her pants and gripped it with both hands, and then rising to her knees, she brought it down on Emily Ray's foot.

Emily Ray cried out, hopping on her uninjured foot as Hans blasted into her and raced quickly past. She cartwheeled over his back and splashed into the cauldron.

With a shriek, Emily Ray sprang from the pot, knocking it from the cinder blocks and sending it crashing to the floor. Scalding water splashed across the concrete and filled the room with steam as the propane tanks and their bright blue flames rolled across the floor.

Greta was crawling through the fog looking for Hans

when a hand clamped onto her ankle. She turned to see Emily Ray squirming towards her. Her face was a mask of scarlet boils, and in her hand, she held the knife.

She dragged Greta closer and leered. "Now, you die."

When Greta looked up, Hans was there. Emily Ray lifted her eyes, and her brows knit in confusion, her mouth forming an 'O' before Hans's kick connected with her face. Her head snapped back before a trickle of blood formed on her lips. Emily Ray's eyes lost their focus, and she slumped to the floor.

Hans took an unsteady step as Greta raced to his side. "Come on, Hans, we gotta go!"

One of the propane burners came to rest at the foot of Emily Ray's desk as Greta helped Hans from the shop. Behind them, flames licked along the walls and crowded the ceiling with smoke.

———

HANS'S MEMORY of what took place in the shop was hazy, though he remembered how quickly it burst into flames. By the time he and Greta stumbled back to the house, found Emily Ray's keys, and unlocked their restraints, the first firetrucks were already on the scene.

Police followed fire, and ambulance followed police until Emily Ray's driveway was a field of flashing lights. The fire was almost out before anyone noticed the two bedraggled children sitting with packed bags on Emily Ray's front porch.

Soon after he and Greta were transported to the Emergency Room, Papa was there.

At first, Hans didn't recognize the man prowling the crisp hospital corridor, peering into one curtained room after another. His clothes were pressed and his hair neat. The man looked like the Papa Hans remembered and not the pale skeleton who'd abandoned them in a hotel room so long ago.

Hans nudged his sister and pointed. "G-G-Greta, do you think that man looks like P-Papa?"

She didn't need a second look. Greta sprang from her seat and, with a shout, raced down the hall. She dove into Papa's arms, and he lifted her into an embrace. Greta said something, and his eyes searched the hallway locking, onto Hans with a wide, eager look. In seconds, Papa was on his knees in front of Hans, begging the children for forgiveness and soothing them with hugs.

"I can't believe I found you," Papa said. "I've been looking for months."

Greta pulled back and met her father's eyes. "What about…" Her gaze fell to the floor. "What about Carla and…and everything else?"

"Gone," Papa wept. "That life's gone forever and never coming back."

"Mr. Gunderson?"

Papa rose and wiped his eyes before considering the uniformed man before them. He was taller than Papa, with dark eyes that crinkled at the corners. He wore a simple tan uniform with a bright gold star on his breast. He held a cowboy hat in his hands and turned it nervously as they spoke.

"I'm Sheriff Blanks." He stuck out his hand, and he and Papa shook. "Let me start by telling you the children will be fine." He reached into the crown of his hat and produced a pair of suckers. He handed a green one to Greta and the red one to Hans.

"How badly were they hurt?" Papa asked. Despite his gentle touch, Hans hissed when Papa touched his bandaged head.

"The boy's got a slight concussion along with eighteen stitches." The sheriff held up his hands at Papa's sharp look of concern. "Nothin' to be worried about. The doctor assures me he'll be fine."

"Now, Greta here," he looked at Greta and smiled, "got out with only a few scrapes. Nothing a bandage or two can't fix. Ain't that right?"

"Your deputy," Papa began. "She was going to..." He looked at the children and frowned.

"Come, Mr. Gunderson," Blanks said. "There's an empty room down the hall. We can talk there." He laid a hand on Papa's shoulder. "Trust me, Mr. Gunderson, the whole county's ready to do all we can to make this right."

Papa followed, red-faced, as the sheriff led him down the hall. Hans watched through the glass pane as Papa and the sheriff talked.

"What do you think they're saying?" Greta asked.

Hans squinted through his swollen right eye and shrugged. "I d-d-don't know." He looked over his shoulder through the glass. Though Papa was usually rattled around police, he was on his feet gesturing wildly to the sheriff and then back at them. The muffled sound of Papa's voice drifted down the hallway as the sheriff nodded, raising his hands from time to time in surrender.

"Hans," Greta said. "Do you think Papa's better?" She met her brother's eye. "Do you think we'll be okay?"

They traded suckers, Hans taking the green one and Greta the red. He opened his Hulk backpack and pushed aside the blanket. He laid his sucker atop the stacks of $100 bills filling the pack and zipped it back up.

"Don't worry G-Greta, it's just like in the s-story." He smiled. "And they lived h-happily ever after."

Jeff is a dabbler in science fiction, horror, and other forms of the absurd. His work can be found in such venues as *The Literary Hatchet*, *Tales to Terrify*, *J.J Outre Review*, and *Mystery Weekly*. When not writing, Jeff and his dog, Edgar, can be found prowling the woods behind their rural home communing with the denizens of the night. Find out what Jeff's been up to on his website. JeffDosser.com or follow him on Twitter @JeffDosser

WHY ARE CHILDREN SO DELICIOUS?

JOSHUA P. SORENSEN

I really love the children
And I watch them every day.
In the morning, off to school.
Or in evenings, out to play.

Now, if you see me talking
To adults, it's just a ruse.
For luring trust of parents
Is why a witch will schmooze.

Some children are precocious
And others stubborn mules;
But just a little candy
Turns them into fools.

I'll fatten up my neighbors
With cookies and with cake,
Chocolate ice cream, custard,
And sweets that I will bake

When they're fat and plump,
With pudgy little toes,
I'll roughly grab and toss them;
In my oven they will go.

Smell that sticky goodness
As those children caramelize.
The tasty youngling morsels
My tongue will mesmerize.

Joshua P. Sorensen has a Masters of Military History from
Norwich University. He enjoys writing poetry and short
fiction; as well as conducting historical research. He can be
found on Facebook: #SorensenVagabondWriter and
Amazon: amazon.com/author/joshuapsorensen

THE WARLOCK OF KAY'S CREEK

BRYAN STUBBLES

The dirt hit the coffin one handful at a time. Johnnie's death made dusk's chill all that more miserable. Sixteen-year-old Mabel looked on from afar as the hushed graveside service quickly concluded. Not even Johnnie's parents attended the funeral. Only the Presbyterian minister, his wife, and the gravedigger attended. None of the Mormons—many of them related to Johnnie by blood or marriage or both—could be bothered. Welcome to 1894 Kaysville.

The Wasatch Mountains (an outcropping of the Rockies) poked up through the rainclouds and stood over Mabel as she trudged to her home, about a half-mile walk from the Kaysville cemetery.

The drizzle of the rain hit the family's roof. The ominously eerie glow of gas lit up the dining room in their upper middle class red brick dwelling. The fireplace crackled an aura of orange. Crisp photographs hung on the walls. A lithographed portrait of Joseph Smith, founder of the Mormon faith, hung on the wall. A fine piano stood guard in the living room. Wooden furniture with plush cushioning lined the room.

Mabel sat at dinner with her parents. Roast turkey. String beans. Bread. The Green family ate well, a reflection of her father Absolam's job at the bank. Mabel's mother Isobel was the linchpin that held the family together, sometimes with delicious food, but sometimes with threats and violence. Mabel picked at her food.

"What ails you?" asked her mom.

Everything ailed Mabel, especially the loss of her Johnnie. A loss her parents would never understand.

"Your mother asked you a question," said Absolam. Mabel looked at her middle-aged parents, worn out by the 19th century reality of Utah. They looked old beyond their years. In the past, Mabel's siblings, all ten of them, stayed with the family. She came last. Until her older sister left. Now it was her and her parents, who were nearly forty-five years older than her. Not only did Mabel have ten siblings, she also had a second mother who had died when she was very young. This was Utah in the 19th century, after all. Second (and third) mothers were more common than anyone cared to admit.

"Eat your beans!" yelled her mother. Isobel slapped Mabel cleanly across the face.

Mabel ran to her room. For many years, the room belonged to everybody. From big brother Jake (nearly 28 years older than her) all the way down to Allie (only a year older). Now, it was hers. Hers for crying. She stared out the window that faced the Wasatch Mountains to the east. The low-hanging clouds could neither disperse nor climb over the mountains. They reminded her that maybe Johnnie's soul was also trapped in an ambiguous state, neither fully in Heaven nor fully in Hell. The melancholy clouds trapped by the mountains reminded her of Johnnie's sad beauty. The rain pittered and pattered. Streamlets run down the window like so many tears. What would she do? She had to *do* something.

Stupid beans. Stupid mother. Stupid bank. Stupid father. Stupid Kaysville.

Johnnie attended a school run by the Presbyterian minister's wife. This was a part of missionary efforts to "liberate" Mormon women from the yoke of polygamy and possibly save little Mormon children in the process. Mormons (and non-Mormons) sent their children to these schools due to a dearth of organized education provided by either the LDS Church or the Territory of Utah. The Presbyterian schools filled that vacuum.

At school, students and teachers shunned her. Everyone except Breckin. His real name was Breckinridge Powell, but when that's your name, Breckin is a distinct improvement. He was gangly and awkward. A good kid, but a bit misunderstood. He carried around a book by Nietsche. He was the closest thing to a friend Mabel had now.

"Old Man Liken," said Breckin. "He could help you."

Old Man Liken? He was nearly eighty years old and the subject of extensive gossip about town. He lived past Gentile Street on the extreme west side of Kaysville. Gentile Street got its name from the two or three non-Mormon families who built homes in the area around 1870 or so. "Gentile" was the old name Mormons gave non-

Mormons. Nowadays, there were a few more non-Mormons in Kaysville, and a few Mormons on Gentile Street. Still, the vast area of farmland on the western reaches of Kaysville presented a culture different than the staid brick homes and orderly grid patterns of the downtown near Mabel's house.

They did things a little differently on the west side. They drank more, worked harder for less money, and were less insular. They accepted outsiders just a little bit more. Besides, somebody had to pull the sugar beets. That was the local industry. Mabel rarely ventured to that part of Kaysville. Gossip said Old Man Liken lived out there in a big house he'd built from pieces of other houses and driftwood from the nearby Great Salt Lake. Kay's Creek ran through Liken's property. This waterway formed from the convergence of three small streams in the foothills above Kaysville and was named after an early local Mormon bishop. It made its way west until it dissipated in the muddy shores of the Great Salt Lake.

Gossip said he was the most Gentile of the Gentiles. The Ur-Gentile. That he shot Mormons on sight. Other gossip claimed he was a reprobate Mormon who believed himself to be his own God and maintained a menagerie of women for his lustful endeavors. Other gossip claimed he was an abortionist. A bootlegger with a home distillery. None of those rumors interested Mabel right now.

The strangest yet most widely-believed rumor was that Old Man Liken was a warlock. A male witch. A man who cast spells for pleasure and profit.

"If you want Johnnie back, Old Man Liken is your best bet," said Breckin.

"Will you come with me?" asked Mabel.

"Of course. It'll be a grand adventure."

Walking there would take nearly two hours. If they rode a horse together, the wagging, judging tongues of Kaysvillites would have a field day. Walking it would be. They'd go separately. It would be a long walk, but necessary. Mabel brought her father's Colt Frontier revolver and some ammunition just in case. The .44-40 ammunition would take care of Old Man Liken if necessary. Breckin, the eternal pacifist, refused to arm himself.

———

MABEL WORE an embroidered shirtwaist and skirt but put on her father's tan duster. She topped her ensemble off with a Stetson. Breckin wore his usual coat with knickers and a flat cap.

"You can't even dress like a cowpoke," said Mabel.

"You're a banker's daughter," said Breckin.

The house didn't quite look like the rumors it featured in. It was ornate. Cute in a creepy sort of way. It even had a spooky little tower.

"It's like the Tower of London!" said Mabel.

"It's just a house," said Breckin.

They walked past the weedy lawn and up the steps to the covered porch. A black metal skull knocker adorned the door. Mabel looked at Breckin, who looked back.

"Scaredy cat," said Mabel.

"Fine," said Breckin. He gave the knocker a pull and a push. The clang was loud enough to wake the dead. Breckin took off running down Gentile like a frightened little bat out of Hell. Mabel knew who the real scaredy cat was. She'd have to catch up with him later. She had business to discuss.

Her heart jumped inside her chest as she waited. She heard slow movements inside, like a chair being pushed across a wooden floor. The door opened.

Old Man Liken appeared. He stood about six-feet four. Emaciated-looking. The type of thinness elderly people get from malnutrition. His long white hair went past his shoulders. He dressed in black—the latest funeral fashions from two generations before. He looked like he hadn't seen daylight in two generations, either.

He motioned for her to come inside.

"Put your weapon on the windowsill," he said.

How did he know?

"What weapon?" Mabel lied.

Mabel could see he knew she was lying. He stared her down.

"You sick girl," he said.

How dare he? He's the one everyone talks about having seraglios and death curses and such. Mabel was perfectly normal, perfectly healthy. Just ask her.

"Looks like you show the effects of a steady diet of dime store novels and penny dreadfuls."

He wasn't wrong.

"Draw!" he said.

"What?" asked Mabel, not believing she was getting into a shooting affray this quickly.

She saw a pistol in his left hand. She moved her hand to draw the .44-40 Colt from her duster.

BLAM! BLAM! BLAM!

He fanned his pistol, firing into Mabel, only five feet in front of him. Each bullet found its mark. That is, each bullet hit the pistol inside her duster, knocking it loose and about ten feet to her side on the porch.

BLAM!

He fired once more, making the pistol on the porch spin.

"Hey, that's my dad's gun!"

Mabel wanted to pick it up but didn't want to get shot trying.

"Go on. Pick it up," said Liken.

As Mabel picked up the gun, she noticed it didn't have a nick on it. She then checked her overcoat. No bullet holes. Old Man Liken was truly not of this world. Liken pointed to the windowsill. Mabel placed her gun on it.

The living room was dark. All the curtains were drawn.

"I need help," said Mabel.

She regaled Liken with tales of how wonderful Johnnie was and how deep Mabel's never-ending love was. She told Old Man Liken of the rumors she'd heard, but she insisted she was certain they weren't true.

"Why wouldn't they be?" asked Liken with a smile.

Mabel wanted Johnnie back. She was willing to do, try, or give anything to make it happen.

"Your love will bring Johnnie back," said Liken.

"Ain't there a spell or something?"

"I'll write it on this paper," he said.

In less than five seconds, Liken wrote on a piece of notepaper, folded it up, and gave it to her.

"Go to the grave and recite this."

"Why do people hate you?" asked Mabel.

"So few people embrace the unknown," said Liken.

"Even the Gentiles hate you," she said.

"Do you hate me?" asked Liken.

"Of course not," said Mabel. "Do I owe you anything for this?"

"Let's talk after the spell works."

Mabel went home, carrying her dad's unscathed gun and the note.

Mabel's folks didn't see her that night because she was at Johnnie's grave, finding her way with a kerosene lamp. A pile of fresh dirt on top. No headstone. She heard something rustle. She saw something move in the dark.

"You killed Johnnie! You won't kill me!"

Mabel fired the pistol once. A voice screamed.

"Breckin?" asked Mabel.

He'd run away from Liken's house just to end up almost getting shot in the cemetery.

"Hey," he said.

"Hey."

Mabel had spent her entire life being put upon by others. Her indifferent and abusive parents. Her bratty siblings. Her cruel teachers. Johnnie's love had been this world's only redemption in her eyes. Bracken had been her friend. Until he abandoned her at the Liken house.

"You ran away once," she said pointing the Colt at Breckin's forehead. "It should be easier the second time." She cocked the hammer. Breckin took off like a bat burnt by the flames of Hell. Mabel laughed to herself.

She read the paper Old Man Liken had given her.

"Welcome, Johnnie, welcome unto me. I call you through He who has created Heaven, Earth, and Hell. The power that made those entities is the same power by which I call you from your eternal rest. You must come and not depart without my license. I have asked you this without any falseness."

Nothing happened. Of course. Mabel's luck in life. Her lot in life. All promise. No reward. Mabel looked around. All still. She moped around a bit. She looked at the paper again. It caught fire and burnt up. A slow drizzle began. Lightning flashed. Thunder smashed. After a few moments of rain, the dirt above the grave began to crumble. A hand poked through.

"Miss Mabel Green!" shouted a voice.

Mabel turned. There in the rain, holding an umbrella, stood her teacher at the Presbyterian school, Mrs. Peck, and her minister husband, the Reverend Peck.

"Hello!" said Mabel, praying they wouldn't see the hand rising from the grave. She walked towards them.

"Do you often come to the cemetery in the rain?" she asked them, not being able to think of anything better to say.

"As often as you do," said Pastor Peck.

Mabel looked back towards the grave. She could see the arm flailing. Apparently, the couple couldn't see it.

"Oh," Mrs. Peck said to her husband. "She's visiting her *friend*."

"We're late for dinner," said the husband, checking his Waltham pocket watch by the light of the kerosene lamp.

"See you in school," said Mrs. Peck to Mabel.

What Mabel didn't say was that the couple had hastened Johnnie to the grave. Nobody in Utah Territory, it seemed, wanted Johnnie and Mabel to be together. So

Johnnie left this world. But now Mabel would bring them back together. She looked back at the grave. Johnnie was free. Mabel ran back. They embraced in the rain. Something felt different. An otherworldly coldness. Well, Johnnie had spent several days in the cold ground.

"Johnnie, is it really you?"

A vague grunt answered Mabel. Maybe Johnnie was tired from being dead so long? Mabel needed to find a safe place for them. She could only think of one place: Old Man Liken's.

Drenched after a long march across town, the duo arrived at Liken's house exhausted at a very late hour. No matter, for Mr. Liken was looking out the window when they arrived. He opened the door.

"I've been expecting you, Miss Green... and..." He looked at Johnnie, "Miss..."

"Greaves," said Johnnie. He readily invited them inside.

This time, Liken's house felt protective rather than foreboding. Mabel knew she was in the house of a friend.

"They thought our love was unnatural before, but now I'm in love with a living dead girl."

"I'll make you some tea," said Liken.

Mabel and Johnnie sat down. Mabel now knew indescribable joy. Even that joy couldn't wash away the hatred she held for those who had driven Johnnie to self-murder.

She needed bloody, brutal revenge.

"Johnnie, you want to make them pay?"

Johnnie nodded. Old Man Liken brought the tea and poured it.

"Thanks," said Mabel.

"You might want to wait for it to stop raining before you exact your vengeance," said Liken.

Mabel had a plan.

"Would you like any spells or incantations?"

"Not this time."

Mabel held Johnnie in her arms. Thoughts of bloody vengeance flooded her mind.

"We need guns."

Mabel drifted to sleep with cold, cold Johnnie.

———

MABEL WOKE up early and walked outside. She appreciated the leaden dawn that came after the storm. The ground was still moist. Utah always needed rain. Mabel looked at the town in the distance. She imagined letting loose with her revolver. They would pay. Forcing Johnnie into the grave. Sure, suicide was a damnable sin, but what about pressuring a youth so much that self-murder becomes the only way out? Kaysville would wake up. America would wake up. The world had to wake up.

"You sure would like to show them," said Liken directly behind her. Mabel's heart stopped for a moment.

"I didn't see you there," she said.

"How many bullets does that revolver hold?" asked Liken.

"Six," laughed Mabel.

"How would you like a gun that holds eight rounds?"

"You're a warlock. Can't you make a gun with unlimited rounds?"

"I'm a warlock, not a miracle worker, you ungrateful child."

"Sorry," she said.

The warlock laughed. Even he had a sense of humor. He handed her a strange-looking gun: the Borchardt C-93. The barrel looked normal enough, but there was some interlocking contraption on the back. The grip was straight. It looked like something out of a futuristic novel.

".32 caliber," he said.

Mabel looked at it. She couldn't find the cylinder. She saw a hole at the bottom of the grip.

"Do they go in here?"

Liken showed her a metal container holding bullets one on top of another. He called it a "magazine." He gave it to Mabel. She slid it inside the grip.

"That simple, huh?" asked Mabel.

Mabel weighed the pistol in her hand.

"Eight rounds," she said.

Liken then gave her several boxes of ammunition.

"Who says you aren't a miracle worker?"

Johnnie stumbled outside. Something still wasn't right. She could move and talk a bit, but not like before.

"Do you want the revolver?" Mabel asked Johnnie.

Johnnie sort of grunted.

"I have just the thing," said the warlock.

He produced a double-barreled messenger's shotgun.

"We're not riding for Wells Fargo," said Mabel.

"Even the undead can use a messenger's shotgun."

He loaded and tossed the shotgun to Johnnie. He then tossed a rusty can in front of Johnnie who obliterated it. Johnnie smiled.

"SHE'S WRONG FOR YOU."

"Her attachment is unnatural."

"She's trying to control you."

"She comes from a broken home."

"She's literally from the wrong side of the tracks."

"Aren't there any nice boys you can meet?"

"Have you tried praying?"

"You can't see Johnnie anymore."

"Heavenly Father is against us because of you."

"You're not my daughter as long as Johnnie spends time with you."

Negative memories drowned Mabel. She opened her eyes. She could see her brick house. Kerosene never smelled sweeter. Burning kerosene smelled even better. The fire glowed in the night. Her parents would pay for all their hate. She stood watch on one side of the house. Johnnie stood on the other. The flames struggled against the brick. Angry and frustrated, Mabel grabbed a stone and tossed it through the window.

"What is that?" yelled her mother. That familiar yell.

BOOM!

Mabel felt buckshot open up wounds in her side. The sting. The pain. She saw her mother. She had gone out the back door instead of the front. Her mom knew how to wield the family shotgun. Adrenaline took over.

"Mabel! What are you doing there?" asked her mom.

"Go on. Tell me how evil Johnnie is."

"Johnnie's dead, burning in Hell," said the mom, reloading the shotgun and pointing it at Mabel.

"Are you hit?" asked her mother.

Mabel didn't feel like answering. Her side hurt so bad. She was afraid to reach for a gun. Her mom had the drop on her.

"We can talk this out, honey," said the mom.

"Can we talk the buckshot out of my gut?" yelled Mabel. Even talking hurt.

"We'll find a good fella for you," said her mom.

Mabel's rage boiled over. The flames were dancing, and Mabel waited for them to not illuminate her. She drew her revolver and fanned the hammer, sending six bullets straight into her mother, who crumpled like a battered rose.

"Mabel…" said her mother.

BOOM!

Johnnie appeared with the shotgun and emptied a load into Mabel's mom's head.

"I saw the whole thing," said Mabel's dad, pointing a snub-nosed Smith & Wesson .32 at Mabel. The two-inch barrel impressed nobody.

BOOM!

Mabel and Johnnie simultaneously opened fire on Mabel's dad. The Borchardt C-93 bullets landed nicely, and the second barrel from the messenger gun did the rest. He fell onto his back.

He tried to speak but could only move his mouth silently.

"The first time you ain't got something to say," said Mabel. She pointed her empty revolver at him. Just pointing it finished him off. She reloaded both weapons and put new shells in Johnnie's double-barreled.

"Where to now?" Mabel asked. Johnnie pointed north.

Johnnie's house. Of course, her parents would suffer next. Johnnie started walking north. Mabel kept up.

"Halt!" yelled a man's voice.

Mabel and Johnnie looked across the street. Bishop Sorensen. Fifty, lean, tall and with glasses and a bowler, he was in charge of Johnnie and Mabel's Latter-Day Saint ward. He was hardly a saint.

"Mabel Green!" he yelled. At least he remembered her.

"Johnnie?" he asked. He looked like he'd seen a ghost. He'd only seen the living dead.

Johnnie grunted in reply and raised the shotgun. Here was their chance to punish evildoers. The pain in Mabel's side ached something fierce. She had to survive. She looked across the street. Sorensen was gone. No doubt to fetch help.

"You still headed north?"

Johnnie shook her head "no." Mabel heard footsteps and whispers. Men were gathering nearby. She recognized Sorensen's voice. An ambush!

She looked around for a sturdy building: the Presbyterian Church. A small, square, brick edifice, it contained a tower, too. Johnnie had died and wasn't too bad for wear. Mabel would give death a try, too. First, she had to take out as many of these bigots as she could before succumbing herself.

"Your destiny," said Johnnie.

Walking backwards with guns brandished, they retreated to the Presbyterian church. Mabel reached behind herself and opened the wooden door. They backed up until they were safely in the vestibule. Mabel felt safe for a second.

Somebody kicked her from behind, sending her face into the door. She landed on the floor. So did her guns. She looked up: Reverend Peck.

"You were supposed to take down the other one!" screamed Peck at his wife, the schoolteacher.

"I can't," said his wife. Johnnie turned. Mrs. Peck finally saw the decomposition on Johnnie's cold, cold face —something Mabel refused to see.

Mrs. Peck screamed and fainted on the floor. Mabel scrambled and grabbed her guns. The Borchardt C-93 was in her left hand pointed at the minister and the Colt was in her right covering the unconscious schoolteacher.

"My God!" exclaimed Peck.

"He's everyone's God," said Mabel.

"She's dead!" yelled Peck.

"And you and your wife will be if you don't do what I ask of you."

Mabel saw the minister look around nervously. Very nervously. Very, very nervously. His fingers stroked the cloth end of his shirt.

"You wanna draw on me, preacher?"

The preacher backed up. Mabel stalked him.

"Imagine you, a supposed man of God. With a weapon."

"I have to protect myself."

"How's that going? Have you liberated many Mormon women from the chattel yoke of polygamy?"

Mabel knew how to twist it in. The church's public

renunciation of polygamy in 1890 had withered the donations of many Presbyterian mission schools in Utah.

"Where were you when Johnnie was being harassed to death?"

The minister was quiet. There was nothing to say as Mabel knew d___d well he'd done nothing.

"Outhouse," said Johnnie, proving her sense of humor survived death.

"Hand 'em over," said Mabel.

"I'm taking out my Derringer."

He gingerly removed the Derringer from his pocket and placed it on a pew. He took out a small box of .41 caliber ammunition.

"Not bad."

"I've got a revolver in the office," he said.

"I'll get it later," said Mabel. "Wake her up," Mabel told Johnnie. Johnnie pushed the shotgun's barrel against Mrs. Peck's cheek. The schoolteacher started to stir. She looked up at the barrel and the rotting face behind it. She screamed. Mabel grabbed her and pushed her towards the minister. He pulled his wife by the arm as he ran in the other direction.

"There's another door?" Mabel asked herself. They escaped out a smaller side door.

After about a minute, they heard voices outside the church.

"I knew they was unnatural, but I didn't know how."

"That was a living dead girl I seen."

They banged on the door like a bunch of drunken gorgons.

"Miss Green, surrender yourself!"

If she'd killed her parents, why should she want to give herself up? Mabel grabbed the Derringer, loaded it, put it in Johnnie's left hand, and put the ammunition in one of her dress pockets.

"She ain't answerin'," said one of the mob.

Mabel spoke to Johnnie.

"Time to rain hellfire and damnation."

She quickly kissed Johnnie before she ran up the little church tower. She reached the top after climbing a short spiral staircase. The place was packed tight…with hymnals and Bibles. A perfect view of the crowd below. Time to find out if the scriptures could absorb gunfire. Mabel knew that after the first volley, it would be open season on her and Johnnie.

She scanned the crowd. She saw women amongst the vigilantes. Several people brought kerosene lamps. Her favorite plaything. She wished she had a rifle. Maybe three pistols would make up for that.

The minister's revolver turned out to be a Smith & Wesson No. 3. Coming in at about three pounds and .44 caliber, it might just have the stopping power of a rifle without the long-range accuracy.

Perhaps a "volley" wouldn't do. Everyone might scatter. She picked up the Smith & Wesson and quickly found a kerosene lamp near her. She figured it was about twenty-five feet away, held by a grinning man with a slouch hat and overalls. His right hand gripped a Winchester '73 while the left hand carried that lamp.

She aimed squarely at the lamp. She saw the flame dance inside her sights. She squoze the trigger.

BOOM! BOOM! BOOM!

One of the shots smashed the lamp, spraying glass and flame everywhere. It lit the grinning man's hat on fire. He began running around like a headless chicken on fire.

A well-dressed man pointed to the window.

"There! The devil herself!"

BOOM!

She fired. His head exploded like a watermelon smashed by a sledgehammer.

Now came the withering fire from below. Mabel watched as the incoming rounds tore into the Bibles and hymnals. She stayed close to the floor. Little bits of Bibles rained on her. She read one, from Judges:

"...Jael, Heber's wife took a nail of the tent, and took an hammer in her hand, and went softly unto him, and smote the nail into his temples, and fastened it into the ground..."

"An hammer" or not, Mabel thought it a splendid idea. Pin every one of these yahoos down with a tent peg through the noggin.

The firing ceased. The gunpowder smelled lovely.

"I reckon she's dead!"

"We pumped enough lead in her to sink an ironclad!"

"Get the other one!"

Mabel heard them banging on the front door. She worried about Johnnie. Would she be able to handle herself? A messenger gun and a Derringer could only do so much damage. She headed downstairs. She waited in the stairwell out of sight. She heard Johnnie open the door.

"We're in!" she heard one of the ruffians yell.

BOOM! BOOM!

She heard Johnnie blast both barrels into the crowd. Her heart skipped a beat.

BOOM!

The Derringer spit its bullet, followed by a scream. She had to provide covering fire while Johnnie reloaded. She fired the minister's revolver.

BOOM BOOM BOOM BOOM BOOM BOOM!!!!!!!!

That also startled the crowd. If they could keep up a fire.

BOOM BOOM BOOM BOOM BOOM BOOM

BOOM BOOM BOOM BOOM BOOM BOOM

BOOM BOOM BOOM BOOM BOOM BOOM

Never mind. The crowd blasted its way into the church, pouring lead into Johnnie, who didn't seem to mind much. Mabel peeked around the corner. Johnnie reloaded her shotgun and held it to Bishop Sorensen's throat. The gunfire stopped. Mabel came out, holding the Frontier revolver and the C-93.

"It's the devil's gun!" said one incredibly stupid mob member. Mabel shot him in the face with it.

BOOM!

"Ohhhh!!!!"

He wriggled around the ground. No mob member returned fire. Maybe he wasn't popular to begin with. Mabel guided Johnnie backwards to the stairwell.

Mabel figured there'd been enough killing. Maybe Kaysville had learned its lesson. They wouldn't dare harass someone to death based upon "strange love" again.

"Let him go," said Mabel. She pulled on the back of her dress. In doing so, she accidentally made Johnnie pull both triggers.

BOOM!

Sorensen's head popped off his neck like an angry

grasshopper. The crowd immediately gasped for a split second. Mabel pulled Johnnie into the stairwell. The gunfire commenced. They retreated up the stairwell.

Mabel took the shotgun from Johnnie and was about to pour buckshot onto the mob when she saw a small cart parked on the grass outside the tower window. A load of hay. She recognized the driver: Liken. She grabbed Johnnie and threw her out the window onto the hay. She tossed her weapons down except the C-93, which she held onto.

BOOM!

She felt a bullet tear into her back and push her through the window. She tumbled but was able to fire two shots.

BOOM BOOM!

One shot hit a female mob member in the nose. Another went wide, impaling itself into a Bible.

"She shot the holy word of God!" someone yelled.

Most of the mob members were inside the church now. The few lounging outside turned their weapons onto the cart.

BOOM BOOM BOOM BOOM BOOM!

She emptied the semi-automatic weapon into the crowd. The buggy sped off, and being driven by a warlock, literally disappeared into the night.

———

AT LIKEN'S HOME, all was oddly normal. He had an expansive meal laid out before them.

Marinated chicken breasts, beef ribs, eggs, cheese,

bread, corn, broccoli, carrots, and peach cobbler. Tea and coffee boiled on the stove.

"It's a feast!" said Mabel. "How did you cook so much so fast?" she asked.

"I'm a warlock," he said.

Mabel laughed. Her side didn't hurt. She touched her side and her back. She was healed.

"You've healed me."

"Oh, what they would think if they knew the value of the outsider," said Liken. "We must get you out of that dress."

Mabel felt a shiver up her spine. Liken disappeared into the other room. What did he mean by "get you out of that dress?"

He came back into the room carrying a bright preternaturally red dress. He tossed it to Mabel. If the gunplay didn't kill the townsfolk, the brightness of that dress would.

"We need to hide her," he said, pointing to Johnnie.

"Can't you make her vanish?"

"I'm not the boss of warlocks. Just a regular warlock. Put her in the closet."

Mabel led Johnnie to a small closet.

"You stay here. Don't be scared."

Mabel stepped into the next room. It must've been a spell or incantation room. Herbs, roots, powders. Bull's skulls. A couple of human skulls. A jar of teeth. No mirrors. Mabel quickly changed. Her slip didn't even have blood on it. Mabel was beginning to appreciate this witching life.

After putting on the dress, Mabel appeared back in the living/dining room.

"For good measure," said Liken. He had a brush and a lip rouge compact in his hand.

"I've never worn lip rouge in my life," said Mabel. "What will people think?"

"You just killed your parents and a not insignificant portion of the Kaysville population. I think they hate you more than before."

"The feeling is mutual."

Mabel recognized what the warlock was doing. Showmanship can be a part of witchery. In Salt Lake City, the only women with painted faces were prostitutes and actresses. He wanted to show them tonight was the night of the painted lips. Mabel understood.

The townsfolk came a-knockin'.

They banged on the door with their rifle butts.

"You gonna answer it?" asked Mabel.

"Of course," said Liken.

"What do you folks want?"

"We want the girls!" came the gruff reply.

"There's only one here."

"Good enough for us!"

The people outside started banging hard, as if to break down the door. Liken unlatched the door. About ten people rushed in, including a few women. Mabel knew them all.

"She looks like the devil himself!" exclaimed Mrs. Lund, wife of a baker.

"The devil wears lip rouge?" asked Liken.

Some of the stern group managed to chuckle at this.

"We want her!" said Mr. Adams.

"She doesn't belong here," said Mr. Smith.

"I've engaged her…" said Liken. A few gasps came from the mob. "…as a maid," finished Liken.

"You don't belong here!" said Mr. Shurtliff.

Mabel knew that Liken had probably lived there longer than Shurtliff, but that was the stupidity of closed-minded folks.

"How soon you forget," said Liken.

Mabel didn't know what Liken alluded to, but she made a mental note of it.

"Mabel Green is a murderess! She shot down her parents in cold blood!" Mr. Layton said.

"I saw the whole thing!" said Mr. Cannon.

"Did anyone intervene?"

The mob looked at one another as if Liken had just spoken Javanese to them.

"Your hatred and ignorance killed her parents."

"No philosophy, Liken. We'll be taking the girl now," said Nebeker, raising his rifle. Liken put his hand on the barrel.

"Your rifle wasn't that hard the last time you visited," said Liken.

"Mrs. Hall, how are things after those herbs I gave you? Feeling better?" asked Liken.

"I don't know what you're talking about!" shouted Hall.

"I'll bet Mr. Hall feels better now," said Liken.

Flustered, Mrs. Hall fled the house.

"You gonna fetch her?" Liken asked Mr. Shurtliff.

Mabel understood everything now. The despised Old

Man Liken, outsider to all, knew everyone's secrets. They'd come to him for help when all their precious churchmates and neighbors judged them. He knew them, warts and all. He also wasn't giving up Mabel and Johnnie. For the first time since Johnnie's self-murder, Mabel felt safe. And bold. From seemingly nowhere, she produced the Borchardt C-93—the first semi-automatic gun anyone there had seen.

"It's the devil's gun!" said Mr. Layton.

BOOM!

Mabel shot Mr. Layton dead. He fell on the floor. His fine-looking Stetson fell off his head, unscathed.

"He won't need this," Mabel said as she put the hat on her head.

"Out," she commanded the others. Cowed, they grudgingly left the house and poured into the front yard.

"We'll be back!" said Mr. Smith, mustering up false courage.

"We'll getcha!" said Mrs. Lund.

Mabel noticed Old Man Liken deep in thought. She felt a connection with him. He was agonizing over something.

"Do it," she said.

"It's done," he answered.

"What did you do, Mister Liken?"

Moooooo.

Mabel looked in front of the house. There were several head of longhorn cattle wandering around. Liken transformed the angry townspeople into moo-cows.

Mabel laughed. She wondered what would happen next.

———

MABEL SLEPT SOUNDLY. She awoke by the dawn's early light. She ran to the window. The cows milled about the front yard. They'd eaten some of the wild grass growing there and deposited a few cow pies.

She saw the dust up the road. A horde of people were on their way over.

"Mister Liken, you better come look at this," said Mabel.

A new mob, mostly on foot and covered in dust, approached.

"Just the way we like it."

"What do you mean?"

Two men on horseback rode ahead of the crowd. They wore dusters and wide Stetsons. Rifle scabbards.

"Mr. Vance Liken, we've come to take you in."

Liken raised his hands. Mabel stood up. She couldn't believe this was happening.

"You're gonna have to unarm me," said Liken.

One of the men on horseback rode up to the porch. Mabel could now see who they were: Davis County sheriff's deputies.

The barrel of a Colt Peacemaker jutted out from Liken's pocket. The deputy took it and unloaded it. He put the pistol inside his coat pocket.

"Since when did you raise beef on the hoof?" the other deputy asked.

"Last night."

"How ya gonna feed them?" asked the deputy.

"Ask them what happened to my husband!" a woman

in the back shouted.

"There were ten people who made their way out here last night. What happened to them?" the deputy asked.

"Must not've made it," said Liken.

"And you ended up with these cattle."

"You might want to count them," said Mabel.

The deputies silently counted the mini-herd. Ten.

Liken raised his voice.

"You folks hungry?"

"We walked nearly two damn hours to get here," said one rigid man.

"And that lake stink is awful."

Liken walked around the porch.

"The womenfolk prepared some picnic items, right?"

Liken scanned the gathering. Sure enough, picnic baskets dotted the crowd.

"We got some stuff in the tater cellar. We got fruit trees. Let's have a barbecue!" said Liken.

"Do we have any butchers?" asked a deputy.

"I'm handy with a knife," said Liken.

"Shouldn't we be looking for the missing townsfolk?" asked the other deputy.

"We should. Let me give Mister Liken his weapon back and we'll be on our way. The townsfolk can stay and enjoy themselves."

"Don't leave," said Liken. "Stay and enjoy the fine cattle."

"We best be goin'."

The deputy reached into his coat to pull out Liken's Peacemaker. Except it was a garter snake. The deputy screeched, and the poor thing slithered away.

Mabel smiled. She liked this Old Man Liken.

"Afraid of a little garter snake?" asked Liken.

Nobody mentioned the fact it had been a pistol when it went into the deputy's coat and was now a snake.

"Reckon you'll be staying for a barbecue?"

"Reckon I will," said the deputy, sweating.

"Oh, gosh! Can I bring Johnnie?" asked Mabel.

"Of course," said Liken.

There was an exceedingly brief but discernible half-murmur among the crowd. That murmur stopped almost as soon as it started. Whatever questions they may have had about dining with the living dead girl, they kept them close to the vest.

Mabel ran back into the house to fetch Johnnie while Liken exhorted the neighbors who despised him.

"Come up, come up, let's have a feast!"

And thus ends the tale about how Kaysville, Utah, became an accepting town void of hate and ignorance.

Bryan Stubbles writes and translates plays, stories and novels. His hobbies include languages, history, movies, theatre, cooking, creating the Utah Gothic subgenre and surviving the pandemic. You can find his awesome theatre blog at unknownplaywrights.wordpress.com and follow him on Twitter @BStubbles

DANARA'S COVEN

C.H. LINDSAY

The clinking of the prismatic windchimes drew Danara's attention to the rainbows dancing across the ceiling. How many times had their magic—her magic —drawn her back? How many sunsets had passed? Time held no meaning for her anymore; only the addition of another presence, another voice. They were here with her now, whispering to each other that another woman would die that night.

She looked around the bedroom at the same faded wallpaper, the same walnut bed and matching dresser, left by the previous owner. On the dresser stood a black candle decorated with silver runes encircled by thirteen small framed pictures of dark-haired women. Thirteen pieces of jewelry lay between the portraits and the candle like spokes on a ritual wheel. Each was in perfect alignment. Her necklace, the one she always wore when she was alive, lay in the back by her image.

Danara knew the other faces in the portraits as she

knew their voices. Every time she returned to this place, they came with her, whispering to her of their lives and their last living memories.

The candle and jewelry were new, as was the arrangement. She moved closer, curious about the light silver runes. She reached out a transparent finger to see if she could touch them. It tingled when it came close to the candle. The tingle surprised her. It had to be Troy's doing, but he knew little about magic.

"Maybe he learned?" one of the ghostly women whispered.

"I doubt it." He knew her windchimes protected from evil, which was probably why they were still there, but he had no aptitude for spell craft. At least, he didn't when she was alive.

"They did not protect from him," other voices whispered, moving closer to Danara.

"No, he was invited here." Much to her regret.

"We loved him. We trusted him."

"So did I." It wasn't her fault—their fault. All thirteen women were taken in by his charm, his sweet words. Danara tried to stop him from killing her, and then, each time she returned, she tried to stop him from killing someone else. But she didn't have the power. However, with each death, each new presence that materialized with her, Danara grew stronger. Now, they were thirteen. A coven. Maybe this time, they could end the cycle.

The bell to the shop downstairs jingled followed by a woman's giggle.

"Too soon," the voices moaned.

It was. The sun was still up, and they'd only just materialized.

The bell jingled a second time. "Oh, Troy, I can't believe we're engaged after only four weeks." Another woman. She sounded breathless and giddy.

"Why not? I knew when you first walked into my shop that you were the girl for me," Troy's familiar tenor voice said.

"My shop." The shop where Danara once sold herbs and potions, homemade crafts, and magical charms. The shop where Troy came to court her every day for two months before he proposed. They visited museums and art galleries, estate sales and pawn shops. He even respected her magic. He seemed so perfect.

"His shop," more voices whispered. *"His magic."*

"My shop," she insisted. She could still smell the herbs and feel the protective magic of her windchimes— although there was a bitter tang of darkness now because of Troy. "My magic."

"Now his magic," the women whispered again.

"Stolen from me." Her shop. Her bedroom. Her magic. Her life. All taken.

"Stolen from us." The final consonant circled the room like a snake stalking its prey.

In that moment, Danara relived thirteen different proposals and thirteen identical murders. Each new death added to the last, the memories and the voices growing stronger. She tried to block them, to not feel the cumulative sorrow. But each time, she failed.

"We failed."

Each of the women died in this room, this bed. Maybe

if she kept Troy from coming in, they might stop him from killing tonight. Her hand reached for the cold of the metal knob, but she wasn't solid enough to turn it.

"And if you could," the women whispered, *"how would you stop him?"*

"I don't know." She wasn't even sure he had to kill in this room or if it was simply more convenient. She only thought that, if she broke the pattern, she could change the outcome.

"Oh, Rita, my darling, we will be so happy here," Troy said from the stairwell.

"I never thought making dolls and wreaths would be so much fun—or that people would actually want to buy them. I'll bring some more over tomorrow."

"Not tomorrow. I've already put up a sign that we'll be closed. I plan to sleep in." His soft laugh was like nails on a chalkboard to the ghosts in the room.

Several of the ghosts moaned.

Rita giggled again. "You're right. It's not every day you get engaged."

It was for Troy. Danara looked around the room. There had to be something she could do to stop this.

Ghostly whispers buzzed around her, becoming more agitated and less coherent until she couldn't think.

All thirteen turned to watch Troy and his fiancée as the door opened. Danara moved in front of them, not sure if she wanted to get out or keep them from entering. Either way, she was stopped by the threshold.

Troy faltered as he carried his still-giggling fiancée through the apparition and into the room. Rita was almost the same age Danara had been when she was alive.

"Run, Rita!" she cried out in desperation.

"They cannot hear you."

Danara barely noticed the voices. Her attention was on Troy, lost in the memory of when he had brought her here to celebrate their engagement. It had been the happiest day of her life.

He set Rita on the cornflower blue bedspread and took the small basket of chocolate-covered strawberries she was holding. "We'll get to those later, love."

The anticipation in his eyes refocused Danara's attention. As soon as he set the basket on the nightstand, she tried to push it onto the floor to distract them.

Several of the women tried to help, but none of them were corporeal enough. Others tried to pull Troy and Rita's hair. They, too, were unsuccessful.

"One more thing." He went over to the dresser and lit the black candle. A light scent of lavender and dill coiled through the room, making the ghosts shiver.

"I've been waiting for this for weeks," he said, kissing Rita.

"No!" Danara felt…stretched. She turned to the window to get away from what she knew would happen next…and then she was part of Rita as he pushed her onto the pillow.

She felt Troy press her into the mattress, kissing her like she was the only woman in the world. After so long, the feeling was intoxicating, multiplied thirteen-fold as the others joined them. Rita's heart pounded, her need burning through them as if they were one.

The thirteen were caught up in Rita's passion, reliving their last moments even as they knew they were also hers.

"Please, let this be different," Danara begged as unful-filled need twisted through her. The fourteen women breathed as one, each fueling the passion until past and present blended with lavender and dill.

Danara felt the woven cord of silk and chain slip behind her neck like before. She screamed a warning, but it sounded ethereal, even to her.

He broke the kiss and leaned up enough to loop the cord together and pull it taut against her throat.

"Troy, what are you doing. It's too tight." Rita grabbed his hands and tugged at them. "Stop it."

"Relax. It's okay, sweetheart." Troy nuzzled her neck, but didn't let go of the cord. "It'll be over in a moment and will make the climax more exciting; more intense."

The ghosts tried to pull away from Rita, but they couldn't break the connection.

"No. This isn't funny. Stop!" Rita thrashed and bucked to get away. Troy only tightened the silk and chain, using it to keep her in place.

With a combined force of will, the thirteen ghosts broke free and formed a semi-opaque circle around the bed. "Let her go," they said as one.

Troy shook his head. "No, I don't think so. I felt you, all of you, last time. I knew you'd come back, so I prepared."

Danara tried to reach for Troy to pull him away, but the burst of will was gone. She couldn't move. The lavender-dill scent filled the room with a purple haze of magic. *The candle.*

She saw the distress of the others as they, too, stood motionless.

He took a moment to smile at the ghosts. "When the

candle burns out, you'll be out of my hair and gone forever."

Rita used the distraction to slip away from Troy. She made it to the side of the bed before he pulled her back. "You're not going anywhere, either." He slapped her and tightened the cord, smiling at her struggle for breath. "Go ahead, fight. I like it rough."

Danara could neither look away nor intervene. Her thoughts were fuzzy and disjointed. The others were fading, their voices almost inaudible. If she couldn't do something now, they would be sent back, and Rita would join them.

If only she could put out the candle. Danara focused on Troy, on her need to stop him. There had to be something.

The prisms clinked against each other, lightening the fog in her mind. "The wind," she whispered.

The others barely made any noise in response.

She drew on the magic of her windchimes and called to the breeze, asking it to help them. It had been done before, but not by her. If she could pull together enough power, it might work. "Help me," she whispered to the others.

For a moment, there was nothing. The prisms clinked together again.

Slowly, the twelve became more visible and joined with her, strengthening Danara and her magic. The force of the wind grew, howling into the room. It tangled the lace curtains, knocked over several pictures, and extinguished the candle. The smoke dissipated.

The thirteen grew stronger, turning the color of soft cream. "Let her go." As one, they touched Troy.

Troy's grip on the cord loosened, and his eyes widened.

"It still won't work. You may touch me, but you can't hurt me."

"I can." Rita grabbed his thumb and pulled it back until it broke, then she rolled off the bed and ran out the door.

He glared at the ghosts and swore, slowing as he pushed past them. He ran out the door and called, "Rita! It was a little BDSM I saw in a movie. I promise I won't do it again."

Danara flew after him, but she was again stopped at the threshold. "No!"

"*We cannot let this happen.*" The others' voices were clearer now, their bodies milk white with a tinge of pink.

She rushed to the window, but she couldn't get past the curtains, even with the magic from her windchimes. She was also unable to penetrate the sunflowers on each wall. The ceiling and floor were equally impassible. "I can't get out!"

"*Can't get out,*" the others echoed.

Someone pounded on the door downstairs. "It won't work." Troy's voice was harsh and ugly. "All the doors are locked."

His words were followed by a thud. Rita screamed.

She was going to die, in spite of everything they tried. This was Danara's room. Her shop. Her spellcasting. There had to be more she could do.

She felt for the magic of her windchimes, the power woven into her dreamcatcher downstairs, and then closed her eyes, remembering how her shop looked, where everything was carefully placed, the power crystals behind the cash register, the protections on the door. She pulled the magic into herself. For a moment, she almost felt alive. It wasn't enough.

"Form a circle." She grabbed the hands of the women on either side of her. The magic expanded, filling the space before them. She reached down to slip through the floor, but the room still held them.

A ripple passed through the room from downstairs, followed by a bubble of magic that engulfed the circle, pulling the coven into the shop below.

It had changed over the years. There were kitschy trinkets and little dolls arranged along the counter, interspersed with candles. Herbal wreaths lined the wall with some of her old power crystals and protection charms. Her dreamcatcher hung at the window between two new wooden bookcases filled with books. Another shelf held a collection of ointments and oils. The scents, blended with magic, were heady.

"*Rita*," the women whispered, bringing Danara's attention back to the woman lying face-down on the floor. Troy again had the cord around her neck. She wasn't moving.

The coven circled Troy, clawing at his hair and clothing until he let go of the cord. Then, they grabbed him and pulled him off Rita's body.

Danara again took the hands of the women next to her and closed the circle.

He tried to push past them, but this time they were too solid for him to get through. "You're dead. You have no right to be here. Go away."

"No. This is my shop, my home." Danara's voice echoed as the others spoke with her. "My magic. You took them from me. They don't belong to you."

He shook his head and laughed. The sound was cold and brittle. "Who is going to say it isn't mine? I have a signed deed. Your deed. A dead woman can't tell the police I stole it. So, you're out of luck, and soon, you'll be out of my shop."

The women keened softly as they glided around him, always facing the center.

The scent of magic was not as strong now. The others less opaque. Without breaking the circle, Danara looked for inspiration. How did a ghost vanquish a living person?

"With fear."

No. Not with fear, she thought. With terror. Danara chuckled softly.

"What poor excuses for ghosts you are," he taunted. "You're already fading. A few more minutes and you'll be gone. Once I tell the police someone broke into the shop and killed my fiancée , I'll sell this place and go where you'll never find me."

Danara could not let him escape. She did the only thing she could think of. She made up a spell. It didn't have to work; he just needed to think it would.

"Ash to ash
and dust to dust.
Vengeance cries
that die you must.
Will and right
and purpose true;
now our fate
we share with you."

Three times they circled Troy, Danara saying the words, the women repeating her. He continued to push at them, to knock them down, to distract them. Each time, he failed. When they finished the chant for the third time, each woman whispered her name, one by one, in the order they were strangled.

Troy was panting with exertion, but the women would not let him pass.

A candle on a nearby table began to burn, filling the shop with the scent of fennel and rue.

"Rita, what are you doing?" He shoved at the ghosts who were now milky white.

She was still on the ground, but she'd turned her face to watch Troy. "Helping."

"I wasn't going to really hurt you, just…" He stopped when Danara hit him on the back of his head.

"Those photographs…" Rita's voice was a hoarse whisper. "You were going to kill me, too."

"I didn't kill anyone. It was the former owner. That's why this place is haunted."

"Liar," Rita hissed.

"*Liar*," the other women echoed.

The candle exploded. A pile of dolls and a basket of dry herbs caught fire, as did a section of the shag carpet.

"Let me go," Troy cried out. "Please. I promise I won't hurt anyone again."

"Like you let us go?" Danara asked. "Like you were going to let Rita go? No. Tonight, you join us." She chanted the rhyme in a singsong voice.

Each of the other ghosts echoed Danara's voice, altering

the words to mock Troy and his distress. A few told him what they'd do when he was dead.

The acrid smoke from the burnt herbs, cloth, and carpet filled the room, setting off the fire alarm and sprinklers.

Danara went to help Rita while the other twelve continued to circle Troy, giggling and whispering promises of retribution.

He was almost as pale as they were, shaking and sweating profusely.

Suddenly, he cried out and clutched his chest. Then, his body went taut. The circle stopped, watching. After a moment, he fell forward.

A *pop* and a sharp, metallic tang indicated an electrical fire somewhere. Rita still lay in the same position on the floor. "Let me help you," Danara said, bending over the woman.

A fire engine pulled up outside. "Go. I'm safe now," Rita whispered.

One by one, the ghostly apparitions disappeared. Danara stayed long enough to see the firemen break down the door.

———

DANARA HEARD the prismatic windchimes a moment before she saw the rainbows dancing on the ceiling and wondered what brought her back to this place. Troy was dead. There should be nothing to keep her here now.

The room looked the same except for a new bedspread. The scent of lavender, fennel, and magic was no longer tainted by Troy's essence. A dark-haired woman stood in front of the dresser, her back to the ghost. "Why am I here?"

Rita turned from the dresser. On the top, a white candle with gold runes burned. The only other items were her necklace and photograph. Those of the other women were gone.

Rita smiled. "I wanted to thank you for saving my life. I honestly thought I'd have more time before he tried to kill me."

"If you knew, why did you stay?"

"Like you, I'm a witch. I joined your Circle a week before you disappeared. When Troy asked me to take some things up to his room, I recognized your photograph. It didn't take long to find out who the others were. I've been looking for proof ever since."

It was a dangerous thing to do, but Danara couldn't fault her for it. "Then, why the black candle?"

"He said this place was haunted and asked me to make him something to help. I said yes because it gave me a chance to search his room. I didn't know it was to catch you. I thought I had more time, that he'd take me out of town before he tried anything. There was nothing to indicate he had killed any of you here."

Danara understood. "I tried to stop him, too. Each time." She paused. "It was your magic that pulled us through the floor." It wasn't a question, now that she knew Rita was a witch. "Thank you." It was then she realized the others weren't with her. It was uncomfortably quiet.

"No need. Without your help, I'd be dead." They were both silent for several moments. "Also, Troy kept a journal.

He wrote about each of you, how it felt, what he took, and where he buried your bodies."

"Then, it's really over." Rita had gone to a great deal of effort to bring her here just to say thank you. "Why else did you bring me back?"

"Troy officially died of a heart attack. He has no family, so, as his fiancée, they're letting me take over the owner-ship of the shop and the apartment. I wanted to make sure it was okay with you first. I'd like to call it Danara's."

The ghost said nothing for a long moment, surprised at the request. "If you're sure you can live here after what happened, I'd like to know something of my life remains behind." It felt...right. Her shop, her magic, would go on with Rita.

"Hearing thirteen women were murdered here will bring the curious. None of you will be forgotten." She turned back to the dresser and blew out a candle. "Thank you."

The breeze picked up. The last thing Danara saw as the room faded away were the rainbows dancing across the ceiling.

C. H. Lindsay is an award-winning poet & writer, booklover, and housewife—not necessarily in that order. She spent thirty years as an event planner, helping organize and run science fiction, fantasy, and horror conventions, and a decade acting in community theatre. Now she prefers to stay at home with her family and write poems, short stories, and novels. This is her twelfth anthology. She's a member of SFWA, HWA, SFPA, and LUW. Mostly blind, she lives in Utah with her "seeing-eye husband," son, and a cat who thinks she's another child.

A LIFE WORTH LIVING

RG HUGHES

—A*hh, you're awake! And there's that inquisitive look I've been missing.*

My name? Jim Berret. You don't know me, but I have a story you need to hear, or at least one I wish to tell.

You see, a year ago, my life had fallen to a rut. A cliché, if you will, and though I don't prefer starting a narrative with waking up, to the best of my memory, that is where life changed for me. So please, accept my sincerest apologies, and bear with me. This won't take long. —

I found myself bound and laid-out in a cellar, my head cocked just a bit. The stiffness in my neck implied I'd been there a while. My feet were numb, and something sharp pressed deep into my back. I didn't remember falling asleep, or even waking up, but there I was, so it must have happened.

— Hey, don't you fall asleep! [Crack] We've just begun. Now, imagine that, will you? Waking with a sharp, numb pain

at your side — intriguingly dull and throbbing. Well, I suppose it isn't something you'd need imagine now, is it? Where were we? Oh, yeah... —

As I remember it, my mind was slow of thought and the surroundings surreal. Perhaps drugged. I didn't care, and that's what bothered me.

The area where I found myself was cool and damp and musty and dark. Not black dark like the clergy's windowless scroll room, but enough for shadows and outlines to appear in lieu of old boxes and dusty furniture. Something akin, I supposed, to the archives of my parish, but without the tall, arched ceilings, mortared stone walls, and barred windows.

Light, at least the glimmer that existed, appeared in flickers of moonlight through barren tree limbs. The branches ponged about outside in a stiff wind, which whistled and clicked through cracks at the edge of a window's frame. This might have offered an escape but was in no way large enough for my figure. I clawed for a clear thought. How had I come to this? How might I escape? Who would do such a thing?

Nothing.

I searched the dark contours and angular shapes. A chair... the head of a child's hobby-horse... but nothing offered hope.

Lying back, eyes to the blackness above, old dust and mildew brought memories of my youth.

— Whoa there! My, My, you do squirm, don't you? It's like you are a three-year-old. [hammering] Now stop it. Ahem, I could ramble at length, you see? Dumping as it were, and thus

help you understand who I'd become, but it's probably best I not do that. Though of particular interest to me, it is not relevant to our story, nor would it offer clues as to why I found myself in such a predicament. I'm sure you'd like to move as quickly through this as possible. Now, stay with me, and let's get back to it. —

I attempted to shift my body leftward so that I could sit but found it impossible. My legs were bound and my hands tied over the front of my belly. Odd I hadn't noticed that.

Where I lay was soft enough. A mattress, I figured, from the way I cradled into it. I imagined lice and centipedes and other nasty creatures crawling beneath, attacking each other without provocation, and protesting their meaningless little lives. It made me chuckle, just a little, something I'm not prone to do. The pain in my side, about kidney level, throbbed, indicating the drugs were wearing thin. I bounced, just slightly, hoping to gain a better angle and dislodge what had poked me, but I stopped short. A quick and terrible agony dug into my back, as if my organs might plop out, popping from me like the pacifier of an irate baby. The poking, perhaps a spring from the mattress paying a quick visit or an errant stick, was relentless. Needless to say, I didn't do that again.

I thought to scream but decided against it. If, per chance, those who'd deposited me in this dungeon, this replica of hell, were still near, it'd be best to keep their secret.

More pain in my side, and my mind began to clear. I snickered, but with the tightening of my gut, I was once again reminded of the pacifier effect.

My hands, though taped, were mobile, and I slid them upward, gnawing like a rat on bacon. I made quick work of it, admiring my ingenuity. I reached, pulling my knees upward in slow, deliberate motion so I didn't conflict with the spring at my back. With some effort, I released my feet.

Footsteps creaked on the floor above. Rather heavy ones, I judged. They were followed by more, lighter steps. Then still more. I could just make out the faintest light from what appeared to be the sweep of a door at the top of a stairway. The thin bulges of brightness crept by in a horizontal line, moving in cadence with the dark shadows of the first set of feet, then disappeared. There were muffled voices and more footsteps, and more dim, glowing light passing by. I counted seven odious figures. Monsters all, deserving of God's wrath. My enemy on the move, I needed to free myself: to find escape and refuge.

I moved to sit, realizing for the first time, it was not a bedspring in my side but rather a tether, like something drilled through a turtle's shell, fastening it to a post. A metal, nail-like shaft had pierced my abdomen and exited my back. The pain wasn't as significant as one would expect, and I felt no blood, now believing this some type of surgical outcome. A cord attached to an eyelet of sorts at the back felt as if it were a braided, flexible type—not something I could chew apart—which trailed off into the darkness, beyond my reach.

A melancholy hymn came from above. Maybe not a song, but something like one, pleasant, as though a group of women had raised their voices during service. My eyes drew weary as I listened until I couldn't bear the weight of my lids any further. I slapped myself across the cheek, keeping the somnolent ebbing at bay, but it crept back, and soon I found myself disoriented. My head tipped from side to side and lolled forward and back. Of the few things I remember, one was the door at the top of the stairs creaking open on its rusty hinges and candlelight descending the stairs. Figures in dark robes stood before me.

"Why?" I croaked.

I awoke again, no longer confined to the dungeon, but within a lighted room bearing no wall art and curtains drawn closed. I lay upon bared plywood, a pillow propping my head for comfort. My hands and feet were bound again, though not to themselves as before but to the rigid surface of the wood. Perhaps in punishment for my earlier near escape.

— *[Fingers snap.] Ughh. Is that too tight? Here, let me adjust it. Don't you cry, now. I'll fix it.*

There. That's better, now back to our story. —

A parade, a procession of sorts, began. I turned my head for a better look. Hooded figures wearing darkened masks and robes chanted in a mystic language. Not Latin, of which I am fluent, but of similar dialect. The language, to my recollection, was one I had never heard. The largest of the cloaked figures was a heavy-set woman, which I could tell by the protrusions at her chest. She led the group in single file, circling about me like crows or buzzards above fresh kill. They carried candles, lit, apparently the same people and candles I'd seen earlier. They sang again, but this song was different. More upbeat in tempo and yet damning in tone. They swished their arms and the candles up and down in rhythmic form, not unlike robed and slowed Sifakas. Dancing monkeys, if you will.

"Why?" I screamed out, only hearing the hiss of wind. I had no voice! The back of my throat hot, as if scalded by an iron, led me to believe they had taken my cords. I jerked left, finding myself bound to the table by something far worse than the tether. I'd been nailed, so to speak, through the side, a foot-long rod driven through me into the wooden top. Something akin, I supposed, to Christ, a sword exiting his side. I tilted my head to one side and then the other, peering at my hands. Each bolted, arms splayed. I threw my head forward and gazed at my feet, knees bent, posed, a single bolt penetrating the center of my overlapping extremities. My God! I was the central player in a crucifixion. Blasphemous!

"Arrrhhh!" I screamed, but the result was merely grunted air. Woozy and disoriented, still without pain, at least not much, I realized there was some sort of drug involved. No! I wasn't woozy at all. Perhaps hypnosis, or witchcraft, or demons!

A genderless voice entered from my left. "Ahh, Mr. Berret. So nice of you to join us."

I looked, straining my bleary eyes, trying reflexively, vainly, to wipe my face. It was the large one. Faceless in a flat-black mask. The eyes, though, were real enough, sparkling and blue, and red lips visible through an oblong hole. Too red and glistening, as if soaked in blood. Was it mine?

"It is always fulfilling when our guests are present and alert," the voice said. I say the voice because I was still unsure of the sex. I remembered the breasts and tried to look again, but someone stilled my head in strong hands and shoved it to the table. Another forced my mouth open, and still another poked a long pair of tongs inside, rattling against my teeth and pinching my tongue. They pulled the meaty thing forward to its length. Did they intend to remove it like they had my vocal cords? I thrashed and pulled at the muscle, but to no avail. I was weak, apparently under their demonic spell and control.

"Hold him still. I need to get this right," the big one said. I could see the chin beneath the mask. No whiskers. Female. Must be.

"This will go better if you don't fight," a voice whispered above my head. A different voice. It was female, feminine, almost sensual. I stopped my struggle, letting myself appear penitent, as if doing so might please her. Perhaps buy time.

The big one said a few words in an incantation sort of way, and I felt sharp pressure against my exposed tongue. I tugged, trying to withdraw into my mouth, but found they had pierced me with another rod, long enough to bridge my lips and teeth, leaving my tongue extended and vulnerable. I twisted my exposed appendage this way and that, wondering at the lack of pain, then turned my head to the side, gazing up at the large, cloaked figure. She held a knife, long and serrated. I clenched my eyes, not wanting to know her intent. Once again, she chanted. I opened my eyes again, unable to resist. Hands straightened my head, holding it rigid. The large woman blew green smoke into my nose and mouth, and the room faded away.

When I awoke again, I found myself still in the room, but the board had been raised and apparently mounted to the wall. I hung like a rag doll, my untethered skull lolling forward and to the side. Inside my mouth, I could feel stitches where my tongue had been forked. I worked to raise my head, sharp barbs prickling the skin of my brow and around the periphery. It was clear what they'd done, but I couldn't fathom why. There were candles set in a semi-circle on the floor. The scent of smoldering myrrh and Frankincense rose from piled twigs on a metal shelf at my bolted feet. I raised my head.

"Awake again, I see," said the large one. Those protrusions were definitely breasts; at least two of the robed figures were female. My mind remained sharp, and yet I still felt little pain. I opened my mouth to ask why but remembered I couldn't speak and thought better of bringing up the pain thing. I peered at the blue marbles behind the mask.

"Why?" I said anyway, but it came out as something quite different. Somehow, she understood, as if the question had been asked this way before.

"You are fortunate to be part of the ritual of the resurrection, Mr. Berret. I'll not call you Pastor, for you are not worthy."

I wanted to decline the forced invitation. To beg they put things back the way they were, but somehow, I knew that wasn't going to happen.

"I'm sure you are wondering—why you? But you needn't," the woman said. "We needed a man of God. Someone with a certain type of background."

I shook my head no and then peered into those blues. What type of background?

"Yes, yes. I see you know what I mean. Witches are God's messengers to people like you, Mr. Berret. It would have been better for you if you weren't of the cloth. We leave that scum to the authorities."

I wept, mouthing, "please."

"I'm afraid there is no bye for what you've done. I have children myself, Mr. Berret. Oh yes. Two. I think you know one of them. Sean. He sends his best. Well, not really."

I gasped and tried to plead, but there was nothing.

"Okay, you got me," she laughed, but it wasn't a kind laugh. "Sean doesn't know you are here or that this is happening, but I'm sure he'd approve. Don't you think?"

I shook my head no, trying with my eyes to beg. Her eyes responded, as if she wouldn't see me.

"We should get started." She whispered a few words, and the candles on the floor brightened. The pain came in waves, undulating with every beat of my heart, dancing against the rhythm of her voice.

It was a long night, and at times I prayed for death, remembering my Lord's dying words. I'm sure none of them, even the one with the nice voice, paid much attention. God, either, for that matter, which left me in guilt for my thoughts against him.

Morning came. I know this because the sun's light slipped in through the side of the eastern curtains. Eastern —the sun was rising.

The large, robed figure appeared in the doorway before me, a small boy herded in front of her. Sean? I worked to focus. To break the crust of my tear-bound lids, blinking, the world blurred.

"Sean," I said, which sounded like a soft "aye", but no more or less than forced air across a swollen throat might. Eyes shut, I tried to envision Sean's parents. To remember who they were. Who she was. But I made no connection. I peered at him again.

"Mr. Berr—?" Sean looked at me, convulsing with nausea, then finished to the floor.

"It's okay, honey," the woman said. "You don't have to look at the bad man."

Sean retched again and again, his black, heavy-rimmed glasses falling from his face and landing in puke. "No!" he said. "Mr. Berret is my friend."

"Friends don't do bad things to little children, Sean."

"He didn't do it. The other one did. The one that looks like Mr. Berret."

There was a gasp from under the hood, and the large figure pulled Sean back into the hallway. "What do you mean, the other one? There isn't another one."

"There is. There is. He comes at recess and after school. He's a priest too. Says he's helping Mr. Berret."

"Oh my God. What have we done?" came a whispered cry. "This is unforgivable."

Everything became quiet except whimpering from Sean, who every once in a while called out for me.

After a while, I heard severe whispering. Several voices. All female.

"Get Sean out of here," one of them said. "And take those glasses."

"What about him?" said another. They weren't using my name, which drove fear deep into my bones.

It was an hour, as near as I could tell, before five of the hooded figures entered the room and lowered my board from the wall, laying it back quite gently onto the table. The large one blew smoke again without saying a word or looking into my eyes. The pain faded as I drifted off.

I awoke to the kind of quiet that happens, I imagine, in outer space, an anechoic chamber, or a coffin. I checked for light, even the tiniest wisp from a teeny crack around my perimeter, but there was nothing. I lay still, sensing small vibrations, thumping in cadence from somewhere above. Not sound, but a trembling, like a lead weight slammed onto hardened soil—far away. Reaching upward, I touched the ceiling of my confinement, perhaps three inches from my prone body. The holes in my palms sore but not painful, pressed against the top.

It didn't budge.

Using my fingers, I searched for some method of opening what appeared to be a fabric-lined box. I would have guessed coffin, except the area around my head and arms seemed disproportionately large, holding claustro-phobia at bay.

The air thinned, and eventually fatigue spread like a soft blanket. I welcomed it, thinking it the end. Eyes closed, I filled my lungs with used air, bequeathing my body to God's tender mercy, apologizing for my earlier thoughts, and allowing slumber to take its gentle hold.

Light tapping and the flow of new air brushed the quiet and sleep away. Blurred light shone through a crack around the edges of my tomb, and I supposed, at least for a moment, it was God, awakening me in resurrection after a thousand years. Dazzling brightness flooded about me as the gap widened, a steel bar wedged through the crack, used perhaps by some unholy thing to pry the lid open. Blinded in light, I covered my eyes. A child's voice coursed through the void.

"Mr. Berret. Mr. Berret. Are you okay?"

Without my cords, I knew better than to reply, but I lifted my body with my elbows to sit.

"We need to go," the child said. "Before they come back."

I rolled, fumbling to my knees and standing, blinded in harsh light. I climbed past crumbling dirt of a shallow pit.

"You guys fill in the hole. I'll get started with him." It was a child's voice, perhaps Sean.

A small hand took hold of my fingers, avoiding the damage to my palms, either through sympathy or disgust, and guided me forward.

"Watch your step here," he said on occasion, but for the most part, I stumbled and bumped into every rock or divot in my path until my eyes became mildly used to their surroundings.

"Sean?" I said, pronouncing his name as 'eye?' in whispered wind.

"Yeah. Me and a few kids from the school came to get you."

"Thanks." Which came out 'ains' but seemed to pretty much cover everything that needed saying at that point in my life.

— *You've got a little something on your shirt. Yeah, right there. Let me get that. I guess a bit of stain won't make much difference now, will it? Ha! You'd think you were my first, but there were three others, you see, and with each my story gets clearer and closer to submission. Amazing what people know and don't even know they know. You look tired. We're almost through, here. —*

We traipsed through trees, through backroads, and over fences to the Church. Though I had concerns about visiting yet another basement, we agreed it would be the safest place and took refuge. The vaulted architecture was home for me. Golden light refracted off stone walls and large cathedral windows set ten feet above the floor. Giddiness crept inward, and I chuckled, which hurt. The drugs or spells or whatever were wearing down. Then, my heart dropped like a hammer driving nails to my abused guts. I could not once again relive that pain! Not the agony I had endured before I was buried. I just couldn't.

"Let's wait here," Sean said. His dark curly hair ran just over his ears with a small, braided tail to one side. His skin, though it carried the look of a child, seemed aged, the way a Desert Willow's skin grows old and marked, though its overall appearance remains sleek and smooth.

I yearned to embrace him in thanks, but given what I had just been through, and the accusations which caused it, I felt it wouldn't be prudent. He led me into the chorus room with its curtained stage, benches to the front, and grand piano centered in the large, oval room.

"Lay on that," Sean said, pointing to a four-legged, thin-top table set near the piano. The similarity to plywood struck me, and I stepped back, memories of drugs and thorned headgear flooding my mind—the pain steadily climbing with each word uttered from that vile woman's mouth.

"It's okay, Mr. Berret," Sean said, as if he could read my mind. "We got you."

I edged forward as he tugged at my fingers. I peered at him, resisting, as though he might leap at me with a dagger, but in the end, I assented, climbing aboard the wooden altar-like table. I lay flat, arms to my sides. Sean hummed a few words, the kind the women had chanted, and I fell asleep.

In my dreams, I heard sing-songy voices, smelled smoke, and felt the warmth of a fire. It wasn't until I heard lapping flames that I realized I wasn't sleeping anymore. I tried to roll but found my hands lashed, rather than bolted, securely to the table.

"Ahhhh," I yelled, which sounded like "Ahhhh," and felt a small hand press against my shoulder.

"It's all right, Mr. Berret. I got you." It was Sean.

My eyes must've appeared horrid, bulging from their sockets and all, but I should be forgiven my concerns and agitation, and Sean seemed to do just that.

"Help," I said, which came out as "Hell," but I think he got my gist.

"Look," he said, pointing to seven metal crosses bolted in a semi-circle to the floor, spread across the oval. The seven witches were mounted, arms extended, to the horizontal bars. Each appeared drugged, as I had been. They were without hood or mask, and I recognized them as members of my congregation. The fires, which heated my skin and blackened the ceiling, were nowhere near me, but on the concrete below the seven.

I looked at Sean, questions pouring from my eyes.

"It's okay, Mr. Berret. They are going to a better place."

The women screamed, flames consuming their robes, and the stench of burnt flesh searing my nostrils. As they perished, one by one, I felt the pain of my hands, feet, side, and head fade. I looked at the hole through my left palm and watched as it closed, healing before my eyes.

"What's happening?" I asked, which came out as "What's happening?"

Sean smiled. "There is a cost for what they did to you, Mr. Berret. One that must be paid."

"What about the bad man? The one who hurt you."

"A ruse, to gain action against a good man. We knew the women couldn't resist."

"But you are just kids."

"We are into our fifth century, young man. We look the age we need to."

Sean cut my ropes, and I sat, my legs dangling above the floor. I looked at him.

"I don't understand."

"We are of the ancient Anasazi. The 'Others', if you will."

"But you're white."

"We appear as we need to."

"Why are you here?"

"These women stole our bones, our souls, using them to achieve their magic. It makes them powerful and dangerous and sickens us."

I considered this for a moment. "What does this have to do with me?"

"Wrong place, I suppose. Wrong time for you, but a convergence for us."

"So, I'm just a piece of meat on the grill?"

"Pretty much, but then, aren't we all?"

I peered into his ancient young face, seeing past the child to what he really was. "What will happen now?"

"We're going home. You should run. Disappear, if you know what's good for you."

I looked at him quizzically.

"It's going to look like this was your doing." He pointed to the witches. "Some might believe you did bad things to the missing children of the area, as well. No, Mr. Berret, I don't see any other way for you to go with this."

"What children? Their children?"

He nodded his head in assent and smiled, fading from existence before my very eyes. Left behind was a small pile of clothes, his glasses, and a child's Zorro-the-Bandit wallet.

— *There! You are back. I thought I'd lost you there for a moment. Now pay attention.*

As you've heard me say, my life, before the witches, had become a cliché—unworthy of living.

Oh dear, you've made a mess again. [Reaching in, wrist twisting. Something gives, snaps, there's a disembodied whine in response.] There, that's much better.

Now, where was I. Oh, yes, yes. I look forward to life now, you see. Lived my way.

It's what brings me here—bearing this tale—to you. I need to learn about those pesky Anasazi, you see. Their bones, the witch-craft those women practiced, and how it works. I am committed, you understand, and will keep looking. Now, you will tell me

275

what you know. What I need to know to improve my story. No more crying and saying you don't understand. Do you hear me? [A twist of the wrist again, pulling at the sutured tongue].

Oh. There now. You've started bleeding again. You really should stop moving about like that. —

New to writing, R.G. Hughes spent the last thirty years on family and business interests. It's time now to run at a new pace and have a little graveyard fun, where good friends are a stone away and there's a story in every plot.

MISS FORTUNE - ANASTASIA

NATASHA MORNINGSTARR

You would expect to see her floating overhead on a broom. Instead, she struts with grace in Louboutin pumps—reminiscent of Meryl Streep, only melanated—she walks with the Devil wearing Prada. With skin the color of mocha, she switches roles like Dorothy in Carmen Jones. The essence of her roots is magick. Her presence pulses with a subtle vibration known to draw people into a trance. One beat of her drum, and you'll do her dance. Her name is *Anastasia*.

Anastasia gasses up her Porsche and throws her Louis Vuitton luggage in the trunk. It's time to hit the open road, away from all the troubles in her life. It's time to check that road trip off her bucket list; a trip she told herself she would take by her golden birthday, only if she was still single with no bun in the oven. In the days leading up to her 25th birthday, she began planning this trip in her mind a million times over, for what seemed like ages. Most important of all, it's time to get away from the vanity and bustle of Los Angeles and head somewhere she can feel more at peace.

Since birth, Anastasia's life was always planned out. She would get straight A's in school so that she could attend an Ivy League University—the education didn't matter as much as the bragging rights for her mom and dad. She would need to keep her beauty and body up to par so that she could land a well-to-do husband and bear him a few beautiful children. All of this was according to her parents' wishes. Anastasia was fed up, tired of always having to be *Miss Perfect*!

From the courtyard, her mother watches as she slams her trunk.

"Where are you going?" Her mother's voice is nearly cracking as she asks.

It almost sounds like she really cares, which is rare. All her mother ever cared about was expensive clothes and pleasing her father. Anastasia's feelings never seemed to matter. Children were an accessory to take out on occasion when family and friends felt like comparing whose family was top tier in the bloodline.

Clicking her tongue in annoyance, her mother repeats, "I said, where are you going, Anastasia?"

She begins to walk toward her daughter, who is ignoring her as she climbs into the driver's seat; the creak of luxury leather seats pressing against Anastasia's body as she shuffles into place do the talking for her.

Turning her Rayban-laced eyes toward the road, Anastasia replies sharply, "Don't worry about it!"

And with a whip of her hair, Anastasia presses her six-inch pump against the gas pedal, and off into the Beverly Hills sunset she drives.

———

SEVERAL HOURS HAVE PASSED since she hit the open road. With her hair flying in the wind on I-15 north, she reaches for the volume on her radio to turn it all the way up. As the soulful sounds of Nat King Cole blare through her speakers, she lets her thoughts marinate. She has no clue where she's going and no real plans other than to just drive until her instincts tell her to stop.

But before her instincts can have a say in the matter, a pothole has different plans. Her Porsche collides with the concrete orifice, causing her tire to blow out. Pulling over to avoid getting hit by oncoming traffic, she looks up to an ominous cluster of storm clouds stirring above. Coincidentally, the news report begins to play on her car radio.

"Tonight, it looks like some heavy rain for us here in Utah," the weather anchor reports. "Please, be prepared. I think I speak for all of us when I say we don't want to repeat what happened the last time it rained here like this!"

Anastasia turns down the volume.

"O-M-G! What happened the last time it rained?" Her voice is filled with curiosity and worry. "And did I really drive all the way to Utah?"

She hops back inside her car, locks the doors, and pulls out her cellphone to check her location.

"Well, I'll be damned," she utters, realizing that she has

indeed driven over 700 miles. Looking around, she spots a beautiful two-story motel. Leaving her car parked on the side of the road, she grabs her luggage and clicks her pumps across the dirt road with plans to rest her pretty eyes.

"This looks like a good place to rest for a night," Anastasia thinks as she makes her way to the entrance. "I'll call for help with my tire once I am settled."

———

"May, I help you?" Behind the motel's front desk stands a petite woman with Rapunzel braids the color of midnight. For a second, her voice leaves Anastasia in a trance.

"Hello, ma'am. May I help you?" repeats the woman.

Blinking twice, Anastasia comes to. "Yes, I would like a room for the evening, please." Reaching into her purse to find her driver's license and AMEX, she looks at the lady and asks, "Where in Utah am I?"

"Oh, this is Ballard, honey." The lady smirks with a pride Anastasia has only seen from women who just swindled their husbands into a shopping spree on Rodeo Drive. "Here's a travel guide, should you want to have a look around or order in for dinner."

Stepping back to examine Anastasia, she asks, "Where are you from, if you don't mind me asking?"

"Beverly Hills, California." This time, Anastasia beams with pride, but that soon fades as she remembers why she hit the road in the first place.

"Well, welcome to Ballard, and I hope you enjoy your stay." Handing Anastasia her room key, the woman turns away to answer an incoming call.

"I'm in the middle of nowhere with a busted tire on my birthday." Anastasia mumbles to herself with frustration. "Why is this always happening to me?"

Sighing with anxiety, Anastasia heads to her room. Flipping through the tourist guide, an ad catches her eye. Written in big bold purple letters—her favorite color—are the words: *Curious about your future and trying to escape from the past? For only $25.00 dollars, let Miss Fortune help you.*

"Hmm! Only twenty-five bucks," thinks Anastasia. "I wonder if I should entertain this? After all, it *is* my 25th birthday, so this *must* be a sign."

With a slight pause but excitement flying through her bones, she reaches for her cellphone to make an appointment with Miss Fortune.

———

AFTER A DRIVE that feels like an eternity, Anastasia hops out of the Lyft and onto the dirt road, clutching her Hermes Birkin bag. As the driver's brake lights become more distant, she can see the flicker of what looks like porch lights ahead.

"Okay, this is spooky…" Anastasia straightens her back, and while holding her head high, she continues walking toward the flickering lights. "Here goes nothing."

As she nears the front door of a beautiful vintage home painted in black, the front door opens slowly, and there stands a lady who can't be much taller than five feet, with braids that drag the floor, cheekbones that would make Maleficent red with envy, and skin the color of mocha.

"Welcome, Anastasia." Her eyes are piercing yet warm and inviting. "I have been waiting a long time for you!"

———

WITH ONE SWOOP of her arm adorned in gemstone bracelets, Miss Fortune gestures for Anastasia to have a seat across from her.

"How are you, darling?" Miss Fortune asks with what sounds like sincerity, but Anastasia shoots her a look of skepticism and confusion.

"I don't know what I am even doing here, honestly." Anastasia turns her head to take in her surroundings and notices hoodoo dolls gently nestled in rows that line red walls, beautifully scented essential oils stocked on wood shelves, and tarot decks by the dozen.

"I'm not usually into *these* kinds of things," Anastasia leans in to whisper to Miss Fortune.

With a smirk and a smile, Miss Fortune leans in to whisper back to Anastasia, "Well, I am happy that you are finally here, darling."

"What do you mean by *finally*?" At this moment, Anastasia's worry begins to cloud her judgment. "This is the second time you've said this, and I don't understand!"

Reaching across the table, Miss Fortune grabs Anastasia's hands and turns them over to read her palms. "Hmmm. What are you running from, darling?" Miss Fortune looks at Anastasia with concern. "Why are *you* really here to see *me*?"

"Well, isn't that what *you* are supposed to be able to tell *me*?" Anastasia snaps back, taking her hands away from Miss Fortune's grasp.

Grabbing her hands again, Miss Fortune replies, "It looks like you are searching for a rush of happiness and joy that has died a long time ago."

Looking into Anastasia's eyes, Miss Fortune smiles, but her eyes fill with sadness.

"You have come to the wrong place for that, darling." Rising from her chair, Miss Fortune turns her back to Anastasia. "And if I were you, I would hop back in that pretty car and go back home while you still can."

Anastasia stands up in a rush. Grabbing her Hermes bag, she pulls out a wad of cash and throws it onto the table and speed walks out the front door. Oddly, there sits her Lyft driver, waiting for her. The next stop is back home and the hell away from this weird town.

————

BURSTING through the front doors of the motel with panic and worry in her voice, Anastasia calls out for the petite lady with the Rapunzel braids.

"Hello, ma'am!" Pacing from one end of the lobby to the other, she reaches for her cellphone when she notices a note on the front desk counter.

"Dear Anastasia, your car tire has been fixed. I am away for the evening and hope that you have enjoyed your stay."

Anastasia makes a dash to her room, grabbing her bags, she makes her way to her Porsche. As she approaches, she notices a small owl-shaped symbol made out of what looks like mud on the driver's side door.

"Who did this to my car?" Reaching in her bag for a makeup remover wipe, Anastasia begins to wipe away the symbol. "This is so gross."

Hopping in, Anastasia turns the volume up on the radio to drown out her racing thoughts from the events of the evening.

Just then, the voice of the same news reporter from earlier booms through the speakers, "Good evening, residents of Utah, and welcome to tonight's news report."

Anastasia begins to reach for the dial to change the station but notices something peculiar standing in the middle of the road. Hitting her brakes, she squints, trying to get a good glimpse through her high beams.

"Is that a deer?" Anastasia smiles, as she loves animals, but her smile soon fades as she notices the deer isn't moving across the road to safety from oncoming traffic. "Maybe it's just as scared as me and wants to go home."

Putting her Porsche in park, Anastasia contemplates waiting a few minutes for the deer to cross the road.

Rolling her window down, she yells, "Okay, you can move now."

The deer turns its head in her direction, and Anastasia pauses, rolls her car window back up, and puts her car in drive, but it won't move. Something hits the car with a loud thud, causing Anastasia to freeze. Not sure what to make of everything that is happening, she reaches for her cellphone to call for help and notices her battery is sitting at only one percent.

"O-M-G! Now, what am I going to do?" Anastasia

decides that making a dash back to the motel would be her best chance at getting help, but when she opens her car door and tries to move her feet, nothing happens.

A wave of paralysis washes over her body as she falls facedown into the muddy road.

———

"Hello, Anastasia."

Coming to, Anastasia looks up to see three women, each a different race, each with Rapunzel hair, and each dressed in all black.

Looking down at Anastasia, frightened and covered in wet mud, they speak in unison, "We are here for *you*."

Anastasia tries to run, as she realizes she has gained back her movement, yet something is stopping her.

"What do you want from me?" With tears streaming down her cheeks, she realizes she isn't going to make it back home. "Who are you?"

"Some call us skinwalkers, some call us aliens, darling." Anastasia recognizes the voice and turns to see *Miss Fortune* walking toward them.

"Miss Fortune?" Shocked and confused, Anastasia begins to grow angry. "Is this some kind of sick joke?" With a shrill shrieking voice, Anastasia yells, "Let me GO."

"NO." All three women yell in unison as they begin to form a circle around Anastasia. "We are here to take you back to the happiness that you seek."

They begin to chant in a foreign language that Anastasia cannot understand. She falls back down to the ground, shaking violently.

Anastasia can hear them singing in unison, "She is one of us/Thank you for bringing her home/Here she must die to be born again."

As her life begins to flash before her eyes, she wishes that she had time to say goodbye to her mom who never paid attention to her. She wishes she had gotten married to the guy of her dreams and had those beautiful children she was expected to have, and she wishes that she had never left home.

Anastasia's body continues to shake and twist like that of a contortionist. She begins to foam at the mouth, and as she reaches for her pulsating heart, everything begins to slowly fade to black.

She has finally found the peace she had been running away to try and find. It was buried six feet down in the dirt of Ballard, Utah.

Natasha Morningstarr is a creative writer with a proclivity for all things horror. She is a member of the Horror Writers Association, enjoys glasses of white wine, rituals with her husband during the new moon, and speaking to the dead with her family of Wanderers. Follow her journey into darkness at NatashaWrites.info/other-works.

UNFRUITFUL WORKS

D. J. MOORE

I first met her outside the gates of Temple Square. In the spot where you usually see a bagpiper playing Amazing Grace for loose change. Arianna Plemmons. With jet black hair piled atop her head and piercing blue eyes surrounded by cerulean eye shadow. She wore mostly black with a deep purple bodice and a short necktie to match. Both arms were raised high above her head, fingers twitching as if playing upon an invisible instrument.

She'd attracted quite a crowd. Other than the occasional musician, you usually don't see street performers in Salt Lake, although a few do come out this time of year due to all the foot traffic. At first, I wondered what her act was. She didn't seem to be doing anything particularly interesting. But then, following the gazes of several people in the audience, I saw a young man dressed in a white shirt with a red tie jerking about in a kind of marionette dance.

The woman lifted her right ring finger, and simultaneously, the man lifted his knee in a puppet-like motion, his lower leg left to dangle lifelessly. Since he was already standing on the tips of his shoes, this left just one toe touching the ground. His lower arms hung limply from the elbows, and his head was slumped down on his chest. Like a puppet dangling from unseen strings.

The woman then moved her fingers in a flurry of motion. The man came alive, dancing a jig that defied gravity with high leaps and sudden spins. His head whipped back and forth violently, threatening to turn all the way around. His arms jerked as frantically as the conductor of a symphony orchestra. He kicked his legs in opposite directions, doing the splits as effortlessly as a gymnast before bringing his legs back together in time to touch pavement.

Finally, the woman lowered her arms to her sides, and the spell was broken. The young man looked about himself as if he'd just came out of a trance, embarrassed at all the attention he was getting. Several people clapped, and some put change and bills into the plastic Halloween cauldron she used for tips. There was even a sign with a QR code on it for people who wanted to send money but didn't have any cash on them. The young man disappeared inside Temple Square, his friends joking with him and hassling him along the way.

The woman timed the ending of the performance perfectly. Seconds after she lowered her arms, the light for the crosswalk came on. The audience dispersed, about half entering Temple Square to see the Christmas lights, and the rest crossing the street to shop at the mall.

I don't know why I didn't move on with the rest of

them. Something about the woman transfixed me. I wanted to stick around for at least one more performance. I wondered if the same young man from before would circle back around to do his athletic demonstration again or if she had a different confederate standing close by.

She didn't make eye contact with me as I waited for her to start again. She stood perfectly still with hands clasped together and head bowed. Combined with her black clothing, she looked the part of a graveside mourner.

I couldn't keep as still myself. Although it was an unseasonably warm December, it was still chilly enough, and my shoes were thin enough that I had to stamp my feet to keep my toes from freezing. The smell of cinnamon filled my nostrils as a little girl skipped past me waving a freshly-baked churro in front of my nose. I was suddenly reminded of how hungry I was and decided to cross the street to the food cart.

However, before I could step into the street, the red hand lit up. Pedestrians caught in the middle of the cross-walk rushed to get out of the way amidst the honking of cars. People leaving Temple Square began to pile up, waiting for the light to change again.

The woman I would later come to know as Arianna Plemmons was once again alert. She slowly stretched her arms out and then proceeded to pantomime a person handling rope. She wrapped the imaginary rope around itself, tying it into a knot. Then, she spun it over her head like a lasso and tossed it into the crowd.

I was surprised to discover I was the lasso's target. She hadn't acknowledged my presence before, so her singling me out came as quite a shock. I've always been a wallflower by nature, preferring to blend into the background rather than be the center of attention. I decided now was the time to discreetly make my exit. She'd have to find a different person to participate in her act.

I turned to walk away when she pulled the imaginary rope taut. I actually felt it press into me. It wrapped around my arms just above the elbows, tight enough to be uncomfortable. How could this be possible? I could clearly see there was no rope, yet it felt just as solid as anything. Had she somehow hypnotized me? I reached up as best as I could and tried to pull the rope loose, but I was unable to make any headway.

She yanked on the rope with a strength I wasn't expecting, and I was pulled forward violently. A few people in the audience laughed. One woman gasped. They must have thought I was her confederate and this was all part of the show. Just as I had at the previous performance. I would have shouted "This is real!" to dissuade them of their misperception if I thought it would help.

I leaned back to prevent myself from being pulled any closer to her, but she was strong enough to pull me forward anyway. My shoes skidded across the cement. She dragged me towards her without my taking so much as a single step forward. There were several impressed oohs and aahs from the crowd. People asking each other how we did it.

Once I was next to her, she grabbed the hair on the back of my head and pulled my face close to hers. She gave me a quick peck on the cheek, and suddenly the spell was broken. I no longer felt the rope around me. I could once again move at will.

I backed away from her quickly.

The light changed and the crowd dispersed, some dropping coins or bills into her cauldron. That should have been the last time I saw her. I should have left. Turned around and walked away, never to see her again.

So why did I stay?

————

Arianna gunned the engine and swerved around the car ahead of us, barely missing its bumper. However, her attention wasn't entirely on the road. She gave me a significant glance, even as she was passing the other vehicle. My eyes, meanwhile, were glued to the road in order to compensate for her not paying enough attention.

"I don't like that particular shade of blue," she said. "We'll have to get you something more suitable on the way."

"Didn't you say the party starts at eight?" She'd invited me to come along to her friend's holiday party. I said yes even though I didn't know her at all. I didn't even know if she thought of this as a date or not. "We don't have time to stop along the way."

"Of course we do. We'll just be fashionably late. In order to make you more fashionable." She laughed at her own joke. "Everyone will understand."

The headlights of Arianna's truck illuminated countless snowflakes, each individual one disappearing as quickly as it appeared in a mad rush to get out of her way. We were fast approaching another car, and she wasn't watching the road.

"Watch out!" I braced myself for impact.

Arianna flicked her eyes casually to the dark road ahead and swerved around the car at the last possible second. "I saw him. You don't need to tell me how to drive."

"Why are you in such a hurry anyway? You just said you don't mind being late. There's no reason to drive so fast."

She glared at me. "I said don't tell me how to drive."

"But you get to tell me what to wear? This shade of blue is just fine. How about this? You don't tell me what to wear, and I won't tell you how to drive."

She looked to the road for a moment and then back to me. "No. I still don't like it. We're getting you something else."

Arianna had slowed down a bit while she was talking to me, which gave the car she'd just passed time to speed up and pass her. She was not happy about that.

"Fiddlesticks!"

I'd expected a stronger swear word to come from her mouth, but the way she'd said fiddlesticks made it somehow worse than one of your garden-variety cuss words.

"Just let it go," I suggested.

She, of course, ignored me.

She sped up, trying to pass the car again, but it sped up too. We were both going way too fast for this stretch of I-15. I could see traffic beginning to pile up in the distance.

I braced myself for impact once again when Arianna inexplicably relaxed and slowed back down. I let out a sigh of relief.

"See? You don't have to..." I began to say when she suddenly flicked her fingers like she was brushing away a crumb. The speeding car immediately swerved off course and ran right into a concrete barrier with a loud crunch. Another nearby car squealed its tires and crunched into the back of it. The speeding car now appeared to be half as big as it was before, crumpled up like an aluminum can. There was no way anyone inside had survived that.

Arianna laughed.

I couldn't believe it. Someone had just died and she laughed! I looked at her in horror.

"What?" She said. "Karma's a biatch."

We drove on in silence for a moment, then Arianna said, "Oh, right. Your shirt." She suddenly swerved across four lanes of traffic to get to the exit ramp, eliciting several angry honks along the way.

I guess we were headed to the mall.

———

WHEN SHE PARKED THE TRUCK, I wanted to get out and run as far away from her as I could. But something stopped me.

For one thing, we were clear across the valley. It would be hard for me to get back home from here. Also, I wasn't entirely convinced she was that bad. Sure she'd laughed at the car crash, but there was no way she had actually caused it.

Was there?

She did seem to have some kind of telekinetic power when she'd lassoed me, but that had to be a trick. Surely, she couldn't actually move objects with her mind. And if she could, trying to escape wouldn't do any good. For now, all I could do was try to get through the night. I just had to put up with her for a few more hours, then I'd never have to see her again.

So, I followed her inside.

The mall was packed with last-minute shoppers and kids in line to see Santa. Storefronts festooned with Christmas decorations and ads advertising sales. Mannequins with perfect bodies staring sightlessly through glass cages. A Christmas song in which a woman sang, "no, no, no" drowned out by the chatter of the crowd.

People moved aside to let us pass. Shoppers standing obliviously in the middle of the aisle would suddenly take a step back. A group of teenagers clustered together would inexplicably arrange themselves in single file until we walked by.

More tricks. It had to be.

If Arianna did have a supernatural power, she was wasting it. Instead of using her ability to do good in the world, she was squandering it on banal trivialities. Self-ishly using it to prevent inconvenience to herself.

The mystique that had initially drawn me to her was completely gone by now. Why do people who seem so amazing upon initial evaluation turn out to be so depressingly ordinary once you get to know them?

When we got to the clothing shop, up on the second floor, Arianna took her time holding up different shirts in front of me before finally deciding upon one.

I paid for it. I didn't want to owe her anything.

She then insisted I change into it immediately, so I went to the restroom.

When I came out, I found her leaning over the railing, looking down at the people below. I watched her flick her fingers. A shopper carrying a lot of bags tripped right next to the fountain, almost hitting her head. While the shopper scrambled to retrieve the items that had slid across the floor, Arianna laughed at her. A mean, spiteful laugh.

That was it. No matter how awkward it would be for me to leave right now, I couldn't stay with her any longer.

I spun around, intending to disappear into the crowd, but Arianna froze me with a glance.

"Leaving so soon?" she asked. "Don't you want to go to the party?"

"I'm actually not feeling that well," I said. "I think I'll just call it a night."

"Right after buying a shirt for the occasion? Nonsense. Let's go."

She started walking off, but I didn't follow her.

"Oh? Is that how it's going to be? Very well."

She made a walking motion with two of her fingers against the palm of her hand. I felt my legs start to walk towards her.

I looked around for help. No one paid us any mind. Couldn't they see what she was doing to me? I must look weird with my feet not obeying me. However, upon seeing myself reflected in a window, I was surprised to find that I was walking quite naturally.

"Hey!" I shouted. "Somebody–" But my protest was cut short. Arianna silenced me by snapping her fingers against her thumb. Like a mouth closing.

"Nuh-uh," she chastened me, wagging a finger. "None of that."

I continued trying to scream, but with my mouth firmly shut, my protests were muffled. People walked past. Some ignored me, some looked at me curiously, but none helped. My eyes pleaded with each face that floated past me. I couldn't speak, but surely, they could see the look on my face. Surely, they could see I needed help. I wished for a Good Samaritan to step in and do something, but no help came.

I guess it's easier to ignore other people's problems than to risk getting involved yourself.

————

ALTHOUGH IT WAS NEARLY CHRISTMAS, her friend's holiday party looked more like a Halloween party. Many of the guests were dressed in black. Ancient tomes, specimen jars, and a human skull adorned shelves around the room. Fragrant incense burned, and candles provided scant light. There was even a witch's broom hanging above the mantel.

Arianna greeted her friends cheerily, barely introducing me except to point out how good I looked in my new shirt. I didn't even try to remember the names of all her friends.

Someone handed me a cup of punch. I took a sip. It was fruity but alcoholic. Thinking it best not to partake on this particular night, I discreetly set it down upon the coffee table. However, someone else, seeing me empty-handed, gave me a replacement. I decided to hold onto the second cup lest someone else give me another. I pretended to sip from it every once in a while to blend in.

I gravitated towards the kitchen to separate myself from Arianna. I was planning on leaving the party through the front door as soon as she left the living room, but I also had an eye on the back door in case she stayed there. It was dark outside, snow was coming down in clumps now, and I had no idea what neighborhood I was in, but anywhere was preferable to here.

The hors d'oeuvres consisted of bacon-wrapped asparagus, focaccia crackers with a soft goat cheese, and homemade jelly squares. Since I didn't know anybody, I pretended to be interested in the décor and nibbled upon the snacks while keeping track of Arianna.

Her friends wanted her to play a song on the upright piano. After some feigned reluctance, she eventually agreed. She crossed the room, seated herself primly upon the bench, and began to play *Lacrimosa* by Mozart.

In addition to thoughts of escape, I had also been mulling over ways I could stop her from controlling me. Since her power was seemingly inherent in her being, there was no wand or book or crystal I could snatch away from her. She didn't need to chant any spells, so gagging her wouldn't keep her from working her magic. However, I'd noticed every time she worked her magic, she flourished her fingers.

Watching those delicate fingers tickle the ivory keys, I saw a chance I might never have again. If I slammed the fallboard down upon her hands hard enough, could I break her fingers and thus prevent her from controlling me?

No. It wasn't worth the risk. She'd surely notice if I sidled up beside her and stop me before I could do it. My best chance was to leave the party now while she was distracted.

The people in the kitchen moved towards the living room to better hear her play. I had a clear path to the back door, but there were enough people around that someone would see me go out that way. I wasn't a smoker, so I had no good explanation for going out back if someone should ask. Besides, the backyard was probably enclosed, so I would need to climb a fence to get out.

I headed for the front door instead. I could claim I left something in the car if anyone questioned me. The living room was crowded with guests listening to Arianna play, so I had to go slowly, careful not to bump into anyone holding a drink. I squeezed myself between groups of people, awkwardly stepped over an ottoman, and at one point slid against the wall, all while inching my way closer to the exit.

Arianna finished her piece and everyone clapped. I was almost to the door. I waited for her to start playing something else so I could continue my departure, but instead she stood up and scanned the crowd.

She locked gazes with me.

"There you are," she purred. "Darling, show our friends how well you can play."

People backed away from me. I was once again the center of attention.

"Me? I don't know how to play." I held my hands up in protest.

"Of course you do. Come here." She made a come

hither motion with her index finger which I was powerless to resist.

I crossed the room towards her just as I had when she'd lassoed me. My feet weren't obeying me, but I could still move my hands. I flailed about, trying to find something to hold onto. I knocked a plastic cup from someone's hands, and it flew through the air right towards Arianna. The cup had been full. Red punch soaked her hair and dripped down her face, reminiscent of the famous scene from *Carrie*.

Some of the guests laughed, but most of them, probably knowing better, remained silent.

Arianna was furious. She released her hold on me to punish the merrymakers. Each person who'd laughed found themselves lifting their own cups above their heads and pouring the contents out upon themselves. Several expensive-looking outfits were splashed with bloody stains.

One of the women who'd laughed wasn't holding a cup, so Arianna walked her over to the punchbowl and made her submerge her head in it.

"Who's laughing now?" she demanded. The woman, whose head was underwater, couldn't have possibly answered, and perhaps couldn't even hear the question in the first place.

There was nothing I could do to help her. Sometimes, the only thing you can do is save yourself. So I used the opportunity to get to the door. As sickening burbles issued forth from the punchbowl, I clasped my hand around the metal doorknob and turned. Biting cold and howling wind rushed in as the door creaked open.

Arianna turned her attention back to me. She slammed the door with a swipe of her hand. "Where do you think you're going?"

"I, ah, left something in the truck," I stuttered out.

She brought her hands together as if about to clap but stopped short. I felt pressure on my skull as she pressed her hands closer together. I instinctively reached up and tried to pry her hands away, even though she was on the other side of the room.

The pressure was so great, I was unable to keep my mouth closed. My jaw dropped open. I must have looked like Edvard Munch's painting *The Scream*. A moan of pain escaped my throat. I had the worst headache I'd ever experienced. My brain throbbed like techno. It felt like my cheekbones were about to crack. Maybe there were hairline fractures already. Viscous liquid began to trickle from my nose. My vision blurred as stinging tears filled my eyes. Blood pounded loudly in my ears. How much longer until my eardrums burst?

"Arianna! Stop this!"

A man in the crowd bravely stepped in front of me. Immediately, the pain ceased. Maybe Arianna couldn't attack someone if she couldn't see them?

I wasn't going to stick around to make sure. I bolted out the door, ran as fast as I could, and never looked back. There was nothing I could have done to save the others. I mean, how can you defeat someone who can kill you as easy as pointing at you?

I've been looking over my shoulder ever since, especially when I'm on the freeway. That night has given me a whole new set of phobias. Whenever I bump into something or stumble over a crack in the sidewalk, I'm paranoid that it was really Arianna pushing me. The sound of a woman laughing terrifies me. And forget about mimes. I can't go anywhere near them.

I also can't stop thinking about the party and what happened after I left. I felt incredibly guilty when I read about the deaths the next day, but I also felt relieved I wasn't one of them.

Call me a coward if you like, but cowards live.

D.J. Moore's fiction has previously appeared in the ETA Hoffman tribute anthology *Machinations and Mesmerism* as well as the steampunk anthology *Put Your Shoulder to the Wheel*. He's also a fan of quality cinema and was an extra in Sharknado 4. His website is maniadelight.com.

VICE

DONALD EVANS

I think this is a confession. Isn't that what you do when you've done something bad? There is no word or category to define my bad. I'll start here, even though it's not the beginning.

The phone rang.

"You have no idea how hard it is to get up this early in the morning," I said as I picked up the phone.

"Dude, it's almost three."

I knew it would be Jeff. He's probably the only person who calls me and definitely the only call I answer.

"Eat me."

I hung up then. Jeff is my best friend, but a man's got to sleep. About five-thirty, I woke up again. The sheets were wet and rumpled. Must've had a nightmare. I had a cooling shower. Time to work.

I sat at my desk and turned on the lamp. I grabbed the first envelope on the top of the slush pile. What kind of life do you have when you spend your day looking through a slush pile? I read about ten pages and threw it in the trash. Why is it that when people mentally masturbate on paper, they feel the need to share it with others? After reading it, I felt like washing my hands to get the icky off. The next story had something to do with toast and a guy who stares at the toast, for like nine pages. I picked up the next package, and I felt cold run up my wrist. I'm too young to have arthritis, so I thought I must have slept on it wrong. The packaging was nondescript, but it bothered me. I couldn't tell you why. I didn't want to open it.

I opened it.

In it was a book. An old, dry, dark book. I held the book in my right hand and peered into the empty envelope extended in my left. I guess I thought it was a joke or expected to find a note. I put the wrapper on the desk and placed the book on top of it. I sat there, staring at it. I had no idea what to do with it, and I didn't want to read it.

I read it.

When I finally looked up, the clock on the wall read six-thirty. I looked at the window and could see the sun beginning to rise. I stood up with a start. I had read for nearly eleven hours. I don't remember getting water, going to the bathroom, or thinking about sex for that whole time. Women and scientists will tell you this is a theoretical impossibility.

I got in the shower. I started at the usual temperature then ran it up a little until it was lukewarm. I tilted my head back as the water sprayed on my chest. I opened my eyes. There was a little black spot on my white ceiling. It kind of looked like mildew. I told myself to remind me to scrub the ceiling in the bathroom to keep the paint clean. I forgot about it and went back out to get some breakfast. On my way to the kitchen, I looked at my desk. The book was sitting there, open. I sat down and read.

At ten-thirty, the phone rang. It was Jeff.

"What the hell are you doing up this early?"

Without waiting for my response, he continued.

"I met some girls. Come have a drink."

The address Jeff gave me was on the edge of an old residential section that had been there for what seemed like a hundred years. Some of the houses looked that old. The further I got down the tight, car-less streets, the more derelict the buildings appeared. I parked, but then I had to keep walking further away from everything. I got the impression that I was slowly descending deeper and deeper into a hole. At its nexus, I found myself standing outside of "The Pit." The name seemed a little on the nose. It was eleven in the morning, but the building hid in shadow. I stalled on the sidewalk. In a town with such a rich history of debauchery and underground bootlegging tunnels, one would expect to find a decent bar near downtown.

Jeff had been a little different lately. He had always been a little different, researching all kinds of crazy people and odd histories, but then he had become even more off, interested in local folklore to the exclusion of any other subject. He hadn't written anything or at least hadn't submitted anything for me to publish in a year. I gotta admit that made me nervous. Jeff kept me in business when everything else I tried to push languished.

I must have just stood there for a couple of minutes thinking all that stuff, and no one had gone in or come out, and nothing had moved on the street at all. The building was still shrouded in sunlight and revealed nothing of meaning.

"Why did you pick this place? How do you even know this is here?" I said to no one.

The door opened. I strained to see inside, but I could not. I stepped forward until the building swallowed me. The door closed subtly behind me. I felt like leaving. I felt like screaming into the tactile silence. I waited for my vision to adjust.

I saw Jeff. He was near the back wall at a table with two girls. One of them was laughing and drinking. The other one just stared. I guess I don't mean stared, but she looked at me *intently*, you might say. You know those people who don't blink much? Her black dress caressed her skin like lustful fingers as she shifted in her chair, and the color made her pallor seem ghoulish and luminous in the brooding darkness. Jeff introduced me, and I sat down. We drank.

Jeff asked about business. I told him about the book. He asked who the author was. That was a good question. The writings bothered me.

Could she read it? is what she asked me, the girl with the unblinking eyes.

I stared back at her.

I told her she wouldn't want to read it because it's sick. Demons and suffering and that kind of stuff.

She did want to read it, she assured me.

When Jeff and his woman got all suck face, I took the wide-eyed girl back to my house. I offered her a drink. I offered her food. I offered to do some cunning linguistics.

She would politely say no and ask about the book. I gave up for the moment.

I pointed to it, and that's when the excrement hit the electrical cooling device. Not in a literal sense but more like a fatalistic way. Like I said, I don't know where anything starts. It probably started earlier. Doesn't matter now.

That night, after she left, I took a shower. I felt unclean somehow. I wanted her, but I didn't want her to read the book, but I let her read the book because I wanted her. I turned it up until my skin began to tingle and turn pink. I rinsed the conditioner out of my hair and tilted my head back. I saw the mildew spot. It had grown. I needed to do something about that before it got out of hand. I put on my clothes. I looked in the fridge. I grabbed a pitcher of orange juice. I closed the door, and as I turned, I saw something. I dropped the pitcher and it shattered, embedding glass in my ankles. Nothing there.

I hadn't expected to see her again, but there she was on my doorstep the next day. I saw her through the fish-eye view hole placed in the door. I don't know what they're really called, and I won't look it up. She was moving her hands and muttering something. Great, I thought. But she looked good. She looked better than I remembered the day before. I was hungry.

I let her in.

I told her I was going to take a shower. She went to the damn book, ignoring me totally. I took a shower. I wiped the steam from the mirror. Looking up into the mirror, I saw the spot on the ceiling. It was spreading quickly. If I left it much longer, I was going to have to repaint. She came in as I was staring at the spot. I hadn't even noticed she was there until her hand caressed my hip. It was so cold compared to the steaming bathroom.

Or maybe it was just cold.

She stood behind me, hands wandering in front of me. She was breathing on my neck, and my mind could not quite finish a thought between each breath. She leaned close to my ear and asked if I was going to publish the book.

"Who would buy something like that?"

Her lips touched my ear lightly as she told me that she would and so would others. That was a good point. In my current state, it was the only relevant point. I would have cut off my foot and put it on a chain if she said it would bring her luck. She left me there, leaning on the counter, staring into a fogged-up mirror.

After I dressed, I went out to talk to her. To seduce her actually. At this point, I actually believed she wanted me, and being an old fashioned kind of girl, she wanted me to make a move. so she kept talking about the book as an excuse to hang around. It amazes me that men have survived as a species.

Anyway, she was gone. I looked at the book. It felt like a blackhole. No matter where I looked in the room, my eyes were pulled back down to it.

I shivered.

She didn't come back for five days. On the fourth day, I started to get antsy. Would she come back? I called Jeff and repeatedly got his voicemail. I got tired of hearing his prerecorded jubilation at being unreachable.

I was desperate.

I started having more violent and frequent nightmares. On the sixth night, I woke up screaming words I had never heard before. I had to go into the bathroom to towel off the sweat.

It was dark outside and inside. I decided I wanted a snack, so I slammed something in the microwave. It lit my face as it irradiated my frozen burger. I could swear I saw some hideous monster in the door's reflection, but on closer inspection it was just me.

For a time, I had toyed with the notion of burning the book or throwing it away, but it was a part of my life now. Everything seemed out of control. It was like she had me in a vice. I wanted her there reading the book and touching me, but if she wasn't, then maybe I could bury it away and move on. I was conflicted. And then, on the seventh day from first meeting her, I woke up with her in my bed.

She just lay there. I didn't know what to do. I reached out. She grabbed my hand and gently pushed it back down to the bed. Silently, she slid on top of me. I went numb all over. I could feel what she was doing and see it in a third person kind of way. I got the impression that she was amused by it all. I could not have cared less. Do I sound pathetic yet?

She was on top of me and she was digging her knees into my side like, get this, like I was her horse. I got this crazy image of myself buck naked wearing a saddle. I started to chuckle. I guess she didn't find the situation as humorous as I did, and she raked her nails across my chest so hard that when she raised her hands, the fingers were dripping with blood. Then, she started to giggle. Now, I've been with some sick chicks before, but this floored me. She spoke some gibberish and made some weird signals with her hands. Then, she licked the blood from her fingers.

I was so weirded out, I didn't even realize she was talking to me now. She was asking me if I'd publish it. Publish the book. She kept asking me over and over as she squeezed her thighs around me and rocked.

I wanted to cry.

I wanted to scream.

"Yes." I moaned.

I had just been saying, "Yes." That's what you say when a woman's doing what you want. I may read manuscripts all day and write in my spare time, but when it came to sex, my vocabulary shrank to "Yes" and "Oh, yeah." Once in a while, for some disturbing reason best left for Freud, I would say "Oh, Momma."

She believed I had said yes, that I would publish the book. My ears popped. I looked down at her hand, gently caressing my bloody chest. Its absentmindedness told me what I needed to know. She had no further use for me.

She got out of bed. She dressed quietly. She wiped her hand on her thigh as if she just looked through the neighbor's trash without a glove. She stared. More like glared. She warned me that I had promised to publish the book, and she had completed a cycle of spells. If I didn't do it, someone else would, and there would be suffering.

There's always suffering. So, I published it. This is going to seem anticlimactic, but apparently, they were all part of a cult, coven, whatever. Her and Jeff and the bartender and ten other people. They wanted me to publish the book so that other people would read it and it would have an amplifying effect. I know this because Jeff left me a voicemail. They performed a ritual from the book and achieved their goal of being the first to be eaten by the returning Elder Gods. Yay for them. I know this because I saw their livestream on YouTube.

At first, everyone blamed me for what those supposedly college-educated morons did. I didn't make them do it. I was waiting to get sued by everybody, but that's when more Great Old Ones returned. It seems people around the world decided to replicate the process using the book to summon more beings who were so hungry after their long slumber that they started by devouring whole cities. People literally saw for themselves how awful the consequences were for messing with the book and got together with their friends to try it for themselves. I blame 2020. I'd die laughing if I weren't already dying of some virus. The CDC doesn't have a clue what it is, just that it is from one of those things. Either its DNA or a virus or something. It's changing me, and it's not good.

I sit at my desk and type this for no one to read. The window is open, and I can see Him covering the hillside. The sky is a putrid brown. Fires still erupt sporadically from destroyed buildings. His slumbering thoughts fill my waking hours. Still, I can't stop thinking about her.

Donald Evans is a lifelong Californian but spent childhood summers in Monticello and visits Utah at least once a year for FanX and family. 2020 has allowed him the excuse to stay home with the things he loves. His wife, new baby, video games, movies, music and books hold his attention as well as the frozen food section at Costco.

WHAT HAPPENS IN SALEM

ANGELA HARTLEY

S he's crazy. Psycho. A freak of nature like that should have never been born.

I can hear their thoughts as I walk down the hall of Salem High. Hate rolls off them in waves as they give me a wide six-foot berth. Even the teachers keep their distance as if my presence were a dangerous pathogen.

Catching.

They aren't wrong. I am dangerous, especially to small-minded humans in a little town like Salem, Utah. I disrupt the neat little narrative they've been fed for a hundred years. It's all bullshit anyway, but no one likes to be shown the truth.

I am a mirror. That is my fate and their downfall.

I can only be what they expect me to be, and in this space, I am the storm.

I want to rage. I want to turn their energy back on them. They think I am evil, but they are truly the wicked ones. They deserve a taste of the misery I can inflict.

But I can't.

Not yet.

I barely manage to keep my frustration in check as Mr. White pokes his head out of the philosophy classroom. The coven assigned him to watch over me during the day because he already works as a teacher at the high school.

Convenient.

I roll my eyes and prepare to play the part of a misunderstood schoolgirl.

No sense adding more fuel to the fire they are already trying to burn you with, Cailee.

The very first craft lesson Mr. White tried to teach me was how to shield—as if I didn't already know. I let him believe I was as weak as all the other girls.

When he catches my eye, his thoughts enter my mind as if he's spoken aloud.

"Control is the key to mastery."

Yeah, he should get right on that.

We lock eyes, and I read an opportunity. He expects me to push back against his intrusion into my thoughts, but instead, I open the door into my mind. With a devilish grin, I project exactly what he hopes I'm thinking about: What it would feel like if I ran my fingers through his curly black hair.

He eats it up like candy.

Our energies sync.

There's a soft moan in his mind as he probes for more, and I indulge. I imagine our clothes tossed on the floor, our bodies becoming one in an entangled sweaty heap. I let him feel it all as I search for the back entrance into his mind. I want to discover his greatest desire and twist it to give me what I want.

There!

I open the door and plant ideas into his subconscious.

Sex. Magick. Communion.

Yes!

Perfect.

His freshly shaven cheeks flush before he slams the mental door, but not soon enough. I know he wants me. Satisfaction twitches the corners of my mouth. This is fun. I push more enticing images of me spread out on an altar, completely helpless. He could do whatever he wanted. He could use my blood as a sacrifice, but as my thoughts continue to broadcast, his hazel eyes turn to blue ice, and I know I've gone too far.

That is quite enough.

The whip of authority in his thoughts is to remind me that I won't like what follows if I don't fall in line.

Shit. He knows I'm messing with him.

A show of defiance and injured pride has me turning on my heel and walking away.

It's what any self-respecting schoolgirl would do.

After school, don't forget. I expect you here. We need to work on that shielding, young lady. I just waltzed right into your mind.

What he wants holds very little interest for me unless it furthers my agenda.

Whatever, Mr. White, I send right back.

As I walk away, I shield my laughter. He called me young lady! Oh, the impudence. I wonder if he'd still entertain his desires if he knew how old and powerful I actually am. Without the coven's leash, I'm twice as powerful as the whole lot of them put together.

Sure, I feigned innocence when I got snared. The high coven lapped up my young girl's sob story when they caught me unleashing destruction on a global scale. So a few people got sick. Big deal. I convinced the coven it was an accident. I'm just a foundling all alone in the world; how was I to know that I was causing a plague with my sad, sad thoughts?

They decided my inexperience made me dangerous but valuable. I just needed proper training. In time, they said, I could be an important member of the coven. The high witch herself opened her home to me, and Mr. White was assigned as my mentor the very next day. For my own good, of course, but I know there's more to it.

There is a talisman hidden in Mr. White's secret room in the school, the one nobody is supposed to know about. The coven chained me to it—taming my raw power into something *manageable*.

Without these chains draining me, no one could make me do anything.

And gee, I wonder where this is going?

The talisman pulls enough raw energy from me to light an entire city, and the coven is using the power for their spells and to feed their souls.

I slip into the alcove outside the school doors and cast a quick glamour so no one can see me. Lighting up a smoke, I try not to think about that night. The memory of them siphoning off my power makes me want to puke.

Fucking vampires.

I should've been more careful. I wanted to ride the

storm and watch the world burn. I was free for the briefest of moments, but right now, escape lies beyond my abilities. The coven is squeezing me tight.

If I could get to Mr. White, perhaps that could change.

I take a drag, enjoying the hit of nicotine. Sad that no one smokes anymore. I guess it's bad for you. The butt barely grazes my lips for the second time before it's plucked out of my hands. Surprised, I turn and frown when I see Mr. White again.

Of course, he has to ruin my smoke break. He's spoiled everything else.

His eyes change color so often that it's hard for me to land on a definitive shade. Right now, they remind me of a stormy sea. I like that.

He shakes his head no, clearly annoyed that I walked away and intending to put me in my place. I try to play it off with wide-eyed naiveté, but he doesn't soften. I open my mouth to spout off the first sarcastic comment that comes to mind but realize, nope, that's not going to fly either. Instead, I close my lips and moisten them. His eyes lock.

Men are so easy.

"How did you find me?" I ask, as if I don't know they can track me anywhere with their fancy little energy collar around my neck.

Tag me and call me Fluffy.

"You are not nearly as clever as you like to think," he says.

I let him believe that as he draws my cigarette to his lips.

I study him for a moment. Smoking changes him into a

less stuffy version of himself that's almost tolerable. In his neatly pressed grey slacks and blue sweater vest, I wonder how old he really is. How many centuries has he preyed on innocent girls like the face I'm wearing? He appears to be twenty-five, but looks can be deceiving. If I've learned anything in my considerable time on earth, it's that nothing is ever quite what it seems when dealing with a coven of witches right in the heart of Mormon country. I wonder how many members are in the coven.

Whatever. They can keep their secrets. I still have a few up my sleeve, too.

"Tell me something, Cailee."

Ooooh, he's practiced the way the vowels roll off his tongue when he says my name. Ironic, really, that he hasn't made the connection. He is Irish, after all.

He takes another puff. "Are you attempting to try my patience personally or is it the world in general that pisses you off?"

The nicotine works its magic on him. With each drag, I can feel the tension in his body release. I decide it is best to say nothing. The question feels rhetorical anyway.

Yes, I am pushing his buttons. It is in my nature to do so. Be true to who you are—isn't that written in *The Book of Shadows* somewhere? I never have liked being molded, and if they think they're going to turn me into 'let me send you positive vibes' girl, they are so, so wrong. And really, if that's the coven's agenda, they are no better than the assholes walking the halls in the high school behind me.

As I finish this thought, Mr. White chuckles.

Shit. My opinions about kumbaya shadows and petty teenage bullshit are blaring through psychic radio. Busted! As I shield, I think, *Oh, well. Those particular thoughts weren't of anything out of normal for a seventeen-year-old girl.*

At least, I hope.

He says, "Cailee, you're more of a Kali. I can't think of a more fitting description. You truly are a goddess of chaos, my dear. And no, I wouldn't want to change anything about you." His words feel like a warm caress. His eyes are soft firelight now, glowing with influence. He is patient; his eyes encourage. He understands; his eyes assure. He is in control... or so he thinks.

Reaching into me the way he does psychically leaves him open. He's shown me what he sees when he looks at me, and my, my, my, he's close to uncovering the truth. I'm glad my sexy, smitten schoolgirl thoughts reached him. Now I can use that energy to become exactly what he expects.

Chaos power tastes like mother's milk. It invigorates me like a cold winter night as I siphon his lifeforce through his persuasion link.

"I know what you want, my dear, but you are treading through dangerous territory," he says, crushing my cigarette out on the pavement. He didn't even finish it. "You need to earn your power back instead of trying to seduce it from me. The unruly magick you wield comes at a terrible cost."

Oh. My. Gods! Is he really that full of himself? This is going to be easier than I thought.

I lift my chin in stubborn defiance, pouting my lips. "Want my opinion? This whole 'cost to magick' thing is bullshit. Long before the coven found me, I manipulated energy with no consequence at all."

"Maybe not to you, but what about others? Energy manipulation is not to be trifled with. The coven's rules protect everything and everyone," he explains as if he's speaking to a child.

Puh-lease.

"But what if they aren't? What if the coven is controlling our energy for their own agenda?"

There's enough truth in what I'm saying to have him questioning. I go in for the kill.

I say, "Don't you want to be in control of your destiny? You and I, we could be together."

I'm careful not to touch him but add a little extra to my voice. Not too much. The last thing I need is to get busted for using his own energy against him. I plant the thought in his mind to kiss me, and he obliges. He tastes of tobacco with a hint of mint. I deepen the kiss, raising the heat slowly. I have him exactly where I want him. He'll be boiling before he even knows what happened.

By then, it will be too late.

I can feel desire pulsing through his fingertips, and even as he steps back, my lips curl with anticipation.

He's so conflicted. Chaotic energy swirls around inside of him. I breathe it in.

But I need more.

I always need more.

A war rages inside of him. The funniest part is, he isn't even aware of who he's fighting. He thinks it's against himself, his higher nature versus his baser desires. I watch his eyes carefully for any sign of awareness as I raise the heat another degree with my gaze.

He can't resist. He reaches for me just as a couple of girls pass by.

Three… Two… One, and… gasp!

"Mr. White!" one of them exclaims.

"Oops," I say, my eyes widening in surprise. "My control's not so good. The glamour slipped."

"Damn it. You did that on purpose," he croaks.

This is the tipping point. What will he do? I half expect him to jump out of the pot. That would have been wise. But frogs and toads are stupid. Instead, he grabs my arm and pulls me back inside the school and in front of a shocked audience. He reaches out with his energy to make them forget. Tsk, tsk. That's against the coven's rules. Free will and all. I wrap them in a shield as they run toward the office to tell.

It's all I can do not to laugh my ass off.

Aww… Poor little frog. He's already cooked.

I almost feel sorry for him.

Almost.

Not really though.

He thinks I'm Kali; I'll show him Kali. I've been mistaken for her before. Worship is worship regardless of the name. Power is power, and he's handing me his. Twisting my arm, he drags me behind.

Yes! Glorious pain.

"This is all your fault!' he shouts.

Anger makes him vulnerable.

I reach deeper and devour his thoughts.

He's young, possibly the age he appears. How incredibly stupid of the coven to assign someone so inexperienced. I'm better at masking my true self than I thought.

"Once I get you alone in my workroom, you'll be sorry for all of the trouble you've caused," he seethes through clenched teeth.

I feed on his emotions as if they are the most delectable candy and grow stronger with each lick. I'm good at creating anarchy. All sorts of ideas are brewing in that small mind of his, but I focus on the ones that feed me best. As he pulls me into his empty classroom, I add even more fire under the pot.

Oh, yes. Take me to that hidden chamber of yours, big boy, and show me exactly who's boss.

He bristles as he hears my thoughts, but I can taste that this is exactly what he wants. He longs to strap me to that alar of his and have his way.

Too bad you're too much of a pussy to go through with it. You want to do all sorts of fun things with me. Admit it. But you can't because the coven has you by the balls.

I push his buttons. Hard. I'm goading him. We are so close to his sacred space. I just need to be invited in.

"Stop." His voice is quiet but firm. Dropping his grip on my arm, he reaches for his head.

As if holding it would get me out of there. Ha!

But the calmness I feel wash over him is worrisome.

"Stop what, Mr. White? I'm not the one who got caught kissing a student," I say, all sugar.

Ah, yes. There.

I see exactly what I need flash through his eyes.

"Don't even try that bullshit with me!" he hisses. "I know you're in my head!"

"Ah, there's the sweet spot. You see, you're the one who broke the rules. Someone or *something* can place thoughts in your mind all day long, but if you actually do the deed…. well… not cool, man. That's basic Witch 101. You should have known better. Taking advantage of an innocent girl like me."

His jaw sets. Oh, the conflict.

So much shame lies in his center. This is the dark core I've been seeking. There will be no love in the act that will follow, and that's exactly how I want it. I need his hate.

I say, "Weak. Pathetic. The whole town will turn on you. Why not take a chance on what I'm offering? Perhaps we can both find a way to be free."

Bingo! Mr. White nods, resigned. He stands before the chalkboard and brings his hands together and then pulls them apart in a sweeping motion. The veil masking the chalkboard entrance to his secret chamber is brushed aside.

The secret room is carved out of black onyx and inlaid with luminescent gold. Seven steps lead down, each engraved with magical symbols. A giant altar is in the center of the room.

"Welcome to my workroom," he says. "I always knew I'd bring an apprentice here, but never imagined it would be like this."

He reaches his hand out to me, and I willingly take it.

This is everything I'd hoped for. Without his permission, I could never get past the warding without him seeing my true form.

As I walk down the steps, Mr. White murmurs an incantation to veil the room again from prying eyes on the other side.

Who knows how long it will take for the principal or school security to come storming in.

I guess it depends on how fast the girls talk.

In the chamber, I'm drunk with anticipation. Energy tells me the talisman's within my reach. Looking around at the shelves of books and all manner of magickal trinkets just ripe for the picking, I wonder where and when the talisman will appear.

There. It's right there.

Oh, my.

The coven was quite clever. They hid the talisman where I couldn't find it unless I was in the chamber, but it's not in the chamber at all.

Exciting.

I run my fingers across the cold surface of the altar, feeling the energy thrum through the stone like a living pulse.

It welcomes me.

I hop up on the edge and lift my black skirt to expose creamy thighs.

"Is this where you want me?" I purr.

Mr. White is completely transfixed. I doubt he could put two words together if his life depended on it, and believe me, it does. He should recognize me for what I am, shout out an incantation, and trap me where I sit.

It's rather disappointing that he's made this so easy. I'm tempted to flash my true form for the briefest of moments to liven things up a bit, but I hold my chaotic nature in check. This next part needs to be of his own choice. Best to stick to the plan. I'll show him my true self once I have him inside me, right before I bite off his heads.

It's more fun that way.

I beckon him forward with my eyes, melting the last of his barriers.

I begin the ritual. "I offer myself to you freely."

The next line is his. I remove my shirt, exposing my plump, perky breasts to sweeten the pot and wait on pins and needles.

"I do this of my own free will," he parrots. Ritual is so ingrained in every fiber of his being that I doubt he realizes the power of his words.

But I do!

With that phrase, he's all mine.

I pounce, tearing off all of his clothes and offering up everything that dreams are made of. After we are both naked, I lay out on the altar exactly the way he'd pictured.

I start with a kiss and inject my venom with my wasp-like tongue. He's completely helpless as I roll over, trading places with him on the altar. I move my stinger here and there, lapping up blood and negative energy. Paralyzed, he moans in fear and pain, but also pleasure.

Funny, how all three intertwine so delectably.

The sight of his naked and bleeding vulnerability nearly throws me into a feeding frenzy, but I hold myself in check.

Slow.

It's sooo much more satisfying if I draw it out. I take a deep breath of him and fall into an erotic rhythm.

Pleasure.

Pain.

Fear.

Torment.

Over and over and over and over again. His energy rises; I pull it in, building, depleting, in an endless torturous tantric orgasm.

"Shhhh," I whisper into his ear as he whimpers. My hair softly brushes his cheek. I straddle and take him inside of me, my second set of teeth grazing ever so lightly. His eyes widen, and I smile as he tries to wrap his mind around what he's feeling and exactly what a Chinese finger trap means.

I slip off the young girl's mask and show my true demon form. I think it's quite lovely, but by the sudden miasma of fear rising from his body, Mr. White, well, he finds it rather unsettling to have an insectile creature who looks like a praying mantis mating with him.

I taunt, "Isn't this everything you wanted, baby?"

Ohhhhh.... The delicious screams. I breathe them in as I move up and down, pulling and tearing him apart as I go. I can feel his lifeforce draining as I grow stronger.

The amulet is nearly mine. I can see it glowing where his heart should be.

Clever. Just not clever enough.

I reach my pincer into his chest and pull it out with his last breath.

Red drips, bathing the stone in Mr. White's blood, but I couldn't care less. The talisman is beautiful, and it is mine.

Finally! I am free.

The coven can no longer control me. Transforming back into my schoolgirl form, I gleefully consider all of the terror I can now unleash. I start up the stairs, one step, two, but on the third, I am thrown back. I try again with the same result and look closer, this time studying the Latin spellwork.

Fuck.

On the third stair is my true name, 'Cailleach,' wrapped in a demon trap. The only person who could free me from this prison lays dead on the altar, his blood binding me.

I guess Mr. White wasn't as much of an idiot as I thought.

Angela Hartley resides in Midway, Utah. Through the years, she's built and managed writing organizations, entertained and educated at schools, symposiums, and conventions. In her down time, she enjoys studying religion theory, psychic abilities, the art of tarot, and psychology to gain a better understanding of the human condition.

MOMENTO MORI

C.R. LANGILLE

UTAH TERRITORIES, 1863

Evelyn Horn sat at the bar in a dusty saloon. She had left Manti a week ago, crossing the mountains on her way back east. Evelyn wasn't headed anywhere in particular, just trying to keep her mind occupied. She eventually found a town that wasn't on any map, but that didn't mean much out west. Towns came and went like leaves on a tree. It had a saloon. That was all that mattered.

A lock of red hair fell in front of her eyes, and she blew it away, only to have it return almost immediately. She grumbled incoherently and motioned to the bartender for another shot of whiskey.

The bartender raised his eyebrows and gave her a look that was becoming all too familiar these days. It was that disapproving, *are you sure*, kind of look. She hardened her stare, which did little, so instead, she pulled out a stack of greenbacks.

The man's judgment never faltered, but he poured the drink. "A bit early isn't it?"

Evelyn looked away. "Not if you haven't gone to sleep."

The bartender ambled to the other side of the bar and began cleaning glasses with a dirty rag. A young cowboy with an expensive, gold-plated pocket watch (in another life, Evelyn would have had that watch by now) and a fancy burgundy vest sat at a table in the corner. It was a stark contrast to her clothes which were wool, heavy, and practical.

His hair was black and slicked back. A soiled dove with dirty blonde hair sat on his lap, doing her best to entertain the young dandy.

Situated near the door was the town's marshal, an older man with a salt-and-pepper beard and balding hair to match. He had shuffled in early in the morning to get a cup of coffee and hadn't left.

Evelyn downed the whiskey. It didn't burn going down anymore. She wasn't sure if that was a good thing or not.

Raymond wouldn't have approved of her newfound habit. Just thinking about him almost brought tears to her eyes. He had died in that damned cave nearly a year ago. Shot by the bastard, Buford O'Henry. Evelyn had once planned to marry Raymond, fool that he was.

Now he was dead.

There was something else in that cave. Something dark, something evil. Something that wanted her.

Whatever it was had used Raymond to try and lure her deeper into the depths. She could still see Raymond's lifeless face, twisted by that dark *thing*.

Shed the lies and embrace the darkness with me. Embrace the truth.

Evelyn shuddered and motioned to the bartender for another shot. Before he could respond, two men in dark coats busted through the doors. They dragged in a young woman behind them, her hands bound with rope and her mouth gagged.

She couldn't have been more than eighteen with sky blue eyes and strawberry blonde hair. Her dress was disheveled and covered in dirt. One of her eyes was swollen shut.

The marshal stood from his table and put a hand on his gun. "What's the meaning of th—"

One of the men drew a pistol and shot the marshal in the head. He fell back into his chair and toppled to the floor.

The other man sauntered up to the bar. "Two beers."

The bartender wasn't new to the game of death. He poured the drinks and kept his mouth shut.

The man was tall and had a scar that cut up his lip. His face was covered in dark scrubble. Scar looked over at Evelyn and then grabbed his drinks before returning to the table his accomplice had acquired. The man set the drinks down, rolled the dead marshal off the chair, and claimed it as his own.

The man's friend was short and stocky. He wore his brown hair in a greasy ponytail. A red bandana was tied across his forehead, and he had a wild, thick mustache that poked out in every direction. The girl sat between the two, eyes downcast.

The young dandy stood and pushed the working girl

from his lap. He produced a billfold from his coat pocket. He grabbed a few bills from within and handed it to her.

"You had better run along now before my associates take an interest in you," the dandy said. He had a British accent. Unlike some of the young men Evelyn had encountered in her lifetime, this man's accent was real.

The soiled dove took the money before disappearing upstairs.

Evelyn weighed her options. Three against one, and who knew if there were more outside. She was a good shot and wasn't afraid of violence, but these odds were against her. She cursed every shot of whiskey she had downed throughout the night.

The young dandy walked over to the two men and the girl and sat down.

The man with the mustache and the bandana began speaking. "We got her boss, just lik—"

The young man raised his hand, silencing his companion. His gaze was locked on the girl's face. He reached out and gently brushed her hair back.

"Did they do this to you?" he asked, his fingers grazing across her swollen eye.

The girl looked away but nodded.

"It's okay, child. Which one?"

"Aww, come on boss. She put up a fight. Damn near bit my ear off!" the mustached man said.

The young dandy didn't turn his attention away from the girl but spoke in a low tone. "One more word, Theodore, and I will hamstring you and leave you in the wilderness for the coyotes."

Theodore stopped talking, his face a shade lighter than it had been moments before.

Evelyn drew her Colt Police revolver from her holster. The bartender caught her eye and shook his head.

"Now, my dear, tell me which one of these ruffians hit you," the young man said.

The girl looked up and glanced over to Theodore.

The young dandy nodded. "Theodore, your hand please."

"Come on, boss, it wasn't nothing."

The young man nodded toward the table. "Your hand. Now. Or I will take more."

Theodore glanced over to his companion, but the other man feigned interest in his beer. Finally, Theodore took off his buckskin glove and rolled up his sleeve. "I'm sorry, boss. I wasn't thinking. You know how I get sometimes!"

The young man nodded. "I know."

In a flash, the young man produced a knife. Evelyn's mind raced on where it had come from, but before she could figure it out, the dandy stabbed the knife down onto the table.

Theodore let out a yell that shook Evelyn's eardrums. He snatched his hand away and blood flew across the room. The knife stuck into the table, and next to it was Theodore's bloody finger.

The girl screamed and burst from her chair, but Scar manhandled her back down.

Evelyn had seen enough. She pushed away from the bar and pointed her gun at the young man. "Let her go."

The young man turned towards her as Scar drew his

pistol. Theodore fumbled with his gun but was having trouble drawing the weapon with his new wound.

The dandy smiled. "Gentlemen, allow me to introduce Miss Evelyn Horn. A Pinkerton, if I may add."

Evelyn's mind screamed for an answer. This man knew her, and she had no clue who he was.

"If you know what's good for you, you'll let her go and be on your damned way." To emphasize her suggestion, she pulled the hammer back on her pistol.

The young man smiled. "You're not going to shoot me. Even now I can see the sway in your body, the fight to focus your aim. If you miss, you might hit poor Miss Huntington here."

The girl's eyes were wide, pleading with Evelyn, although she couldn't tell if they were pleading with her to shoot or not. In Evelyn's moment of hesitation, the young man produced another knife.

He was fast. Faster than anyone Evelyn had ever come across. Or perhaps it was the whiskey giving her doubts. One moment he was at the table, and the next he was behind the girl with his knife at her throat.

"Now let us be civilized, Miss Horn. Put the gun down, or the girl dies while you watch."

Evelyn weighed the options. Perhaps her aim was instinctual, and her body would take over. Or perhaps she would accidentally send a round through the girl's shoulder. Or maybe she would spend too much time overthinking things and miss the fact that Scar had moved in behind her.

Evelyn spun, but Scar was already there. He caught her wrist and wrenched the weapon away. She reached for her hairpin dagger, but Scar headbutted her in the face.

The room wobbled as loud footsteps that shook the earth thudded up to her. The young man crouched down and lifted her face. "Bring her along. Perhaps two will make *it* happy."

Evelyn's world went dark.

With the darkness came the whispers. It always started as a buzz, like a swarm of flies that had found a rotten corpse bloating in the sun.

However, those whispers began to coalesce into something sensible. Evelyn placed her hands over her ears to block out the noise. She didn't want to hear the words.

The gesture was futile. Raymond's voice burrowed into her mind.

"I'm waiting for you, Eve. We're all waiting for you. Sleeping in the dark. You should join us."

It was Raymond and it wasn't. There was something *off* in his voice. A subtle rage that was unlike the man she had loved. She'd heard that rage before in others. Drunken imbeciles in the saloon; men with a taste for whips and whipping; men who found a knack for teaching via the school of knuckles and blood.

"No," Evelyn said.

"We can wait. But can you? Embrace the truth."

The darkness wrapped itself around her and began to shake violently. She screamed until someone slapped her in the face.

All at once, the whispering ceased, replaced with the crackle of a nearby campfire. The young man crouched down in front of her.

"I apologize for striking you, Miss Horn. However, we can't have that kind of noise," he whispered. "There are things in these woods, things that very much want us dead."

Her cheek stung where he had slapped her. Evelyn opened her jaw wide and there was a pop. Eating would be uncomfortable for the next few days.

"You know me, but I don't know you," she said.

The young man smiled and put a hand to on his chest. "Heavens! How could I be so rude? I am Robert Chamberlain Jr."

He said it like the name was supposed to bear weight, but Evelyn didn't recall ever hearing of a Robert Chamberlain, senior nor junior.

"And what is it we're doing out here, Mr. Chamberlain?"

He smiled. "Well, Ms. Horn, you see, we're about to change the course of history. For too long, the heathens and non-believers have gone about their business without ever knowing the truth of what really exists in this world."

Do you seek the truth?

"So, you're some sort of religious zealot?" Evelyn asked.

"Oh my, no! Don't confuse me with one of those Christian fanatics. I'm not about to dance around and play with snakes. Let them take false comfort with their insignificant god. What I seek to awaken is much older."

Evelyn hoped the man was crazy. However, given what she had witnessed lately, she had a feeling in the pit of her stomach that told her he was serious. She nodded to the girl. "What role does she play?"

"Miss Theresa Huntington? She's a witch, from a long line of witches tracing back to Salem."

Theresa's mouth was gagged. Her eyes went wide, and she shook her head and tried to speak. Chamberlain reached over and removed the gag. "No screaming, or it will go right back on."

"I'm no witch!" Theresa said. "You got it all wrong."

Her voice had a southern drawl that Evelyn was familiar with. Evelyn looked at Theresa and then to Chamberlain. "This little thing, a witch?"

Chamberlain gave her a devilish grin. "Oh indeed, yes. Don't let her pretty face fool you. Underneath that façade is a twisted soul. A soul with the power necessary to awaken the Voracious One. Now, if you'll excuse me, I must prepare."

Chamberlain stood and walked back to his compatriots. Evelyn glanced at the girl. "Don't worry. I'll figure out a way to get us out of here."

She tried to move her hands, but they were bound with rope. Her legs as well. The knots were tight. These cowpokes knew what they were doing. They had taken her gun and her hairpin dagger as well.

Chamberlain sat on a log next to the campfire. He poured some coffee into a tin cup and took a sip. Theodore reached out to grab a wooden ladle but knocked the handle with his cut finger and let out a howl. Scar chuckled from the other side of the fire.

"How many times you gonna do that?" Scar asked.

"Shut yer yap," Theodore said, nursing his injured hand.

"Gentlemen." Chamberlain wasn't looking at his

buffoons. His gaze locked onto something beyond in the trees.

Scar drew his gun. Theodore spun in a circle, looking out into the pines that surrounded their camp. A branch snapped in the darkness, followed by a tree falling to the ground.

Theodore fumbled for his pistol. "Shit boys, it's coming! It's gonna kill us!"

Chamberlain stood and crept back toward Theresa. "You can feel it out there, can't you?"

Theresa looked at Chamberlain and then past him to the woods. "You have no idea what's out there."

The fire burned hot, but its light ended at the tree line, unable to pierce the shadows. There was another snap of a branch, closer this time.

What followed chilled Evelyn to the bone. A low wail, almost like a crying woman. The wail grew in intensity until it turned into a gravelly, wet croak.

Theodore ran a hand through his greasy hair. "No, no, no!"

He struggled before he was able to get onto his horse. Scar pointed his pistol at him, but Chamberlain shook his head. "Let him go."

"Boss?"

Chamberlain smiled. "Good luck, Theodore."

Theodore spat and then spurred his horse forward. The horse fought against his command, but Theodore finally got the beast to move. He galloped out of camp and into the darkness.

From the timber came the crack of trees and the rumble of earth. Whatever was out there moved fast.

Two things happened. First, the horse let out a scared whinny. Then, Theodore screamed.

Gunfire echoed through the pines. Four shots, then nothing.

"What was that?" Evelyn asked.

"Some things are better left unnamed, Ms. Horn. To give them names garners their attention." Chamberlain returned to the fire with Scar. "Keep this burning hot through the night.

"Okay, boss."

As the night drew on, Chamberlain read a book while Scar snored loudly. Evelyn couldn't sleep, nor could Theresa. Every time she looked over, the girl's eyes were wide open, scanning the trees and shadows.

"Do you know what's out there?" Evelyn whispered.

Theresa shivered and hugged her chest. Evelyn got the idea that it wasn't from the chill. "That *thing* out there. I can feel it. Its presence is…I don't know how to describe it. You know when it's hot outside? I mean the sort of heat that just drains you and there's nowhere to get away from it. It's like that."

Evelyn looked out into the woods. As if in response, an unkindness of ravens took flight as something disturbed their slumber. Evelyn didn't feel anything crazy out there in the darkness, but then again, she wasn't a witch.

"Is it true?" Evelyn asked.

"That I'm a witch? Does it matter?"

"What does he want with you?"

Theresa shrugged. "What do nasty men want with any woman? To dominate them, I suppose."

Evelyn couldn't disagree. But there was something else. "Your power, what's he plan to do with it?"

"I think he plans to awaken something."

"Can you do it?"

Theresa looked away. "I think so. That's what scares me. When I was young, my power sort of just *manifested*. One day, I was playing out front of the cabin. Ma and Pa were busy chorin'. Well, to say I was bored would be an understatement. So I needed some friends. Needless to say, I found them. Gave my Pa a huge fright when he came out and found me playing with a bunch of forest critters like they were pet dogs. I think it was the maybe the bear that scared him the most."

Theresa's grin was infectious, and Evelyn couldn't help herself. By all accounts, there was nothing to smile about.

Just as fast as Theresa's smile came, it disappeared. "It scared my Pa something fierce. He got angry with me. Started arguing with Ma about bloodlines or some such nonsense. He never looked at me the same again. He thought he could beat the devil out of me." Theresa turned her head and wiped her cheeks. "This stupid *gift*, as my Ma called it, ain't been nothing but trouble. So I keep it buried deep."

"Well, let's make sure this bastard can't do whatever he plans to do," Evelyn said.

Evelyn was able to untie the girl, taking care that Chamberlain's attention was elsewhere. Once Theresa was untied, she helped undo the knots in Evelyn's bonds. Before they moved to leave, a raven landed on a nearby rock. It cocked its head to the side, staring at Evelyn and Theresa with a curiosity only known to animals.

Theresa smiled and held out her arm. The raven immediately flew over to her. Theresa stroked the bird's head.

"My mama used to tell me that ravens and crows helped usher the spirits of the dead to the other side. If that's true, maybe this one has Theodore's soul." Theresa said. "She told me she had the power to rip my Pa's soul from that bird before it flew away, but she was more than happy to see that bastard burn in hell." Theresa ushered the raven back into the night sky.

Evelyn made her way over to the horses. Her chestnut mare, Oats, was with the others. Evelyn snuck over to Oats and patted her head. Oats shook her mane and nipped at Evelyn's ear.

"I know, I let those horrible people mess with you. I'm sorry," she whispered.

Evelyn dug through her saddlebags looking for her gun, but it wasn't there.

"Looking for these I presume?"

She spun around and found Chamberlain. He held Evelyn's gun belt in one hand. In the other, he spun her hairpin dagger effortlessly.

With a flick of his wrist, he sent the dagger flying through the air towards Evelyn. She turned away, but it still caught her in the shoulder. She cried out and fell to the ground as the blade bit into her flesh.

Theresa screamed and ran at Chamberlain, but Scar grabbed the girl before she could make it far.

Chamberlain smiled and dropped Evelyn's gun belt to the ground. He drew a knife from his coat and twirled the blade on his fingertip.

"Ms. Horn, you are quickly becoming more trouble than you're worth." Chamberlain nodded to Scar.

Scar threw Theresa to the ground and strode toward Evelyn. He drew his pistol as he walked.

Evelyn crab-walked backward to try and create some distance. Scar closed in quickly. Evelyn let out a shrill whistle.

Oats neighed and kicked, catching Scar in the chest. He let out a deep *oomph* as he sailed through the air.

Evelyn scrambled to her feet. Her shoulder blazed with pain as the knife shifted. She gritted her teeth and yanked it free.

Chamberlain rushed her. He was fast, and she was wounded, but her body ran on instinct. Evelyn shifted her weight and pivoted. A half-second slower and Chamberlain would have driven his knife into her heart.

She didn't have time to think as Chamberlain continued his assault with a series of stabs and slashes, all designed to kill.

Evelyn danced back, twisting and dodging. The last one went for her eye, and although she ducked away, the blade still kissed her cheek.

Blood ran down her face and into her mouth. She spat it away, never taking her eyes off Chamberlain. He was a viper ready to strike.

Scar groaned and rolled to his side. Evelyn cursed her luck.

Chamberlain shot her a devilish grin. "It seems your time has come to—"

The telltale click of a pistol hammer locking into place cut him off. Theresa stood behind Chamberlain, Evelyn's gun in her hands. She shook harder than the leaves on an aspen in a hard breeze.

Chamberlain's visage hardened as his lips curled into a sneer. "Now child, put that down before you hurt yourself."

Theresa's eyes burned with hate. That rage spoke a language that few understood but Evelyn was intimate with.

Theresa took a step forward. "You killed my ma."

Chamberlain pivoted so he could keep Evelyn and Theresa in his sights. His eyes flicked behind Theresa. Scar was on his feet and moving towards the girl.

"Look out!" Evelyn yelled.

Theresa turned and screamed. Chamberlain took advantage of the girl's distraction and rushed her. Theresa turned back toward him, and the gun barked in her hand just as Scar barreled into her. The round went wild but clipped Chamberlain in the leg. He grunted and dropped to the ground.

Theresa was on her back with Scar on top of her. She tried to shoot him, but he knocked the weapon away.

Evelyn raced towards the pair, but Chamberlain grabbed her by the foot, and she fell to the ground.

She kicked back and caught Chamberlain in the face. He let go with a growl. Scar had Theresa's arms restrained with one hand and reared his fist back to punch her. Evelyn flung the dagger at Scar and caught him in the arm. He yelled and spun around.

"You'll pay for that," he said.

Evelyn got to her feet, backing away from Chamberlain. "Let that girl go."

341

Scar smiled through the pain. "Or what, you'll kill me?"

"I'm going to kill you regardless, you lump of cow shit."

Scar laughed. He grimaced as he yanked the dagger from his arm and threw it away. "That's a cute little sticker you got there. I'm sure you'll appreciate this."

Scar drew a Bowie knife from his belt.

Evelyn was wounded, weaponless, and facing an opponent who had a knife and was almost twice her size. However, at least he wasn't focused on Theresa anymore.

Scar ambled toward her holding the Bowie knife in a downward grip. He gave her a grin that promised horrible things.

The campfire went out as if someone had doused it. The woods fell silent. Scar stopped his advance and stared at something behind Evelyn.

She turned.

Standing in the meadow was Theodore. His eyes were milky white, and he cried tears of blood. He opened his mouth as if he were about to say something, but the sound that came from him was like a wailing cat mixed with a bullfrog.

His movements were jerky, as if he didn't know how his legs were supposed to work. Extending from his head was a tendril of darkness, pocked with burning dots that resembled stars in the night sky. Evelyn followed the tendril back to the trees and found its source. She instantly wished she hadn't, as her mind splintered under the strain of what she saw.

Crouched in a large branch was a massive shadow with

eyes that glowed with azure hate. It hopped down onto the ground and stood. The thing was easily over ten feet tall. Its body was thin, emaciated, and coated with black fur. Covering its head and face was the skull of a large elk, its antlers stark white against the creature's dusky body. The tendril that connected to Theodore came from the creature's back.

Scar made a move for the horses and snapped a twig. The creature's head lolled to the side, and another tendril sprouted from its back with a wet popping noise. It sped through the air and speared Scar through the mouth.

He dropped to his knees and tried to fight against the tendril, but soon his body went limp. Scar's eyes turned white like Theodore's. He convulsed as the tendril began to pump something dark into him.

The creature stared at Evelyn as it strode from the trees toward her. It lifted the two men with ease and placed them at its side like they were pets.

The thing crouched down so it was eye level with Evelyn. Rancid breath rasped from under its skull helmet. Evelyn was afraid if she moved, she'd end up like Chamberlain's lapdogs. The thing cupped her chin with a skeletal hand. Theodore and Scar reached out in unison, mimicking the creature's movements.

It pulled her closer. Evelyn's instincts kicked in, and she tried to break its arm, aiming for the joint like she had been taught. Evelyn would have had better luck trying to snap a fencepost.

If the creature even registered her attack, it didn't let on. Its eyes bore into her. They were swirling galaxies, the centers of which were massive stars that burned black and cold. It spoke to her, drilling into her mind with the precision of a monkey using a stick to dig termites from a mound.

The words were foreign, their sound making her vomit. Theodore and Scar's mouths moved, teeth clattering as they tried to mimic the creature's tongue.

From their mouths came the whispers of a legion of sleeping beings. Entities waiting for the universe to align in such a way that they could awaken and spread their truth through the cosmos. They slept in the dark caves of a blasted planet, deep down where the suns of a million galaxies could never touch. As one, they stirred.

Yet, the stars were not right, so still they slept.

A tendril wrapped itself around her throat before forcing its way into her mouth. She tried to scream but couldn't make a sound.

The chattering of the two outlaws grew louder, and somewhere deep down in her primal brain she wanted to join their chittering. Then, from behind her, Theresa's voice cracked through, driving the noise away.

"Back to the darkness I command thee, leave this place, turn and flee!"

Over and over, Theresa said the words. Each time, her voice boomed louder.

The creature hissed. It dropped Scar and Theodore to the ground. Everything went dark as Evelyn's eyesight began to blur. Soon, there was nothing but the wet hiss of the monster and Theresa's voice.

Then, there was nothing.

———

EVELYN FLOATED IN A DARK PLACE. Her stomach lurched as if she were falling. Before she could scream, she was swooped up into the air. Faster than she thought possible, the darkness melted away and the trees of the forest sped by underneath.

She had the sensation that she was flying. In the distance, a large mountain loomed that seethed with hate and dark energy. It seemed to pull her closer.

Evelyn fought against the pull, but it was useless. Near the top of the mountain was a figure silhouetted by a large bonfire that stood at the entrance of a massive cave. It cast an inhuman shadow that moved of its own accord.

Evelyn awoke screaming and in pain. She was on her back with Theresa crouched next to her.

Evelyn's stomach turned. She rolled to her side, spewing out a brackish liquid the color of mud. Her throat was raw and it hurt to breathe, but she somehow found words. "What happened?"

"I drove it off," Theresa said.

"How?"

Theresa shrugged.

Evelyn nodded. For a while, she lay on her back, staring up at the sky. The clouds shifted, offering her a view of the stars, and deep down in her gut she couldn't help but think about the vast army of...*things* that were waiting to awaken and destroy everything.

Evelyn knew the truth. She didn't seek it, but it found her, and it would haunt her until she died, and perhaps even after.

Evelyn turned her head and looked at Theresa. "So, you're a witch, eh?"

"I told you so."

"Thanks for saving me. Without you, I think I would have died."

Theresa hugged her legs to her chest. "You did die."

Evelyn's heart skipped a beat. "What?"

"The thing killed you. But I was able to bring you back."

Evelyn propped herself up on her elbow. A lock of hair fell into her face, and instead of being red, it was whiter than snow. It was just a strip as far as she could tell, but her hair wasn't what bothered her. It was what Theresa was trying to tell her.

"You have to be joking."

Theresa's eyes went cold. "Death is no joke." The girl handed Evelyn a feather. It was a raven's feather, but instead of being pure black, there was a strip of white.

———

CHAMBERLAIN HAD SLIPPED AWAY to live another day, although he was now on Evelyn's shortlist of outlaws to find.

Evelyn and Theresa rode out. During the day, the forest wasn't threatening. They followed a game trail that led them to another small town. Evelyn was elated; however, that elation melted away. Behind the town was a large mountain. Evelyn knew this mountain. It was the same one she had seen when she had died. She knew that at the top, there'd be a cave, and in that cave, there'd be answers.

There'd be the truth.

C.R. Langille spent many a Saturday afternoon watching monster movies with his mother. It wasn't long before he started crafting nightmares to share with his readers. An avid hunter and outdoorsman, C.R. Langille incorporates the Utah wilderness in many of his tales. He is an affiliate member of the Horror Writer's Association, a member of the League of Utah Writers, and received his MFA: Writing Popular Fiction from Seton Hill University.

ACKNOWLEDGMENTS

This anthology would not have been possible without the generous support of our Kickstarter backers:

Adam Alexander

Alice Ramona Font and family

Amanda Rock

Ashleigh H.

Brock Poulsen

Brooke Clonts

Charity Ponton

Christina Berry

Daniel, Trista, and Eleanor Robichaud

Donald Evans

Drew Lettner

E. Storey

Ed Varra

Eric Estrada

Ernesto Pavan

Frank Lewis

Fyodor A. Pavlov

Gayle K

Ian Tubbritt

James H. Duke IV

Jane Font

Jason Miller

Jason Smith

Jennifer Langille

Joe Costa

John M. Portley

Johnathan Shiverdecker

Jonas Sværke

Jordan Albrecht

Jordan Howard

Joshua P. Sorensen

Kari Blocker

Kasie Mumper

Kelley Bhridha Morgana

Kelly Burt

Kenneth Skaldebø

Kimberly Ingols-Iverson

Kirsten Kowalewski

Kylee Robinson

Leaves

Lee W Smith

Levi's Mom

Lisa J Gessini

Lisa M

Lori Lynn Sadelack

Luna Corbden

Lyndsay Carder

Matthew B Alexander Jr

Meg Young

Megan O'Sullivan

MeriAnn Boxall

MH McFerren

Michael Darling

Michael Fowler

Nathan Wainwright

Nicolas Mandujano III

Niki

Noora Hautapaakkanen

Peggy O. Reed

Rich Jeffery

Rick & Connie Pope

Ruth Ann Orlansky

Ryan DeMoss

Sandra Halladay

Sariah Horowitz

Scott Kruckenberg

Sergey Kochergan

Shane Burley

Steve Matney

Susan Jessen

Theresa Ferraro

Tracey McKiernan

TyRee Scott Olsen

Vanessa Debroeck

William P Davis

Yoko O. Olsen